purplepeng

HIS MOTHER

Set in the attractive seaside town of Southport, HIS MOTHER is a contemporary psychological thriller about a secondary school teacher: Mr Rimmer.

A teenage female body is found face down in the Marshide marshlands. Detectives Inspector Folkard and Sergeant Shakespeare strongly suspect Mr Rimmer to be *their man.*

Unfortunately, it proves challenging to find the much-needed evidence that would link the death of Mary-Eloise Chambers to their suspect.

Mr Rimmer has many secrets; although he appears to live alone, he in fact does not. The closer Inspector Folkard and Sergeant Shakespeare get to their killer, the more the reader learns of Mr Rimmer's relationship with his mother.

It is only when Inspector Folkard looks back at similar attacks on young females, that she begins to make some much needed headway. Inspector Folkard knows there is at least one other body close by; finding it could be the vital piece of the puzzle, but where to look?

17th March
2016

To Wendy:
Happy Mother's
Day

HIS MOTHER

SALLY-ANNE TAPIA-BOWES

Copyright © 2015 Sally-Anne Tapia-Bowes

purplepenguinpublishing

FIRST PUBLISHED 2015

ISBN-13: 978-0993191909
ISBN-10: 0993191908

Cambria font used with permission from Microsoft

With thanks to family and friends (Julie in particular) for their support,

but especially to my daughter Teresita.

For Rose, my greatest fan and my best friend.

1

DIRECTORS ARE SO clever, how they make it all look so real – the close-up shots of the knot fastened around the victim's neck, some of her flaxen hair caught up in it. So clever, so real. The small details are the best; there she was, dangling in such a nonchalant manner, one shoe still on, the other had supposedly slipped off, off onto the wet kitchen floor.

Sunday evening – nine-forty, Mr Rimmer's favourite television programme confines him to his much-loved armchair for a further twenty minutes. He leans forward every now and then, pushing his spectacles back onto the bridge of his nose. Mr Rimmer then shakes his head from side to side whilst laughing quietly to himself, before he settles back down - so clever, so real - how anyone can lay on the slab of a morgue looking so dead, keeping so still.

At ten-thirty precisely Mr Rimmer gets up, tidies all about him, cushions in their place, curtains drawn, television turned off, a portrait of his mother adjusted. Bedtime – upstairs with a cup of cocoa, upstairs to sleep.

Mr Rimmer's clammy hands turn on the green floral bedside lamp; for a while he sits on the edge of his three-quarter bed, thinking of his mother, before turning on the electric blanket and clambering into bed. Mr Rimmer flicks through the seaside's town's local paper, The Southport Visitor, before he finds a horticultural article that is of interest to him. He begins to feel tired not long after he has begun to read.

Eventually Mr Rimmer falls sound asleep; he sleeps for most of the night.

2

SUNDAY - NEARLY MIDNIGHT. Inspector Folkard closed her eyes and pictured the crime scene, again; something was missing, possibly something obvious.

Despite having worked in the police force for over twenty years, the harrowing photographs still had a habit of distracting her early in the morning. Worst was the one that had captured the victim face-down in the marshland, her shoes, both missing; at times like these, days turned into nights and nights into more nights.

It was true too that on these days Chief Inspector Folkard could be more of a disciplinarian about the house. Her three children would mockingly, yet affectionally, refer to her as the *Chief* instead of mum or mama; her loving yet militant manner kept them all trundling along in some sort of necessary and collective routine. Her husband, Walter was the wind beneath her wings – constant, dependable and above all, very patient. Some mornings she left before six; some nights, she'd arrive after midnight.

At forty-four she had achieved much. She had worked hard, far too hard in her earlier days to get where she wanted. Harry, the eldest, had had it the hardest – as he reminded her - the girls got away with murder.

3

IT IS MONDAY morning. Mr Rimmer gorges his breakfast; food is a comfort to him – the drink is not. At precisely seven-thirty he clambers into his reliable light blue classic car and sets off to work – *Mr Blue Sky* all the way. At the top of Marshide Road he keenly eyes with both irritation and disparagement the young mother who pushes a pram with two small children inside whilst pulling along the third.

At precisely eight thirty, Mr Rimmer arrives to work. He parks where he has always parked; he surveys the building ahead with some distaste. Mr Rimmer has worked at St William's High School for Girls since he graduated. He completed his teacher training in 1978; he is still here – 34 years later. Mr Rimmer's mother had always wanted to be teacher.

Mr Rimmer shuffles along the corridors in the fashion of one who drives around on automatic pilot; he pushes his spectacles back onto the bridge of his nose. During the journey, as always, Mr Rimmer gathers himself, implements a smile and mentally rehearses the half-term's events – visiting an aunt in Wales, yes, the weather was fabulous this weekend, yes, I too like a bargain – even to rummage amongst the belongings of someone or another at the local car-boot.

By the end of the school day, Mr Rimmer is exhausted. The teenage insults are still ringing in his ears, arrogance worming its way under his skin. Once home, Mr Rimmer hangs his work suit in the closet. There are two other suits; they hang alongside some of his mother's favourite outfits. Mr Rimmer takes off his polished shoes and places them carefully next to his mother's. Wearing her peach sheep-skin slippers makes him feel better.

Naked now, Mr Rimmer heads for the shower; he pulls back the peach frilled curtain, removes her slippers and proceeds to shower – Mr Rimmer is already feeling better. Children have made comments about his weight for as long as he can remember. Mr Rimmer washes as far as he can reach. He concludes that for a man of fifty-six, he is in reasonable health – with the exception of his diminishing eyesight.

Mr Rimmer finishes off the sticky toffee-pudding before setting up the back-room come kitchen, for tonight's private tuition. He fretfully tidies some sweet wrappers from the previous lesson before placing a jug of high-juice on the table with a plate of fresh custard creams. Mr Rimmer has always liked parting the biscuit before sucking on the cream – his mother disapproves.

Mr Rimmer likes to wait for Eva in the front porch. Sometimes Eva's mother will drop her off late. Mr Rimmer will busy himself with his rabbit's foot, tickling the stamens of a favoured young fuchsia, just like he had been taught to, as a child, by his deceased grandfather.

Only one long half-glass, half-brick Victorian greenhouse survives in Mr Rimmer's impressive back garden. His grandfather would take him there to help pollinate all sixteen varieties of fuchsia. He looks with affection at his grandfather's rabbit foot before hanging it back on its hook behind the *mother-in-law's tongue* sitting prominently in the windowsill.

4

INSPECTOR FOLKARD TOUCHED affectionately a portrait of her family before leaving. How much younger she had looked then. It was rare she ever wore her hair down any more, certainly her untameable mop of thick highlighted brown hair required some grooming on a daily basis. She looked into the mirror in the hallway and fastened her navy raincoat. Her thick brown eyebrows needed plucking; she often told herself this at the same time every morning but rarely did anything about it.

Her roots needed doing too. That was a priority. Thick eyeliner to the top eyelids belonging to her greenish-brown eyes and some tinted Vaseline to her cheekbones and lips, had been Inspector Folkard's make-up routine for as long as she could remember. On the occasional night out, she would wear a brownish lipstick.

Only the two Labradors accompanied her to the front door; there would be no walk on this bleak Monday morning, not at this time. Upon closing the black metallic gate, she looked back at her idyllic life, her family caged in domesticity, caged from the outside world – the children were getting older by the minute.

Gathering focus, Inspector Folkard dialled for the lab report. Confirmed. The victim had been strangled, not drowned – not many signs of a struggle – no, no signs of anything else. Her shoes? No – not found.

Yesterday, her corpse had been identified by both her mother and father. Mary-Eloise Chambers. Sixteen. The parents' smiles attempted to disguise their uncontrollable dread - she had been missing for one night. It was hard for the victim's mother to stand straight; she wasn't sure what to do with her hands. After a few moments she looked into the helpless blue eyes of her husband. She whispered something inaudible before approaching her body.

Mary-Eloise Chambers looked at peace. A poppy bruise above her wrist, a scarf about her neck, her eyes closed, closed forever.

Mrs Chambers nodded before slowly fingering her daughter's wrist, then with more confidence her daughter's hand, each finger, around each nail, her slender arms, her freckled cheeks, her blue lips. 'Derek. Derek,' she repeated.

Mr Chambers didn't think he could touch his daughter; she already looked so different: he would try to remember her alive – quirky, adventurous, intelligent and kind – that letter-box smile.

Mary-Eloise Chambers went out this last fine Saturday after consuming most of her evening meal. She promised her parents that she would be back by ten; her parents did not question this, she was rarely later than half an hour.

Kate Chambers had looked out of the front-room window; her hazel eyes proudly followed her daughter until she was almost out of sight. With a contented smile, she returned to the lounge to watch television; she held the hand of her husband for a short while before taking up the remote and changing the channel.

Derek Chambers was caught up in the memory of a time gone by. He had recently been diagnosed with Alzheimer's. Although the disease was still in the early stages, he felt frustrated by episodes when he would become confused. Just the other day, he had headed for the local supermarket for some cat food; he pulled over. He couldn't remember the store's location. He was filled with utter disbelief. He cried. When he returned back home, he spoke to his wife. Together, they had agreed that it was not the right time to tell Mary-Eloise; her AS results imminent – such a long and cruel disease, there would be plenty of time.

Kate and Derek took it in turns to look at the time. By half-eleven, Derek was fumbling about looking for his mobile. Neither had received a text. Mary-Eloise was not picking up her calls. She was not replying to their messages. Mary-Eloise would have rang. Mary-Eloise would have texted.

The voice of Police Constable Stanfield assured Mrs Chambers that there would be a perfect explanation – that teenagers lost their mobiles all the time – that their daughter was probably at a friend's and would contact them at any moment. They were not to panic – she was probably trying to contact them right now.

Tired, and for the next five hours, Kate and Derek remained on the sofa they had acquired when Derek's mother had passed away. Derek held his wife closely. Every minute or so they would look up at the clock. Nobody would accuse the Chambers of being negative people – their pint glass was always half-full. Kate and Derek sat in the gloom of the room, silence all around them. They knew they would never see Mary-Eloise again. They knew her, like the back of their hands.

When Inspector Folkard and Sergeant Shakespeare knocked at the door, Kate and Derek were filled with mixed emotions. The Chambers needed to know where Mary was, wherever she was; they needed to see her. Sergeant Shakespeare, looking worse for wear, offered to make them all some tea. 'Do you have any family or friends who live nearby? Is there someone who could sit with you?'.

Derek's chest was hurting now; his left arm tingled, the muscles tightened around the top half of his arm, a numbness in his index finger prevailed. They held hands, like they used to when they were teenagers – clammy, frightened, needy.

Kate had cried like a baby on and off throughout the night. She couldn't stop playing those videos in her mind. When Mary-Eloise was about to be born, the midwife had asked her if she wanted to look into the round mirror because the head was about to come through – what a lovely head of hair - no – not at all – please - just get her out - the pain was too much.

Kate didn't know why she hadn't felt *all maternal* during the pregnancy. None of that mattered now. She was so tired after giving birth, she was desperate for some sleep. She was ravenous too - scampi and chips with lots of vinegar and a large mug of tea with lots of sugar.

Kate couldn't take her eyes off the baby – she was *her* baby. Derek had laughed when she described her emotions at the time – it had been like falling in love all over again. 'Yes. Mary, after Derek's mother - and Eloise, after mine.'.

Inspector Folkard spoke slowly and with care in her voice. A teenage female body, fitting the description given by Mr Chambers last night had been found amongst the Southport marshes; the victim had been strangled. Inspector Folkard watched their reactions, filmed them.

Sergeant Shakespeare continued. She asked for either Mr or Mrs Chambers or both to identify the body, as soon as they felt able to do so. The Chambers would attend together, they could go right now. Sergeant Shakespeare held the front door open; they entered the back of the plain vehicle in unison, still holding hands.

Inspector Folkard looked across at her colleague – she was looking a tad pale. For years they had sported the same hairstyle – hair brushed away from their face, pony tail. Sergeant Shakespeare's plain yet attractive features of medium length brown hair very much complemented her pale blue eyes and matching skin. Yet today she looked weary and unusually lifeless. Inspector Folkard decided she would wait for her colleague to speak to her first. The timing was not suitable. Her attention returned to the Chambers, who sat like ghosts.

Kate and Derek returned home that evening to be greeted with sincere condolences from the police doctor. Two other P.C.'s were checking the bins and placing items in plastic bags and wallets. Indoors, a police doctor apologised and explained in a quiet voice that the next twenty-four hours would be crucial – that their assistance was crucial if they were to catch the person or persons responsible for the crime.

Dumbfounded, Kate and Derek stood still whilst upstairs officers rummaged about in their daughter's room. Kate couldn't look into Mary-Eloise's room yet; she called for the two P.C.'s twice, asking them to be careful with their daughter's belongings. Several items were removed before they finally headed back to the lab.

Truly alone for the first time in what seemed to be a long while, Derek and Kate took to their bed. There they lay, awake for most of the night, memories rocketing back and forth – the pain, unbearable; was there really anything left to live for?

Back at the station, Inspector Folkard was listening to Sergeant Shakespeare who was summarising the autopsy report. 'No blood alcohol content. The murder could have been pre-meditated; the killer clearly knew how to kill the victim and was most likely known to the victim.' Sergeant Shakespeare then demonstrated with both her hands. 'He or she, had grabbed Mary-Eloise from behind, like this, and had pressed firmly on her external carotid artery, like this, on the right side of the neck.' .

Sergeant Shakespeare then stood behind her colleague, as if to reassure herself that she was getting things right. 'In less than ten seconds, following a firm pressure, right here, Mary-Eloise would have lost consciousness, the oxygen to the head, brain and face prevented. Following that, more pressure on the artery, possibly another two minutes and dead. Just like that.'.

Inspector Folkard looked over the autopsy report. There had been no broken nails and no scratches on the victim's body. It would certainly explain why the victim had not fought with her attacker. The motive though was eluding them both. No evidence of any sexual interference – nothing at all to go on.

Inspector Folkard asked for the estimated time of death. Sergeant Shakespeare paused for a second before reading out loud that the autopsy report placed her time of death at around eight-thirty in the evening. Inspector Folkard agreed with Sergeant Shakespeare. Mary-Eloise had either been strangled on the way to town before she had had the chance to meet up with friends, then the killer later, and most likely, drove to the marshland to dump her body or, Mary-Eloise had travelled, more likely walked away from town, in the direction of Churchtown, for whatever reason, and had conveniently been dumped by her killer who possibly lived nearby.

At the moment in time, they had little, if nothing to go on. In a small town like Southport, CCTV was regarded necessary only by the larger stores. Between the many marshes, the coastal road and Churchtown village, where she lived close by, there was no such technology visual to the residents. Both the Inspector and her Sergeant knew they would be relying heavily on door-to-door enquiries, and on

willing witnesses coming forward. Most likely, a reconstruction and an appeal would be needed in order to gain answers to the questions that troubled them most.

5

EVA IS LATE. Mr Rimmer is sure she has never been this late before. From his porch he observes the gulls ahead; a curlew's cry startles him. Mr Rimmer, is tired from fiddling with one thing after another and is about to make a call when she arrives in a taxi. Eva saunters up the path, her dark pigtails swishing to and fro. Eva has her blue boots on today. Eva has size five feet.

Again and again, Eva apologises; her mother was running late, she'd lost track of time - she smiles. Mr Rimmer is disarmed by her sincerity; his frustration disappears, they are friends again. 'I completed the work you set me too! I told you I would.'. Mr Rimmer smiles. He waves his left arm forward and invites Eva in.

As customary on a Monday night, Mr Rimmer leads Eva into the back-room and offers her the wooden chair with the red velvet seat. She sits by the window that looks out onto the impressive back garden. Mr Rimmer sits opposite – they always sit like this. He pours her a glass of high-juice then raises the roof of the porcelain green and white biscuit container.

Jennifer, a past pupil, had bought him this jar as a gift some time ago. It had reminded her of Mr Rimmer's house, window-boxes below every window – the windows like eyes framed by shutters. Mr Rimmer never closes them.

Custard creams. Eva's favourite. Mr Rimmer's mother liked shortbread; Mr Rimmer's mother used to ritually repeat the phrase *100% best butter* shortly after opening a packet. Mr Rimmer reflects on the benefit of the adjective *best* as he brings down the lid of the house with a clank. The lesson goes as planned, that is, until Eva reminds Mr Rimmer that her examination is on Tuesday next week and that today is to be their penultimate lesson together.

Eva's dark eyes narrow as she informs him that she has changed her mind about studying A' level English. Eva is clearly nervous; she keeps tucking an imaginary wisp of dark hair behind her right ear which, like the other, protrudes outwards, just in front of her two customary pigtails. Eva explains that she is worried that she will not be able to manage the workload and wants to try a BTEC course in Film Studies instead.

At times like these, Mr Rimmer can be very patient – it's a natter of confidence. He explains slowly and carefully to Eva, why this course of action is not the best route for her to take. 'You are more than capable. The workload is not that much if you keep up with it.'. Eva's letterbox smile puts Mr Rimmer in the picture.

Eva has made her mind up. She thanks Mr Rimmer in the customary manner before pressing the crumpled stash into the palm of his hand.

Mr Rimmer watches Eva leave in her mother's car. Eva waves with nervous enthusiasm. Her mother waves without even looking at him; she is doing so with her right arm outstretched across Eva's chest - her head is turned in the opposite direction, she is looking over her left shoulder before pulling away.

Indoors, Mr Rimmer busies himself tidying his back room. He affectionately brushes his right palm across the warm velvet-red seat before composing himself. He walks about the kitchen unaware his left hand has made a fist. On occasions like these, Mr Rimmer's mother would sit him down and give him a nice cup of tea with plenty of sugar. As a child, this was often on school nights. Mrs Rimmer's mother believed a nice cup of tea could solve most things in life.

Sitting now in the front-room of his house, in his favourite armchair, Mr Rimmer decides against watching television. He picks up the Radio Times; as customary, he pushes back his spectacles onto the bridge of his nose and is about to circle his favourite programmes for the week when something catches his eye. Mr Rimmer catches sight of the local paper beneath, the Southport Visitor; he gazes momentarily at the headline: **TEENAGER'S BODY FOUND IN MARSHLAND**

Mr Rimmer hesitantly picks up the newspaper and reads the front page:

THOUSANDS of tributes have been paid to the family of a teenage girl whose body was found face down in the middle of the Marshide marshland .

The grim discovery was made at 7a.m. by an elderly dog walker. Detective Sergeant Shakespeare from Merseyside C.I.D. later confirmed that 16-year-old Mary-Eloise Chambers had been strangled.

Mary-Eloise Chambers was a sixth-form student at Stanley High; she was due to return this week to continue her AS studies. Headteacher, Caroline Hart made this statement earlier today: *'Mary-Eloise was about to complete her first year; she was a much-loved member of our school community. She was bright, intelligent and had a bubbly personality. Mary-Eloise had a zest for life and often looked out for others. Her friends and teachers are deeply shocked by news of this tragedy; our hearts go out to her family and friends.'.*

A tribute page on Facebook, R.I.P. Mary-Eloise Chambers, has already attracted thousands of comments; the posts were made by the many devastated friends of the popular teenager - one described her as 'the life and soul of any party.'.

Forensic officers arrived at the scene before the area was cordoned off for investigation. It is believed a small number of items were found near the body. Officers are trying to ascertain if they are in any way connected to the teenager in question. Detective Inspector Folkard from the

Merseyside CID made this brief statement to the press: *'We can confirm that a post-mortem examination was carried out earlier today and that the deceased has been formally identified. The investigation is on-going. Anyone with any information, however insignificant it may seem, should call Merseyside C.I.D. on 0151 777 2263 or Crimestoppers on 0800 555 111.'.*

Mr Rimmer shakes his head from side to side; he thinks of Eva and other past students who have dedicated so many hours to their studies. Jennifer for example, is now at Ormskirk University; she is not far off completing her final year. Jennifer is training to become an English teacher, like Mr Rimmer. Jennifer is very intelligent; she still calls on occasion.

Mary-Eloise. Mary-Eloise was different; she was quite capable, and very loyal. Sadly she was naïve too. Mary-Eloise wanted to eventually settle down and get married and have children. Mr Rimmer tuts three times before shaking once more his head from side to side. 'Mary, Mary quite contrary.'. Mr Rimmer is standing now. He looks ahead, out from his wide bay window. 'And now Eva. What a waste. What a waste of my time.'.

Mr Rimmer decides to take a walk before his evening meal; he takes the binoculars from the kitchen window-sill and leaves through the back door. His mother warned him there'd be days like these – days when all his planning and hard work would come to nothing.

6

'HER-MI-O-NE JANE CUM-MINGS! Where-are-you?'. Her mother would often bellow, stipulating each and every syllable. Inspector Folkard smiled to herself recalling an almost forgotten memory of a time when her mother had castigated her following her deliberate disappearance under a large, round, white table-clothed counter at her Aunty Jones' wedding. Although her brother Philip had also hidden beneath the counter too, he had managed to escape, as usual, unnoticed. Her mother had smacked her backside good and proper.

Seven times. Seven times, a smack for every syllable: 'Her-mi-o-ne Jane Cum-mings!' How times have changed, she thought to herself. Inspector Folkard shook her head from side to side. An amused look had temporarily frozen on her ovalish face; her closed mouth made a large smile: the right-hand side of her mouth had lifted upwards making her thick lips tilt.

A light knock at her office door alerted Inspector Folkard to the time: 8:00am – the first meeting of the week: feet down off the desk, a job to be done. Sergeant Shakespeare, looking a little worse for wear, entered in a hurry making her usual cut-throat gesture to signal the arrival of the Chief Superintendent. Briefing over, roasted and peppered for the day's investigation, Inspector Folkard emerged from her office amused by her sergeant's trance-like manner. Sergeant Shakespeare ignored the jibes from the less ambitious crowd lolloping like punch bags in the corner of the incident room. A sidelong glance was sufficient; the pack, without more ado, settled back to work.

The drive along Southport's sea-front promenade was truly pleasant for the time of year; recently, there had been nothing but rain. May showers had followed April showers; these had followed the February and January showers – so many showers, so much rain. Today, the sun was almost shining; at times it hid shyly behind greyish-blue clouds – peeping in and out, playing a game. Seagulls flickered noisily about the shore – the tide was in.

Door to door enquiries had so far flagged up sweet nothing: today's interview, Mr Bernard Rimmer, English private tutor to the deceased. Although Mr Rimmer no longer taught Mary-Eloise; he was one of the last people to see her alive, something about her calling in the night before she went out to ask for a reference – a job at a newsagents, somewhere in Churchtown village.

Inspector Folkard pointed to the left, Blackpool Tower; Sergeant Shakespeare nodded but did not look up. She rarely made much conversation before 9:00 a.m.. Inspector Folkard learned that her colleague had recently been out on a hen-night – her younger sister's. Despite it having taken place two nights ago, she still wasn't feeling so good: her younger sister had referred to her as a light-weight. Inspector Folkard instinctively pulled the vehicle over at the very moment Sergeant Shakespeare had suddenly grabbed her left forearm. There was no need to apologise.

Turning right, down Marshide Road by the disused sand factory, the Sergeant alerted Inspector Folkard to the marshland on both sides. Mary-Eloise's body had been discovered on the left bank, not too far from the pavement. About a quarter of a mile further down was Mr Rimmer's attractive mustard-like bungalow.

Homely, thought Sergeant Shakespeare. Very homely, thought Inspector Folkard. The restored outer brick wall prevented passers-by from treading on the spectacular sight of the mediumish rectangular garden. A large pond was to the centre of the lawn, two large glass balls bobbing up and down in the cool water; to the left, a little higher, another two much smaller ponds, a smaller bobbing ball in each.

For a few moments they leaned on the wide metallic mustard gate to the very right of the brick wall, the diagonal view even more captivating – koi carp fish skittering about, flirting close to the surface.

Inspector Folkard knew little about gardening, but she wished Mr Rimmer could come round to her abode and paint a similar picture onto her own orderly, practical and unadventurous landscape. Those oriental lilies, wow... beautiful, red but not quite like a poppy... beautiful. Below each of the two bay windows at either side of the front porch, window-boxes, stained tastefully with a medium green paint similar to the green colour they use job lot around France. Both boxes contained a variety of plants that had only just recently been introduced into the soil – green foliage mostly. By summer, Inspector Folkard knew instinctively the window-boxes would be packed with impressive, trailing flora. The matching shutters at either side of the windows looked as old as the property. Lovely.

No-one in. They glanced up and down the road in unison, a double-act. They were about to turn away when an all too friendly, distant voice beckoned them both. The male voice was coming from the house to the right of Mr Rimmer's abode, when facing it directly. The elderly neighbour waved with some enthusiasm. Neighbours, thought Inspector Folkard, everybody needs good neighbours.

A smiling man of more than sixty years of age, short and a little stocky – bald on top except for the sides, came trundling through the far-too-small porch of his semi-detached abode, along the garden path and directly up to the single wooden gate, his left arm outstretched – an open palm – probably sweaty.

'Albert Conway, President of the Neighbourhood Watch.'.

Mr Conway attempted to casually lean on his thin wooden gate. Sergeant Shakespeare began to take down some details – Mr Rimmer, secondary school teacher – Walton. 'Should return between 4:00-4:15 p.m.'. Inspector Folkard thanked Mr Conway for taking the time to speak to them. Mr Conway, feeling much happier with himself, was about to walk away, along with his air of importance, when Inspector Folkard wiped the smugness from his face and made enquiries about his whereabouts on Saturday night.

Sergeant Shakespeare failed to hold back a grin; she then opened Mr Rimmer's well-oiled gate, walked up the paved path and posted the usual C.I.D. calling card through the porch's lower letterbox. In the windowsill, a pretty young fuchsia caught her eye, coral pink and purple, exquisite; behind. a gruesome plant, a mother-in-law tongue cacti. Behind it, was a rabbit's foot or tail or something furry hanging on a nail. Sergeant Shakespeare father had possessed a few of these over the years – they were meant to bring good luck. Not for the rabbit, she used to insist.

Later, despite the Sergeant's mocking comments, Inspector Folkard reminded her that nosey neighbours were one of the most reliable sources of information, often filling in the gaps needed to make an arrest– every detail mattered, no matter how small – if she had wasted time at university watching television, like she had many moons ago, she'd know that everybody needs good neighbours. Sergeant Shakespeare nodded in agreement – she was already feeling a lot better.

7

DESPITE HIS MANY years in the teaching profession, Mr Rimmer believes the job doesn't get any easier. Mr Rimmer always leaves school as soon as he can. Already feeling more relaxed, Mr Rimmer heads back home. The back roads wind and bend through various small villages until he passes Formby. He is short of a mile from the coastal road that will lead him directly home. Today, Mr Rimmer can clearly see Blackpool Pier; presented like a postcard, it is an impression of a town framed in two circular snapshots – the fairground to the pier's right, snaking its way amongst the landscape.

Mr Rimmer's grandfather used to work at Southport's fairground, before he was born – Mr Rimmer doesn't like fairgrounds, they make him feel nauseous. His grandfather warned him not to go on The Great White – all wood – not safe – one day there would be a fatality. The Great White has since been demolished. There was a long-standing protest, it made front headlines in the Southport Visitor.

As a teenager, Mr Rimmer once went to Southport fairground with a school friend. Mr Rimmer didn't have many friends, but Thomas Dutton had been a good friend – he never teased him about his weight. Mr Rimmer remembers sitting neatly inside the Caterpillar Ride, on the outer side. The green canvas-like roof came over them, from right to left before fastening tight-shut.

For a while Mr Rimmer smiles to himself. He remembers that he really enjoyed himself, mostly because of the undulating movements – and despite the dark, he felt safe and secure. When the ride quickened the plastic seat forced Thomas to slide adjacent into Mr Rimmer. They were sitting closely, in near darkness – not scary at all – safe, like the rocking motion of a train journey. All Mr Rimmer could see going round was a variety of footwear.

Mr Rimmer is now thinking about how much one can tell about a person from just their choice of footwear. His mother went through a phase of wearing the wrong footwear – blisters day in and night out. Then Mr Rimmer remembered how his father later told him that The Caterpillar was a ride for babies. Mr Rimmer closes his eyes before opening them again; without realising his left hand has changed into a fist. A few moments later he is feeling calmer. His mother loved the fairground.

After the ride, they ran into a group of other kids; Thomas had talked for an ever so long while with two older girls he knew from the year above. Mr Rimmer leaned uneasily against a blue bin, shuffling; he wished at the time he had had pockets, he didn't know what to do with his clammy hands.

Mr Rimmer remembers some of the words to a song in the charts. There was a spinning ride directly behind the laughing girls: *'...someone get me out of here...get me out of here...'*– number one in the charts, Top of the Pops: *'IIII... woon't let... youu down, woon't let... youu down again...'*.

Mr Rimmer cannot recall either of their names now; he can't even remember *her* name, the laughing girl with the teeth. The ride kept spinning round and round and the seats moved up and down, up and down. When the laughing girl with the teeth as straight and as white as a picket fence suggested a ride, he declined – Thomas didn't.

The one he liked least, wore an electric blue biker-type jacket; she had long ropy hair, it looked messy. Mr Rimmer wanted to make conversation; he wanted to be more like Thomas. He tried to speak on at least two occasions but the words just wouldn't come out.

Frustrated by these memories, Mr Rimmer shakes his head from side to side – the sky is losing its brightness; a passer-by, being pulled by an over-weight Dalmatian nods as his car nearly passes his own home – 260 Marshide Road. His parents had lived there all their lives, his father's parents had lived there too, most of their lives – they were all dead now, dead as doorposts.

Mr Rimmer parks his car up the drive before shutting the mustard gate; he pauses momentarily with his back resting on it to look over the large pond, almost the width of his quaint bungalow. From this angle, the bobbing balls look menacingly at him. He admires the red-oriental lilies for a short while; the decorative koi carp are glittering as they skitter occasionally to the surface. Mr Rimmer decides that the porch could do with a lick of paint – he needs to move the *mother-in-law's tongue*; it's getting too big for the windowsill.

Albert Conway and his mother Nancy, next door neighbours, are not sitting as usual at their single front-room bay window. Albert has never really left home; he once married his next door neighbour, Miriam; he was her god-father at sixteen. They are now divorced. Poor Albert. His daughter Anne never visits, not even on Father's Day. Mr Rimmer remembers unintentionally overhearing a few conversations between Mrs Conway and his mother about the divorce, something about a court order, an unpleasant judge and social services had been involved. When Mr Rimmer asked his mother years later about his family, she just shook her head and said it had all been very unpleasant – that Albert had not seen his family for a long time. Mr Rimmer cannot remember whether he had overheard in the past, something about him playing away. The gruesome thought leads him to indoors.

Mr Rimmer looks ahead as he closes his porch door. Stanley High School is almost directly opposite his home; Mr Rimmer went to Stanley High and hated it. In the first week, he had his face punched in. By the end of the second term he was being bullied almost every day: *'fatty, fatty, mama's little pig...squeal home, squeal home fatty, mama's little pig.'*.

Mr Rimmer squealed home, five years on the run.

Mr Rimmer's father died of a heart-attack when Mr Rimmer was in his third year at Stanley High. The bullies went easy on him for a while. Mr Rimmer had come home from school early to a hushed silence; strangers shook his palm and handed out condolences. His mother blubbered between angry, tearless sighs. Mr Rimmer decided then and there not to trouble his mother any further.

The Rimmer abode has now been restored to how he best remembers it, when his father was alive: the happy photographs helped. There's the one of them all together, the one with grandfather Rimmer, a few years before he died. Mr Rimmer's mother is looking at his father, leaning into him, he is smiling, his arm around her. Mr Rimmer is in a cardboard box – apparently the only way of keeping him still at the time. The house looked good, all the wood stained a dark brown and the rest – mustard. The windows with their shutters though didn't have boxes at the time. When they had been added, he could not recall. He did remember however, after his father had died, a painter coming round a lot and that he was the one who painted the shutters and window-boxes in a French herb-like green.

Mr Rimmer looks away from the school. He is now looking out onto the front garden. He smiles as he acknowledges his own efforts: he is re-united with his haven. How beautiful the garden will look come spring. His mother used to spend a lot of time in the front garden – she preferred it. His father tendered the back garden, took him hours,

Mr Rimmer's thoughts turn to another photograph; he isn't quite sure why he still keeps this one – he is sure he had thrown this one away once. It is a photograph taken both after his father had died and after the painter came along. His mother stands not far from the front porch – the two smaller ponds are now filled in with a variety of common manageable plants. Despite his age, Mr Rimmer is clinging to his mother's upper sleeve – in turn she holds him close but her eyes are not upon him – she is smiling at someone else.

There have been too many visitors to the house in the first five years or so, following his father's death. Mr Rimmer was always on his best behaviour. Living so nearby to the school wasn't easy – everyone knew everything about everyone – especially the bullies. Mr Rimmer was glad to have later attended Christ the King's Sixth Form. It was at least two bus rides away from where he lived.

Much later, Mr Rimmer is feeling tired: time for bed. Time seems to have passed quickly; this happens from time to time. It is a little like when one is driving and suddenly they realise they are close to their destination – not knowing how they got there in the first place. Mr Rimmer heads upstairs with his customary cup of cocoa – he is weary and feels distressed, his left arm is hurting a little. Upstairs, he looks into his mother's bedroom before removing his spectacles with his left hand, he turns his fist forward so that he is able to wipe his eyes with the back of his wrist.

Tomorrow is Tuesday, no students on a Tuesday. Once undressed, Mr Rimmer remembers the *mother-in-law's-tongue* in the porch. Determined to move her, he retraces his steps, walks down the staircase that runs through the middle of the house, through the front room, to the front door that leads out into the porch.

As he reaches for the cacti with its very long sharp leaves, a white rectangular business card catches his eye. Mr Rimmer puts down the monstrosity before casually picking it up. He reads it and, for a few moments looks outdoors. It is a quiet night, streetlamps both to the left and right of the house stand silently in an orderly manner amongst the darkness.

Mr Rimmer surveys the business card once more: Detective Inspector H.A. Folkard: Merseyside C.I.D..

He forgets the cacti with the sharp tongues; instead, he returns indoors to converse with his mother; his mother always knows what to do.

8

TUESDAY. SERGEANT SHAKESPEARE pointed to the left towards Blackpool Pier; she had always detested fairgrounds. As a child, she had been sick on almost every ride, especially on the ones that go round and round. She was feeling a lot better now; sitting in the driving seat she made a gesture to her Inspector about an advancing vehicle from behind. A yob on a motorbike semi-circled around their unmarked car; his passenger giving them the finger. Charming stated Sergeant Shakespeare. I did that once, thought Inspector Folkard.

The marshes looked eerie at this time of day, eerie yet beautiful, noisy too. Birds flickered about in unison, making different rah-rah shapes, much like a synchronised swim. Inspector Folkard liked this early hour of the evening, especially in late May; there was something mysterious yet magical about it all, like the birth of something yet to come. The photographs had somehow captured the beauty that enveloped Mary-Eloise's corpse that morning, much better than the ones taken at the local tip where a female body had been discovered last August. In Southport, even in not so nearby towns such as Blackpool, murder was generally uncommon. Inspector Folkard could count the total number of murders that had taken place in the last five years on one hand.

Mr Rimmer, approximately five foot ten inches, dark-haired male in his fifties, stout, wearing spectacles, dressed in what seemed to be his work attire, stood framed in his left-bay window as though he had been expecting their visit.

Sergeant Shakespeare was amused by the scene coming from Mr Conway's downstairs only front window. Mr Conway sat at a table by the window with a somewhat older female version of himself – she too had little hair. They watched the arrival of the detectives like a pair of Siamese cats, upright and static – only their heads moved. Inspector Folkard casually exited the car ignoring the curious passer-by with the over-weight Dalmatian. Once on the path, she quickly glanced into Mr Rimmer's classic car – very nice, sky-blue with wooden features both inside and out – doors that open like shutters at the back - very clean, very clean both inside and out.

Mr Rimmer greeted them both in the manner one does when a pre-arranged engagement has taken place. First entered the Inspector, then Sergeant Shakespeare. Mr Rimmer shook hands with them both, first with the Sergeant then with the Inspector; he then proceeded to invite them both into his front-room – the one on the right, if one faces the house. A plate of custard creams was at the centre of a small rectangular coffee table. The Sergeant declined a hot drink whilst Inspector Folkard remarked that she was gasping for a nice cup of tea. Mr Rimmer was about to say something when he changed his mind.

As soon as Mr Rimmer exited, Inspector Folkard gave her the signal for the Sergeant to follow. Inspector Folkard paced herself about the room, filming with her eyes, at times stopping to look out from the front window - a large school, almost opposite, loomed menacingly over two of the neighbouring abodes.

Although unstirred, Inspector Folkard had not noticed Mr Rimmer standing directly behind her, tea in hand, small chip to the handle. Mr Rimmer informed Inspector Folkard that the nice Sergeant had gone off to use the toilet, apparently hadn't been feeling too good recently. It reminded Inspector Folkard of a scene in Jurassic Park - one of her daughter's favourite Jurassic Park movies. In a later scene in the movie, the dinosaur outwits the expert – who, impressed by the beast's intelligence, compliments it by calling it a clever girl, that is, before he is ripped painfully apart.

Impressed by Mr Rimmer's stealth, Inspector Folkard began a pointless conversation about the weather before casually stepping left and picking up a framed photograph of an attractive woman wearing a red dress from the top of the television set. Inspector

Folkard sensed a fragment of discomposure in Mr Rimmer's voice as he informed the Inspector that the portrait was of his mother. For a very short time, Inspector Folkard was arrested by her deep brown penetrating eyes; she was beautiful – large lips, thick dark curled hair – plenty of cleavage.

Mr Rimmer offered the Inspector a seat; he consistently sipped his tea before responding to each question. Mr Rimmer was happy to help; he sat in what seemed to be his favourite armchair before he began. Mary-Eloise had been one of his better students – always arrived on time, rarely cancelled – A* candidate. Mr Rimmer was very sure when he had last seen Mary-Eloise. It was only this Friday; she had called in to ask him for a reference – a reference for the post of a part-time weekend counter assistant at Colin's Newsagents in Churchtown – the one on the corner, by the traffic lights.

Sergeant Shakespeare entered the room, tea-cup now in hand. 'Smashing cup of tea, just what I needed.'. Sitting opposite across from Mr Rimmer, the three sat like the Bermuda triangle, the striking antique clock above the fire place ticking, ticking away. Mary-Eloise's visit had been a quick one, Mr Rimmer continued – his eyes glancing at his mother's portrait - he'd told her that he'd let her know when the reference had been completed – he was more than happy to help – lovely young lady – tragic.

Mr Rimmer had been shocked when he had seen the story splashed all over the Southport Visitor. 'Shocking – her poor parents.'. Closing his eyes, Mr Rimmer shook his head from side to side before he opened them again. Mr Rimmer was very sorry that he couldn't help more – he pushed his spectacles back onto the bridge of his nose.

Inspector Folkard sat back at the point when Sergeant Shakespeare asked Mr Rimmer about his private tuition - making notes, dates, times – all in all, Mr Rimmer had taught eleven students over the last four years. At present, there was only one – a year 11 female student – Monday's at seven.

Inspector Folkard sat perfectly still, her gaze transfixed on Mr Rimmer. She had already noted his large chunky hands, and long fat fingers with neat nails – maybe too long for a man - no sign of a wedding ring. Although he was probably in his fifties, he still looked strong enough to strangle – if his hands were anything to go by. Inspector Folkard thanked Mr Rimmer for his time. Mr Rimmer stood up. He adjusted his mother's portrait before offering a steady hand to the Inspector – steady yet clammy, thought the Inspector before he gently prised his palm away from the Inspector's confident clutch.

Inspector Folkard moved towards the porch before casually stopping to ask Mr Rimmer how long he had lived alone. Mr Rimmer immediately replied that it had been too long to remember. For a short and uncomfortable period of time, Inspector Folkard refused to budge from the framed doorway. Sergeant Shakespeare, accustomed to the Inspector's obstinacy, looked to Mr Rimmer for an answer. There was no escape. Mr Rimmer, looked with irritation at the prickly, tall cacti pointing menacingly over the Inspector's left shoulder. Mr Rimmer thought for a brief period of time before responding – Christmas – 2002 – ten years ago.

Sergeant Shakespeare followed Inspector Folkard out into the front garden. Mr Rimmer was about to distract himself by checking on his favourite young fuchsia when Sergeant Shakespeare turned around and called over. 'Mr Rimmer? Did you get round to writing Mary-Eloise's reference?'. Mr Rimmer paused momentarily before shaking his head quickly from side to side. 'No. I did not.'. The metallic mustard gate closed behind them. As they turned about they noticed Mr Rimmer had already stepped indoors – a headache looming in the distance.

Sergeant Shakespeare was sure to wave to Mr and Mrs Conway; Mr Conway, delighted to be acknowledged, waved in return. Mrs Conway gave her a bobbing sort of nod. On their approach to their maroon vehicle, an early evening flourish of midges intermingled ahead. Instinctively, they both scratched at their hair. Inspector Folkard's mother had told her numerous times, especially when she first started out in the police force, that she should wear her hair tied back. 'More professional.'. How right she was. She was right about most things. Untidy snail trails glistened below a pot of holsters. The evening sky reddened and gulls swarmed overhead. The porch door had now been firmly locked behind them.

9

ON WEDNESDAY LATE afternoon, Mr Rimmer receives a text from Rachel, Eva's mother. Mr Rimmer disapproves of her over-familiarity – she always puts a kiss at the end of a text and often uses those silly icons with smiles. Mr Rimmer suddenly sits down in the manner one does when they have an aching back or have been informed of a bereavement, his left arm bent, hand on hip, thumb forward, the rest of his fingers spread backwards, in peacock fashion.

Eva will not be coming for her last lesson this coming Monday. The mother, who knows-it-all, is very, very grateful for all he has done, she would recommend him to anyone. Eva would pop in sometime; she has a gift for Mr Rimmer. Mr Rimmer gazes for a short while out of the window. Mr Rimmer has a gift for her.

Mr Rimmer looks to the back-room; upon entry, he looks at the empty chair with its velvety seat before composing a shopping list. The cupboards are bare – although there are plenty of tins. Milk. Sugar. Custard creams. Eggs. His mother would say: *You have to break a few eggs to make an omelette.* Mr Rimmer contemplates going shopping when it occurs to him that Eva might call in tonight with her gift. He decides the shopping can wait until tomorrow.

Yesterday, and very fortunately, after a long day in school and a visit from C.I.D., Mr Rimmer had walked to the end of his road, to Churchtown Village, in order to acquire a gift for Eva. He had turned left, shutting the gate with a clamber, waved at Albert and his mother in their window, them waving back like muppets. Mr Rimmer was pondering on what to buy Eva, when it began to rain, not heavily really, just a light shower.

With some resistance, he had crossed over and took refuge in the porch of St Patrick's Church, the church his parents were married in. Hushed and rushed his father used to whisper, hushed and rushed. Mr Rimmer can still picture his father saying it whilst holding a newspaper in one hand and using the pointing finger of his other hand, perpendicular to his lips.

Mr Rimmer stopped going to church as soon as he could get away with it. Father Hickey looked like a crow and leaned over you like one too. His monotonous Sunday lectures droned on and on; listeners lived in fear of exiting the church early following communion. You had to shake his hand before you left the front steps of the church. His hands were always ice-cold.

There had been no point in waiting for the shower to clear, Mr Rimmer needed to move on before the shop shut at 6:00. In the cluttered shop, an elderly gentleman smiled politely as Mr Rimmer fumbled for the right gift. Coloured tights. Feather pens. Mr Rimmer examined a mug before rejecting it: *Eva; meaning evangelical, a little angel: loyal, kind and hard-working.* A few moments later and Mr Rimmer had pricked his thumb on the small sharp pin of a silver brooch – a tessellation of circular flowers in a circle, much like a Christmas wreath.

Mr Rimmer stands up from his favourite chair and looks at his thumb, all better now. He looks at the gift wrapped in paisley patterned paper with no card and thinks of past gifts he has given to other students. Possibly a few moments pass before he goes upstairs to shower.

Mr Rimmer is careful to leave his bedroom door ajar so that he may hear any callers. Strangely the evening darkness seems to have consumed the entire house. Mr Rimmer switches on some lights. As he enters his bedroom he sees his wardrobe open. Upon closing the door, he notices one of his mother's dresses, the blue one with the embroidery and long sleeves laid out on his bed.

Downstairs, following his shower he heats some home-made pea soup and divides the contents of the pan between two bowls when the door-bell rings. Mr Rimmer quickly puts the bowls in the oven, onto the bottom shelf, before he rushes to the front door. Albert passes Mr Rimmer a package that arrived today, whilst he was in school; he helpfully points out to Mr Rimmer that he has accidentally smeared something green like onto his spectacles.

Albert is also anxious to learn more about the visit from C.I.D. but before he can say another word Mr Rimmer thanks Albert for his kindness and closes the porch door. Albert often collects parcels for him to save him trundling up to the depot on a Saturday morning before 10:00: Albert is very attentive. Mr Rimmer cleans his spectacles with his handkerchief before returning to his business. Much later than usual, he clambers up the stairs to his three-quarter bed; switching his electric blanket on, brings him much comfort.

Once in bed he opens the parcel; he is quite sure he did not order its contents, yet upon a re-inspection he agrees that the parcel is clearly addressed to him. Mr Rimmer sighs; he's been here before – he is so tired that he feels as though he could sleep for days. He thinks of Eva and her mother who is always saying sorry and sounds so polite but still drops Eva off late. Mr Rimmer thinks of INSET day tomorrow – something about Child Protection Guidelines and Every Child Matters; he falls asleep with his left hand in the shape of a fist.

10

BACK AT THE station the incident board was filling up with information on the murder of Mary-Eloise Chambers. A true likeness of Mr Rimmer had become a recent addition. Until they knew different, he was the last man to see Mary-Eloise Chambers alive. She had called in to ask for a reference about a quarter to eight.

According to the autopsy report, the estimated time of death had been recorded as anytime between ten in the evening to three the following morning - the marsh water not helping with the usual body temperature examinations. If his story was true, and she had just 'popped in' then it would be likely that she had only spent a few minutes at the porch door before setting off to join her friends in town. None of Mr Rimmer's neighbours had seen Mary-Eloise that evening. By seven, the sky would have been at its darkest. Nobody in fact had seen her arrive. Neither had anyone seen her leave. Mary-Eloise may have caught a bus into town, but according to the bus drivers, that were driving the two buses that travel via Marshide Road into town, they believed that she had not got on their bus – although they could not be entirely sure. Coincidentally they had both stated that one teenager looked much like any other.

The newsagent's manager, Mr Colin De Silva, who spoke good English despite his heavy Sri Lankan accent, had not seen Mary-Eloise. He confirmed that he had asked her to gain a reference so that she could be considered for a part-time job and that she had stated she would get one before the end of the week. In reality, the job was hers – he had spoken to Mary-Eloise on many an occasion; she only lived up the road – came from a good family. 'She was a very polite young lady. My wife had cried when she heard of her death.'.

Inspector Folkard left the office late that night. Sergeant Shakespeare had been busy interviewing all day, then co-ordinating statements. Tomorrow they would carry out the dislikeable yet necessary job of interviewing the Chambers. Although neither were a suspect, they could not rule out that Mary-Eloise had in fact returned home. Most victims were after all, killed by someone they knew.

When Inspector Folkard arrived home, she was feeling weary. She knew without even texting her husband, without any prompting, upon her arrival, a bubbly bath would be waiting as well as candles and the offer of a foot massage. A kiss on the forehead from her Walter always made her smile. Although he was a few years younger, some had remarked that he in fact looked a few years older. Her brother Philip often stated that it was her fault – the grey hair – that she worried him sick, staying out all hours.

Hermione Folkard thought she was one of the luckiest women she'd ever known. Many of her female colleagues had expressed bitterly over the years that the chores of the household had rarely been shared – many had ended divorced. Hermione Folkard knew she had it all. Without her Walter, she would not be able to concentrate nor focus on her job; without him, she would not have come so far in her career.

Zita was fast asleep in bed. Hermione Folkard kissed her twice before she stood over her for a short while. She lay on her side with her thumb in her mouth – her wide and thick lips loosely around her right thumb. Underneath, as always, lay her large elephant Ellie who had for as long as they could remember taken the place of a pillow – a small mouse trapped at the end of her trunk which had curled all around it. Her long, thick, dark brown hair matched her large eyes. Like always, her mass of untameable hair would lie in all directions – how very beautiful she was, the baby of the family. She looked a lot like her mother-in-law – a Columbian beauty.

Darcy was still awake. She would more likely join her in the bathroom as soon as she'd got in the bath. There was much to talk about in Year Six – the pressure of S.A.T.'s, her interest in the same boy who was unlikely to ask her out and the latest progress on her newly acquired tablet game: Minecraft.

Before she headed for the bathroom, Hermione entered Darcy's bedroom. As always, Slipper, the female Labrador, was asleep at the foot of her bed. When she heard her footsteps, she awoke - making a notable effort to welcome her home.

This involved remaining still on her side and thumping her tail loudly in response to the usual one sided conversation. Tramp, the male Labrador, must have been outdoors in the garden for he could always be counted upon to welcome her in style. It was a relief to undress without worrying about the amount of dog hair he would leave on her clothing, the thick dart-like hairs impossible to conceal.

As Hermione Folkard turned around, she noticed that Zita had left a picture for her as a present on her pillow. It was a picture of a small elephant crying tears like the rain. The tiny elephant was standing next to the mummy elephant. Inside, the message read: I MIS YU MUMY. Hermione's eyes stung – she tried to swallow but she couldn't. Leave had been cancelled last weekend; she couldn't wait for this weekend; in fact, she couldn't wait for the summer, their long break in France, far away from it all.

Hermione Folkard then headed for the bathroom; not long after Darcy joined her. So much could happen in a child's day; it all meant so much to a child of her age. Darcy would often text her mother during her working day. Sometimes Harry would call into the station. They were in many ways old enough to understand the demands of the job. But Zita, at the age of five, was still too young – to her, when it came to spending time with her mama, everything was unfair.

Despite her age, Darcy, who was ten going on sixteen, and who looked very much like her mother with the exception of her blue eyes, was able to comfort her mother who apologised once more for the lost weekend. They had in fact had a great weekend. Dad had taken them on Saturday to Knowsley Safari Park to see Max the elephant, who had only just been born a month earlier. On Sunday they had gone to the Trafford Centre where they had purchased some new clothing, an item each from the Disney Store and more unnecessary make-up (mostly lip glosses that tasted like what they smelled). Moving quickly on, she needed her mother to listen to her sing; she was after all going to win the X Factor one day. That was one thing about Zita – once asleep, there was no waking her.

By eleven, Hermione and Walter were in bed. Not many series could distract her from the day's heavy workload but the latest episode of Sons of Anarchy would have her both laughing and in shock as the latest plot line was revealed. By the end of the episode she would often state her workload was incomparably easier in the usually safe seaside resort of Southport.

11

MR RIMMER HAS never liked INSET days. He'd rather teach than be talked at. Worst of all are the enforced ice-breaker activities. The last INSET day was the worst ever yet: Snowballing. Everyone in the room wrote a noun on a piece of paper then after a count of three, threw the ball to another colleague. They then added an adjective. The exercise went on until the ice was truly broken alright. As usual, the snowballs headed mostly his way, although that time there were no stones in the middle - small comfort.

Mr Rimmer doesn't much like talking to others outside his department; for years, he has deliberately avoided learning the names of new additions to the staff list. At a quarter to nine, Mr Rimmer enters the school hall. As usual he struggles to mingle amongst the large number of teaching and non-teaching staff. Holding a coffee cup helps - he is less likely to perspire. Mr Rimmer never knows what to do with his empty hands. Eventually he finds a seat next to a colleague in his own department.

At nine, headteacher, Anthony Jessop greets the staff and briefs them on the day's In-Service Training. Mr

Rimmer has never really liked Anthony Jessop. Mr Jessop rarely speaks to Mr Rimmer; he rarely speaks to anyone unless he wants something. Mr Jessop finishes his power talk by reminding his staff that his door is always open. Whilst Mr Jessop speaks, Mr Rimmer recalls unexpectedly a painful memory: the week his mother died.

Mr Rimmer returned to work, following a four week absence; staff at St William's High had been very supportive. That week, Mr Jessop had passed Mr Rimmer on the corridor, on several occasions; he never once offered his condolences. Mr Jessop has since been nominated for an O.B.E. His father used to say O.B.E. stood for Other Bugger's Efforts.

Mr Rimmer feels angry at Mr Jessop's lack of sincerity. Superficial to the core, he stands every briefing with his right leg crossed over his left – waving his hands about. When Ofsted visited a couple of months after his mother's death, Mr Jessop, accompanied by two unattractive female inspectors, was about to pass Mr Rimmer on the corridor when suddenly he stopped and turned towards him. Mr Rimmer was so taken aback that, like a muppet, he responded with grateful enthusiasm, like the child in a short line, waiting and praying to be picked for the team.

At first, the morning is going far too slowly. A Kagan activity requires them all to now work in pairs. Mr Rimmer considers the meaning of the word Kagan; for some reason he thought this to be a form of pelvic floor exercise. The rest of the session has been set aside in order to explore the purpose behind the Child Protection and Safeguarding Code of Conduct. Later, Mr Rimmer is feeling more relaxed. He looks at his watch and smiles when he realises there are only forty minutes before the session will come to an end and lunch will be served. He nods in agreement when his colleague Raymond Belchier, highlights a sentence on the document: *those with regular contact with children and young people are in a position to get to know those individuals well, to develop trusting relationships.*

Following some useful feedback from each table, the trainer from the council reminds everyone participating, that children and young people often share confidences and concerns with adults. Mr Rimmer nods. Mr Rimmer knows this to be true. For a few seconds Mr Rimmer thinks about someone he once knew well. What he remembers suddenly upsets him; he tries hard to concentrate on what is being said to avoid reliving a painful memory. Mr Rimmer's left arm is hurting now – he really could do with a nice cup of tea. Perspiring a little, he pushes back his Spectacles; he makes a concealed effort to breathe rhythmically. Although at first this does not work, he eventually feels more settled. Although some colleagues have looked over on occasion, they continue to ignore him.

The Child Protection Officer continues to click her way through a power point on the Code of Conduct. Unbeknown to everyone else, Mr Rimmer is thinking about an old friend: Alice Lau. Alice had shared several concerns about her step-father – her mother was an alcoholic and her father was living in a flat following a recent separation. Michael Farnsworth, her step-father, has since been jailed. Alice said once that Mr Rimmer had been her saviour.

At lunch Mr Rimmer re-joins the bosom of his department; he sits in his favourite chair drinking out of his favourite mug: *Best Teacher* – a gift from Jennifer. The afternoon is a blur – Mr Rimmer dreams of Jennifer – he is watching a movie with her – his arm around her shoulder – other men look on enviously.

Mr Rimmer waves to the office girls as he passes reception on his way out: as always, they politely wave back. Today hasn't been that bad after all – Mr Rimmer cannot wait to get home. Mr Rimmer clambers into his light-blue classic car; he resolves to play something up-beat on the way home, The Pretenders it is. Mr Rimmer is sure Eva will call round tonight. Mr Rimmer is excited; he has something to show her.

12

THE LAST FORTY-EIGHT hours revealed little for the investigation team; Mary-Eloise was a popular and likeable character, there appeared to be no skeletons in her cupboard. Inspector Folkard's team had the body, but the absence of a motive never mind a rock-solid suspect gave her little to go on. A follow-up interview with the Chambers was to take place later today; it was unfortunate yet necessary to go over every detail once more: something was missing, something obvious.

Inspector Folkard was ready to go; the drive to the Chambers household would only take about fifteen minutes in total. Inspector Folkard hated to arrive late for any appointment; at twenty to one, she picked up her car keys and headed for the stairs where she met Sergeant Shakespeare on her way down. Apology accepted they headed for their maroon unmarked vehicle; the Inspector lobbing the keys over the bonnet just in time for Sergeant Shakespeare to catch.

Sergeant Shakespeare smiled cheerfully at the Inspector; a brief discussion revealed a new woman in Miss Shakespeare's life – a woman she had met on her sister's hen-night. 'Wendy. She's called Wendy.'. Small talk over, Inspector Folkard reminded her Sergeant not to forget to call Blackpool C.I.D. to request the details and statements on a case where a young female corpse had been found in a tip, also strangled, about the same time: last August.

Cambridge Road displayed such large abodes in comparison to other dwellings on the way to Churchtown; many of these detached Edwardian family homes had now been revamped as either nursing or retirement homes, some had been demolished and apartments built in their place. The road stretched from Churchtown village to almost the centre of Southport town – in between was the very large and luscious Hesketh Park. Although not central in the town, the park existed like a large circular lake. Almost any destination could be accessed from here. It was nearly always busy.

Inspector Folkard once knew a cookery teacher who lived in a beautiful coral pink house on Cambridge Road, the Churchtown end. Inspector Folkard remembers feeling some envy when the one time she was invited back for a cup of tea, she had been taken in by literally its rosy exterior. She still remembers walking through the bright and breezy interior – lots of lemon yellow. It sure had the wow factor. Not long after though, she had had to move again - her husband's job – he often played golf – she couldn't have children – he didn't want to adopt. Despite its grandeur, it was in reality a spacious, lonely and silent house. By the time she'd heard her story and had left the house, she felt no envy at all. There were many things in life that money really couldn't buy.

The trees along the length of the road bore a history of their own; large and thick-trunked, their fat roots swelled above the concrete like octopi. The long, confident branches stretched comfortably across the large and wide road, many meeting along the way. Leaves and younger branches innocently intermingled: all together, an arch for the driver to cruise through. Splinters of sunshine successfully pierced the few triangular gaps; golden leaves flickered about, moving to and fro.

Much like Mr Rimmer's, but on a much grander scale, 313 Cambridge Road bore a magnificent garden, one too that immediately appealed to the eye. The Chambers had clearly spent many years building up each distinctive part of their ornamental front garden. Inspector Folkard pictured a much younger Mary-Eloise running about the garden.

The large and heavy black and golden gate clinked open with ease; the two detectives, ambling up the patterned path, gazed at the manicured lawns both to the path's left and right. Neat rectangles bore large and colourful lion-maned flowers and snapdragons leaned forward in anticipation flirting with their visitors. Antique troths were filled with white, thick leaved trailing geraniums. At the front of the house, hanging baskets deceivingly appeared to have just been thrown together – a meadow of colour: lilacs, pinks, greens. This was a garden that would in the coming months come into its own. At the front door a quaint oblong doorbell

waited patiently for their return.

Almost immediately, the detectives were met by Kate Chambers; she was expecting them. Already notably thinner, she directed the detectives across a wide pale blue and white hall before a long corridor; thin side tables, tastefully standing by the odd chair or chaise lounge, held mostly white flowers or plants that stood mostly within their packaging – the messages had not been removed – maybe not even read. Sympathy cards, bearing more flowers, butterflies, crosses and doves littered every surface.

They walked into the mint green and white lounge, the same room where they had sat all night waiting for their daughter to return, the same room where the detectives had broken the news about the body on the marshland, the same room where Kate and Derek had nursed Mary-Eloise on many a night as a tiny baby.

Once seated and as settled as they could be under the circumstances, Sergeant Shakespeare began to go through past details shared by the Chambers. A little later, she suggested they looked together through recent family albums but Kate Chambers felt strongly it would be impossible - too painful. 'It's too soon. I can't do that. I know I can't'. Inspector Folkard smiled before she requested they re-visit Mary-Eloise's bedroom.

After a few moments, Kate stood up and lead the compassionate party out of the room and up the wide royal blue carpeted stairs, left at the turn, second door on the right. It was obviously too painful for the parents to pass the various framed portraits that existed of their one child. At one point Kate Chambers paused by one of Mary-Eloise in her school uniform and looked as if she were about to speak. Finding no words, she continued.

The contrast from the pale blue and white hallway and landing to Mary-Eloise's bedroom was arresting. The peach and mid-blue L shaped bedroom was bright and breezy, almost energetic. Sergeant Shakespeare made several notes about each possession, their significance – probably none – that was, until Derek mentioned Mr Rimmer's name.

Inspector Folkard had become preoccupied with an ornament on one of Mary-Eloise's bedside tables. It was a colourful miniature merry-go-round with horses on what looked like cocktail sticks - teeth gnashing.

Inspector Folkard reflected on the placement of this small, pretty item. She considered that an item placed so close to where one slept was the sort of thing someone did when they had acquired something recently – a gift, or they were fond of the item or even the person. The less one thought about someone, the further it could find itself. Over the years, Inspector Folkard's own bedside table had acquired more and more items – framed photographs of the children, hand-made keepsakes, notes with crying elephants.

Derek had rarely spoken to Mr Rimmer in the last two years. 'He seemed nice enough – yes, nice enough. Mary-Eloise always spoke kindly of Mr Rimmer but then, she spoke kindly of everyone.'. After a short pause he spoke again: 'Yes, the merry-go-round ornament, a gift from Mr Rimmer – her G.C.S.E. exam results.'. Derek Chambers recalled out loud. 'An A* for Literature and an A for English.'. Upon their exit, Inspector Folkard asked the Chambers if a sympathy card had been sent from Mr Rimmer, a phone call or even flowers. There was no real significance. Neither could recall that he had, but then they could recall little about the last few weeks – they hadn't even read the cards properly. 'We'll look through the cards and gifts later and let you know.'.

The Chambers thanked them for their time before the detectives thanked them. Slowly and softly the large heavy door closed quietly behind them. The magnificent garden with its manicured lawns on either side, was as impressive upon their exit as it had been upon their entry. Yet from this angle, the overall impression was more grandeus. In the far left corner, a group of ceramic mushroom-like bells, hidden below a small bench, clanked in the breeze; these stood in front of an old cherry tree.

Sergeant Shakespeare pictured the Chamber girl sitting there, maybe talking to her mother or father whilst they attended to the garden. An empty bird table stood nearby – three nut holders completely empty. The wind was picking up now. Inspector Folkard was already at the tall and large metallic gate. Sergeant Shakespeare eventually joined her. Silently at first, they set off back to the station. Somebody somewhere knew more than they were letting on, but whom and why?

13

MR RIMMER SITS on a bench in his back garden; it is a microcosm of blissfulness. From here he is able to hear the doorbell. Long and wide, private - contained within three very tall walls - the side path runs from the back door to the bottom of the garden. To the left – a large lawn, with an impressive and deep kidney shaped pond to its middle right - an old weeping willow shelters all that lurks beneath.

Borders and borders of meadow, foxgloves and lupines sway at the back, everything else affront; the purposeful disorder is deliberate and effective. Mr Rimmer remembers his grandfather telling him that flour could be made from the seeds that could be extracted from lupines – that he had read somewhere or other and that it was still used for cooking in parts of the world like Australia and South America.

Another very large tree, a chunky silver-birch, leans over from the very left of the garden; at the centre of it, about three-quarters of the way up, a huge thick sprig of mistletoe, once rooted into the trunk by Mr Rimmer's grandfather - the colour of piccalilli. A lonely swing sways from an old thick branch. Mr

Rimmer can still picture his mother laughing, pushing him from the front, tickling him, making him scream.

To the right of the path stands a long glass Victorian-type greenhouse – brick three feet from the ground, the rest, glass – intricate detail to the wrought iron along the top and over the entrance of it. Today, not many varieties of fuchsia remain; some of the space is occupied with some tool or another. In the corner, a rusty garden chair with a large brimmed hat on its seat, garden gloves, a trowel and a bucket.

At the very bottom of the garden is a wooden granny house with rotting window-boxes. This quaint and roomy haven was Mrs Rimmer's favourite place, that and the converted loft. When Mr Rimmer's father was alive, his mother would spend hours reading, drawing, passing the time. Mr Rimmer liked to play with his grandmother's large doll-house. His father came home early from work one day and caught him; he castigated him and called him a sissy.

When Mr Rimmer's father passed away, the granny house remained unoccupied for a long time. Mr Rimmer often squealed home from school to speak to his mother, mostly about the three bully boys. Mr Rimmer had always refused to name and shame the bullies although one day he said that they were called: 'Tom, Dick and Harry.'. Mr Rimmer's mother was often in bed – a bottle of wine with sleeping tablets on the bedside table.

Mr Rimmer recalls feeling initially overjoyed when some years later, sometime in the early hours, he heard his mother's laughter coming from somewhere in the back garden. From his back room window he could see a light in the granny house. Mr Rimmer trundled across the smooth lawn, even skipped a little. When he heard his mother laugh again, he laughed too.

Mr Rimmer had tapped on the window with his long fingernails but he was not heard. Mr Rimmer shakes his head from side to side as he recalls the sight of his mother laughing between breaths, her face buried in a stranger's naked lap.

Mr Rimmer needs to stand and stretch his legs; pins and needles tickle his left palm, his small finger, numb. Mr Rimmer would like nothing more but to knock the damn thing down but what would he replace it with? Mr Rimmer needs a nice cup of tea. As he stirs the tea-bag around and around in the cup with a small chip to the handle, he recalls the many times his mother told him that no-one would take his father's place – no-one. Mr Rimmer knows his mother loved his father with a passion.

For a few years later, there were many male callers to the house; worst was that time when Mr Rimmer caught Albert Conway leaving in the early hours. Seething with anger and frustration, Mr Rimmer goes upstairs for the shower – to wash the dirt away. A few hours later he wakes up on his mother's bed, having fallen asleep. For some strange reason he does not remember going in her room.

Mr Rimmer cannot eat anything tonight. He is still waiting for Eva to call around. Mr Rimmer really needs to do some shopping; he is short on toilet paper, facial wipes, his mother's shortbread - in fact, all the essentials. Mr Rimmer decides he will watch some television, distract himself, keep busy. When Eva calls around he will politely turn off the television; the programme he so wanted to watch can wait for another day. 'Would you like some juice, biscuits?'. Mr Rimmer stops talking to himself at the point he realises he has no more biscuits. No biscuits. Mr Rimmer has a habit of snacking on biscuits in the middle of the night – a visit to the toilet equals a visit to the biscuit tin.

In a quandary once again, Mr Rimmer decides he will nip out in his car and pop to the cooperative: it is only halfway along Marshide Road – he will make sure that he is back in a flash. Mr Rimmer leaves a note on a blob of blue-tac: BACK IN 5 MINUTES.

Mr Rimmer dresses quickly; he is almost as good as his word. The thought of seeing Eva brings much consolation – today has been a particularly long day. Quite unbelievably, Mr Rimmer returns twenty minutes later to a token bottle of cheap Italian wine in the porch, bagged in an obvious recycled gift bag, a card attached. Like his mother's visitors, she probably left in a hurry.

Mr Rimmer sits uncomfortably in his favourite chair watching something on television; the gift bag is by his side, the card in his left hand, on his lap. To open it would mean it was all over; Mr Rimmer means to postpone this for another time. He tucks the envelope down the left hand side of the seat; he will not forget it is there. His father hated cheap wine, especially Italian. 'Useless cowards,' he would mumble. Mr Rimmer knows Eva's mother will have bought the wine, it is not Eva's fault. He must make contact again, find a way of thanking her. Mr Rimmer has something to tell Eva; he has a gift for her too. It sits rejected on the table in the back room. Mr Rimmer is hoping to sit Eva down at the table, then he will talk her round.

His mother looks at him from the beautiful framed portrait on the television; Mr Rimmer is feeling sad. Tomorrow is Friday, only a half-day, a 12:30 finish – the summer holidays are nearly here – six weeks to go - a well-earned rest in sight. Mr Rimmer composes a text; he makes several changes before he settles on: *Thank you Eva for the wine, it was very thoughtful of you. I have a small gift for you too. Let me know when you can call in to collect it. Look forward to seeing you soon. Bernard Rimmer.*

Habitually, Mr Rimmer erases the text after sending; he waits diligently for a reply. Mr Rimmer is entranced with a memory of his mother crying, following the news that his father had died when unexpectedly his mobile bleeps. Mr Rimmer pushes his spectacles back, breathing a sigh of relief at the screen banner that informs him that Eva has texted him back.

Mr Rimmer takes his time before reading the text; when he sees the size of the message, he is most disappointed. When he reads the message he is disheartened: *Will call in soon, promise ☺.* Mr Rimmer has now wasted an entire forty minutes composing and erasing different texts to Eva. In the end an inner thought suggests otherwise and he decides to play it cool – he will lie in wait. His mother too was one for promises; most of the time she kept to them. A long time ago, she promised him that no-one would ever hurt him again.

14

FRIDAY LUNCHTIME, A rare working day from home - Inspector Folkard is settled across the settee, a mobile in one hand and a chicken and mushroom King Pot Noodle in the other: her favourite. She reminded her Sergeant not to forget to drop off the files from Blackpool C.I.D. on the way home. Sergeant Shakespeare confirmed she was already on her way. Highlighter and note-it tags on the coffee table, she was ready to proceed as soon as Sergeant Shakespeare arrived.

Inspector Folkard swapped ends on the settee; she decided she might as well look out of the double doors that led onto the back garden. The garden toys looked solitary – she missed spending quality time with her children! Darcy had come home on Wednesday elated because the boy she fancied the pants off had hugged her after saying yes to her asking him out. But yesterday, Darcy had cried silently on the way home. She sat quietly on the back seat, tears rolling down her chunky, freckled cheeks – Paul Kavanagh had asked her out for a prank.

Walter had comforted their eldest daughter on a few occasions that day. He insisted that he would not have hugged her in the first place if he did not like her and that he had probably ended things because of the jibes of others; he'd suggested that they dated in secret, he was after all a shy boy. Hermione Folkard was about to interfere when Darcy sat upright from the slumber that encumbered her, firmly stating that she didn't want to go out with a boy that was embarrassed to be seen with her and couldn't stand up to others. That's my girl, thought Inspector Folkard, that's my girl.

Boys never fancied Inspector Folkard at that age – Inspector Folkard confidently thought she was still a bit of a catch, but back in school, well, in fact, until she entered sixth form really, she thought she'd never have a boyfriend. It didn't help that she had been the eldest and the only girl. Her mother wouldn't let her do anything everyone else was doing. Inspector Folkard would summarise her upbringing when concerning her mother as cumbersome. When reminding the girls how much they got away with, she'd repeat the familiar phrase: 'my mother sat on me'. Although not intended to be funny, everyone would laugh, that was, with the exception of the matriarch of the family.

Her first boyfriend had been a shy boy too: Daniel Starbuck. Ginger from the top down, freckles, cute as a button, he was a real gent. Walter was a bit of a

Daniel; this time she wasn't going to grow complacent and let this one go. To this day she can recall the ache from being rejected. Although everyone said she'd have to get back on the horse, that there were plenty more fish in the sea, it took a long time before she recovered –and for a short while, she played the field. Inspector Folkard shrugged uncomfortably when she thought of the things she used to get up to; she hoped her girls would be less daring and more thoughtful of the feelings of others.

The sound of Sergeant Shakespeare pecking at the doorbell snapped Inspector Folkard back into the 21st century; the files had arrived. Sergeant Catherine Shakespeare had another big smile on her face; it was about time she settled down, hopefully this one would treat her better than the last. In her arms, she held one large cardboard box. Mugs of tea in hand, they began to exchange information as they wadded through the interviews and looked through the gruesome photographs.

Alice Lau – 22 – body found at the tip in Blackpool, Bristol Avenue, Bispham – discovered by morning staff at 07:50 hours. The body was believed to have lain there for three days before being discovered. Sergeant Catherine Shakespeare remarked that crucial evidence would have been destroyed in the first seventy-two hours. Inspector Folkard shook her head from side to side.

Detective Sergeant Vincent Fenton, officer in charge of the crime investigation Branch, had listed her injuries as 'extensive'. The post-mortem conducted on the body revealed she had been strangled; other injuries were consistent with being hit with a heavy metal pipe. Forensic officers searched the dumpsite for four weeks in total. Only a bracelet belonging to the victim had been recovered from the bin in a nearby unit. Inspector Folkard wanted to see a picture of that bracelet.

Unfortunately the time lapse between the victim's death and her discovery had made matters more difficult for the forensic team. It was difficult to see how exactly she had been strangled, although it seemed it had been done from behind. It certainly looked like she had put up a fight, hence the metal pipe. Forensic tests had been carried out on all of the bins from the area surrounding the spot where Alice met her death. 'Horrific', stated Sergeant Shakespeare just at the point when she found the photograph of Alice's bracelet. Interesting – stated Inspector Folkard – a charm bracelet – only three charms on it, a star, a moon, a unicorn – looked more like solid silver than plated.

With nothing much to go on, Inspector Folkard asked Sergeant Shakespeare to make the necessary arrangements for 'a day out' in Blackpool – a visit to family members and a visit to the tip. Alice had lived alone; she had been living alone for just under six months before she was murdered. Her parents ran a

B&B on the Promenade. Inspector Folkard shared that she liked to be beside the seaside.

15

MONDAY EVENING AND Mr Rimmer hasn't been able to sleep very well tonight; he has tossed and turned too many times. By five a.m. Mr Rimmer has had enough – he is shattered but despite trying and trying he still cannot sleep. His mother's special friend, Javier, the one with a wife but no children, keeps playing on his mind. Mr Rimmer has had enough; he exits his bedroom and enters his mother's bedroom next door. He knows he shouldn't shout but he is just too angry.

Because of his mother, because of him, because of them, because of Eva, Albert and his bloody mother - who did nothing until she knew everything, because of the bullies, Alice in Wonderland and Mary the Contrary, he will probably have to ring in sick tomorrow – as usual he will have to pick up the pieces.

By six a.m. Mr Rimmer's head is pounding. He is filled with so much remorse that he now sits on the bottom step, his head heavy in his bloody hands – he has been crying for a while now. Mr Rimmer is not usually a violent man.

16

TUESDAY MORNING WAS bin morning; Inspector Folkard dragged the heavy grey bin to the front of the gate only to discover it was recycling day. Back with the bin, and twice out with the four separate plastic boxes – some of the tins with paper still on them – some of the milk containers with lids! A long scenic walk with the dogs restored her inner peace. At 6:30 Walter's alarm stirred and the morning madness began. Darcy couldn't get out of bed because she'd struggled to go to sleep the night before – it was like this every night – it was like this most mornings. Zita couldn't get out of bed either; she kept falling back asleep, snoring, curled like a quaver. Walter diligently arose and his robotic routine began; he turned on the shower before making them both a lovely cup of tea.

The girls eventually succumbed to the pleas of both parents; once awake they made far too much noise – time for a sharp harp. Kisses, hugs, more hugs, reminders, more kisses – Inspector Folkard escaped in the nick of time: one of the dogs had had an accident. Feeling a little guilty, she closed the door at precisely 07:40; mobile to her ear, she was about to make a call when Sergeant Shakespeare arrived. Apologies over, they briefly discussed their plans for the day - postcode imputed into the satellite navigation system and off they went – destination Blackpool Promenade.

The Lau Bed and Breakfast stood at the end of a row of similar abodes, a coral red surface to all of the outer walls, the windows white, white and dirty. Three tallish concrete steps led them both to the obvious entrance; window baskets hung at either side of the porch, both packed with oversized plastic red and yellow roses.

From the outside, Inspector Folkard could see an array of business cards cluttering the left-hand window. Sergeant Shakespeare was about to ring the doorbell when the front door flung open; a rough couple made their way out, leaving the door of the porch wide open. Sergeant Shakespeare hollered in before stepping forward.

An overweight man with fast narrow eyes came forward from the back room; he did not smile although he shook hands immediately, welcoming them both before showing them into the front lounge. Eventually Mrs Lau joined them, the bed and breakfast was empty now and they were able to talk. Mrs Lau breathed heavily before she sat down.

Inspector Folkard noticed Mrs Lau had very swollen ankles; they were bulging out from underneath her lengthily pleated skirt. For a moment, they reminded her of her mother's feet. Her mother used to wear the shoes with the wooden soles. Her younger brother, Philip, once threw one of them in temper at her, right across the kitchen; it hit her smack bang on the forehead. Mrs Lau's eyes looked sore. Mr Lau explained that the Sergeant's phone call had ignited an unnecessary row between them – it was still all so hard; Alice would have been twenty-three this Christmas. 'If only she had not moved out – there was no need, she lived rent free at home.'. Mrs Lau added that they would have allowed boyfriends to stay over; that they never really understood why she moved out in the first place.

Sergeant Shakespeare smiled. Inspector Folkard asked if they could firstly see Alice's bedroom, the one before she had moved out – they appreciated the room might have changed since then. Mrs Lau remarked kindly that, to them, time had been one big blur – her room had remained as it was on the day she had moved out, pretty much untouched.

Appearing more at ease, Mr Lau proceeded to the kitchen to make them all a hot brew. Mrs Lau lead both detectives to the top of the stairs and along the corridor to the furthest room. For a Bed and Breakfast, the business seemed quite neglected. The monotonous cream wallpaper was yellowing, especially at the corners. The corridors bore spasmodic dustless prints of tasteless scenes framed in unvarnished pine. Who could truly know the effect on this couple following the death of their only child?

Alice's room was quite plain – many items had been removed during the move and taken by her for her new flat. Following a lengthy inquest, the items had been returned, boxed – but the Lau's had still not managed to unpack these – the need to retain Alice's scent was great, commented Mrs Lau. 'It is all I have of her now.'. Inspector Folkard made a mental note for Sergeant Shakespeare to read through the inventory of these items – maybe there would be some significance – one never knows.

Alice's room was painted a soft lilac colour, lilac on all of the walls; even furnishings such as cushions, although a shade darker were of this colour. An ugly pair of plain purple curtains framed both windows in the room. Outside the window, opposite the door, was the exterior wall of another property – a room without a view. But from the back window, on the right from the door, was a splendid view.

In the distance, the sea. A section of the fairground could be seen when looking left – it seemed so close – the people on the rides snaking around, probably unaware that they could be seen for miles and miles. To the right, windmills – all circling quietly around and around in unison. Most of the walls were still dotted with left-over blue-tac. Alice, like any teenager, had had many posters of different pop groups, her mother stated – she'd thrown them all away when she moved. Only one poster had remained behind, an animation; it was on the second wall to the left of the door, above her bed. In it, a tall beige horse stood in the meadow with its head leaning over a fence; its golden mane and tail, thick with curls. A lighter shade of gold shone on the very tips of the hair. There were three rabbits in the distance – they stood like little grey statues on a hill, their front teeth protruding from their mouth. The sun was shining. On the white wooden picket fence perched a robin redbreast with a wriggling worm in its beak.

Sergeant Shakespeare presumed Alice had had this poster for many years, possibly since being a child. She was about to ask why Alice had not taken it with her when Mrs Lau began to quietly cry. After a brief interval, she sat on Alice's bed and began to speak of a time when she had become separated from her husband – for a couple of years. They had only just re-united, shortly before Alice's death.

Without further prompting, Mrs Lau revealed an extra-marital relationship that led to her new partner moving in for a short period of time. Inspector Folkard detected between the sobs some deep regret. Michael Farnsworth, she stated, was currently detained at her majesty's service for assault following a pub brawl – G.B.H. – two years. 'Alice got on well with Michael. But she missed her father. If I hadn't taken up with him, Alice would have stayed at home. She wouldn't have moved out. All the tension – it must have been awful for her.'. Mrs Lau's spoke more slowly now. To Inspector Folkard she seemed not only quieter but even smaller than before. She looked like she was about to divulge a secret - withdraw into herself. Mrs Lau shared she had drank a lot with Mr Farnworth. She was now a recovering alcoholic. If only she could turn back time.

Mr Lau called from the bottom of the corridor that their brew was waiting. Having made a note of what little had remained behind, they silently moved in unison downstairs. Mrs Lau's eyes were red by now – a handkerchief was held to her nose with her large right hand. How bare the hall looked on the way down – what little appeal there was to the place. One could only hope that the bedrooms were far cosier and more welcoming.

Once they had returned to the front lounge, Sergeant Shakespeare asked about some of the details contained in the report regarding Alice's death. Detective Sergeant Fenton had recorded at the time that Alice had been working at Rossi's Ice-cream Parlour at the time of her death. Mr Lau interrupted. He spoke as if reminiscing some fond memory. As a child he had taken Alice there many times – 'the pink and white ice-cream, with the flake and sherbet, of course.'. Mr Lau also revealed that she'd left her job with them at the Bed and Breakfast for a job there. 'When she received a call about a possible full-time post, she jumped at it. Alice was like a kid in a sweet factory.'. Although she wasn't too keen on the owners themselves, she was really content in her work – she liked the people she worked with too. His mother looked up when he spoke. 'At one point we got the feeling Alice was seeing someone who was working there too.'.

Mr Lau stood up; he began to gather the empty cups. He added that she had only been working there four months before she was taken; Mr Lau hesitated for a moment then sat down, mugs in hand. Mrs Lau looked at her husband for a few moments before placing her left hand on his – the skin bulging from beneath her wedding ring. Inspector Folkard noticed her wedding ring appeared new or to have been recently polished.

Sergeant Shakespeare double-checked the address of the establishment before Mrs Lau added that it was not far from Alice's flat – although it was not Alice's anymore. They still drove by on occasion past both dwellings, still picturing her at the window, handing out ice-cream. Sergeant Shakespeare referred to Detective Sergeant Fenton's report once more; he read the flat's address out loud: Flat 3, 67 Brighton Road. Mr and Mrs Lau nodded in agreement.

Since handing the keys over to Alice, the landlord had never looked in on Alice. Yes, the Lau's agreed; she often referred to him as the ideal landlord. Sergeant Shakespeare asked if they had had any concerns about anyone she had come into contact with – anything they might have thought of, no matter how small – maybe something that they may even have remembered only recently – past boyfriends, people she worked with. 'Did Alice receive any special gifts?'.

Mr Lau swiped the back of his right hand across his eyes. They had been having problems in their marriage; they had separated – a long story. The truth was, other than a few visits at the start, when they helped her move in, they had been content to wait for Alice to come to them. 'We intended to go round more – life was chaotic at the time.'. Mr Lau was crying now. 'I only wish I had paid more attention - called round on Alice more.'. Mr Lau started shaking his head from side to side. His wife began to cry too.

It was when Sergeant Shakespeare asked about Alice's visits to Southport that Inspector Folkard took out her notebook - a few visits, yes, many really but then all her friends went to Southport from time to time – less so, once she had the flat. Inspector Folkard asked if Mr Bernard Rimmer's name rang any bells; had she ever received any extra tutoring? They were both sure that it did not, and tutoring, no. Mr Lau was standing now. 'There'd never been any tutoring. Alice was bright alright but was never the student that went the extra mile. Didn't like school much.'.

Later, standing on the steps, Inspector Folkard asked about the charm bracelet. Her mother could still picture it now about her dainty wrist; swallowing hard, Mrs Lau stated it had been a gift from a recent boyfriend she had met on a few occasions at Southport fairground: 'Imagine!', exclaimed Mrs Lau, 'Imagine going on a date to that dump when you have a perfectly good fairground of your own, on your own doorstep!'. Imagine that, thought Inspector Folkard.

Sergeant Shakespeare double-checked Alice's previous address with her father. '67 Brighton Road – about two miles away, if you head into town.'. Mr Lau saw the Inspector and Sergeant to the door. The coldness hit them as they left. 'Typical British weather,' remarked Mr Lau, 'no good for business.'. The door closed behind them. Deep in thought, they headed to their unmarked maroon car.

Blackpool Tower loomed in the passenger mirror for a long while. The promenade seemed endless. At the front, a merry-go-round seemed to move slowly – as if trapped in a nightmare. The sky had clouded over. Despite this, there was still time to visit the tip. Following that, they had planned to drive by the flat, then to the ice-cream parlour. Today was not a day for ice-cream, even if it was pink and white.

Sergeant Shakespeare questioned the likelihood of Mr and Mrs Lau still using their local tip. Inspector Folkard made no reply. Thankfully, she had no idea what it was to coincidentally lose an only child and relive the nightmare that was exclusive to the likes of the Lau's, and the Chambers, and possibly the Manning's.

How interpretations and language had changed over the years – a blind person now had a sight impairment, a library was now a Learning and Resources Centre and Blackpool Tip was now a Tip and Household Waste Recycling Centre. Inspector Folkard could just imagine Walter saying he would be back in half an hour; he was just popping out to the Tip and Household Waste Recycling Centre.

Surprisingly, the tip was closed. A newish sign related that from Friday to Wednesday, the closing time was 03:45 p.m. Inspector Folkard had never been to tip anything in her life. She may have accompanied her husband on a very rare occasion but had always remained in the car. How orderly it all looked – not a tip at all – unlike the girl's rooms - signs located everywhere – organised chaos.

A voice called over. A tall, very thin male about fifty years in age explained without any prompting that tomorrow they would be closed – they were always closed on Thursdays. 'You'll have to return on Friday.'. Sergeant Shakespeare introduced them both; they displayed their badges before she spoke again. She asked if they could take up some of his time in order to ask a few questions - a past murder - the victim's body was found on the sight. Happy to oblige and without any hesitation, the tall man opened the gates and invited them both onto the sight and into his small, cosy hut.

Mr Warren Jones, aged thirty-eight – foreman and manager to the sight – had been on site that very morning when Alice was found. He sat down at this point and invited them to join him. Sergeant Shakespeare referred to some details in Sergeant Fenton's report. Yes, the body of Alice Lau – he could remember it all. 'I can remember it as if it were yesterday.'.

Mr Jones related that he had arrived on site just before eight in the morning, as always. It was on a Tuesday, following the Bank Holiday weekend - apparently she'd been there about three days - an unforgettable sight - horrible. 'Her body looked awful. She was wet from the rain. Her neck looked broken from the way her body was twisted in the opposite direction to her head.'.

Inspector Folkard asked if he could take them to where the body had been found. Mr Jones remarked as they left the hut, that CCTV had been installed following the discovery of the body. At the back of the tip was a heap the size of a house. The body had been become buried underneath the rubbish - she had been in a heavy duty black bin bag for many hours.

Mr Jones thought initially a dog had been buried from the way the elbow made a shape at one of the corners. He knew something wasn't right but what it was, he wasn't sure. He'd paused briefly before picking a hole in the bag with his nail and ripping it a little open. When Mr Jones saw a woman's head - his face altered. What he'd seen was enough - something he'd never forget. At that point, he called the police. There were officers on site for about a month. 'Did they ever catch the killer?'.

Sergeant Shakespeare, now at the wheel, said very little for a short while; Inspector Folkard looked over the information they had gathered. Like Mary-Eloise, Alice had been strangled but she'd also been hit with a metal pipe – why? Which came first, the strangulation or the blow? 'The blow, proposed Sergeant Shakespeare, would suggest a lack of premeditation, the strangulation to finish her off. Alice was older than Mary-Eloise and possibly stronger. She may not have been as easy to kill as Mary-Eloise. Inspector Folkard added that if they were dealing with one killer, the blow could have followed because the victim escaped momentarily, following the attempted strangulation. Could this suggest the killer was not that strong? Certainly, Mr Rimmer would fit the second profile and both victims could then be fragmentally linked in this way to him – they had both, after all, been strangled from behind.

They needed to find out if Mr Rimmer had taken any trips to Blackpool – but how? Sergeant Fenton would not have looked at the time for any such links – anyone stating she had been seen with an older man would be likely to say it was her father – and they now knew her father had rarely been round to the flat. It was a long shot, as they say, but it could give them the link to promote the investigation in a whole new light – more importantly, one Superintendent Reid would support.

Sergeant Shakespeare nodded. The bracelet belonging to the victim had been recovered from a bin in a nearby unit. It puzzled Sergeant Shakespeare why it had become separated from the victim? Had the killer taken it, then changed his/her mind and then discarded it? The charm bracelet, bearing a star, a moon and a unicorn was, in fact made of solid silver – the killer had surely become attached to the victim – that is if he'd bought it. The killer was more likely to be a man. Inspector Folkard agreed. It was a quality item. A search warrant could uncover the much needed receipt – but there just wasn't enough evidence to get any magistrate to agree to one.

Sergeant Shakespeare suggested that any future interviews with suspects such as Mr Rimmer should also include questions revolving around the subject of *personal disappointment or feelings of being let down*. Inspector Folkard nodded in agreement. Strangulation was often the behaviour of a frustrated and angry killer – rarely done on impulse. Strangulation was not this killer's 'signature' – otherwise why the pipe? The killer or killers had attempted to hide both bodies and had cleverly chosen places that would erase as much evidence as possible. It seemed obvious that the killer or killers of these two girls knew their victim and was reasonably intelligent.

17

NEARLY TWO WEEKS have passed and Mr Rimmer is almost back to his usual self. He has not heard from Inspector Folkard and company; he has not heard from Eva either – the present has since been removed. Mr Rimmer has given it to his mother, they are friends again. His hands have healed.

There are only four weeks left in the term. Mr Rimmer sits at his school desk; he is contemplating a week's vacation in the Lake District. Mr Rimmer recalls the photographs of his mother and father honeymooning on Ullswater – he may have been ten years older but there was no doubt they were very much in love. There were few photographs of them together left now. Years ago, Mr Rimmer burned several items belonging to his mother. He wished he hadn't now. Some of Mr Rimmer's favourite photographs include one of his father and one of his mother. His mother had taken one of his father, rowing the small and simple boat – he was looking at her, smiling. His father had taken more photographs of her, rowing, giggling, in awe of him.

At 12:30 the bell rings. Mr Rimmer is filling in missing registers when Raymond Belchier knocks on his classroom door. As usual, Raymond enters before Mr Rimmer has had a chance to answer; he has a message from the office – it is written on a note. Mr Rimmer thanks Raymond for taking the trouble to find him. At times Mr Rimmer can be a bit of a hermit. Sometimes Mr Rimmer will remain in his room for most of the day; he doesn't mean to be so unsociable, it's just that he doesn't really watch the soaps or reality TV. He doesn't participate in Facebook, he doesn't knit or bake, he has no wife, no children or grandchildren. He can't even discuss his parents with anyone. Mr Rimmer doesn't even like to discuss the news.

Mr Rimmer squints momentarily before pushing his spectacles back: *Jennifer Dwyer 07811431650.* Mr Rimmer's end to the week is already brighter than he had at first anticipated. He is eager to get home; he wishes to speak to Jennifer without interruption. Mr Rimmer only ever had Jennifer's home number; now, he has her personal mobile number. Jennifer is about to complete her 3rd year at Ormskirk University – she will make a fine English teacher one day; she was certainly her teacher's pet.

As Mr Rimmer leaves St William's High, the office girls note his happier than usual disposition. In the car park, he contemplates calling Jennifer from his mobile but decides he will savour the call for when he is sat down, alone. Mr Rimmer drives away; he sings to ABBA's classic hit, Chiquitita. Mr Rimmer is singing loudly now:

'Chiquitita, tell me what's wrong? You're enchained by your own sorrow...

How I hate to see you like this, I can see that you're oh so sad, so quiet... I'm a shoulder you can cry on...your best friend...I'm the one you must rely on...

You were always sure of yourself...now I see you've broken a feather...we can patch it up together.'.

Mr Rimmer arrives home; he parks the front end of his classic sky-blue car unintentionally close to the wooden wall with a built-in door that leads to the back of the garden. He does so before returning to the well-oiled gate; he closes it behind him. Unusually, he forgets to wave to the Conways; although Albert is disappointed, his mother still does the Churchill nod: Mr Rimmer has a lot on his mind.

Once indoors, Mr Rimmer weighs up whether to make the call now or take pleasure in the call later. Mr Rimmer settles on making a cup of tea first; he needs to think about what he might say to Jennifer. He has been very busy; he has a gifted student called Eva now, he is in fact expecting a visit from her any minute today. He still has the cookie-jar she bought for him as a gift years ago. He recently nearly dropped the lid but managed to grab hold of it before it hit the floor.

When Mr Rimmer eventually makes the call, it is nearly eight o'clock. He has thoroughly showered and is sitting in just a dressing gown and slippers. Mr Rimmer wants to appear busy; he switches the television on before he makes the call. Mr Rimmer is unprepared for Jennifer's quick response, three rings and she has already answered.

Mr Rimmer makes polite conversation. It is reciprocated. Jennifer asks Mr Rimmer if he can help her; she has failed her last teaching practice, fallen behind with the paperwork – needed some time off. Mr Rimmer wants to agree immediately but knows he must hold back if he is to fully enjoy the moment. Eventually, Mr Rimmer agrees to meet with Jennifer; he is really busy at the moment, maybe they can catch up and have a coffee sometime – she can fill him in – he can fill her in too.

Jennifer is relieved when he agrees to speak to Mr Jessop; he is sure he will be able to arrange at least a six week stint in the first Autumn half-term – she is to leave it with him. Mr Rimmer will call Jennifer soon – he is glad to be of any help. Already Mr Rimmer is thinking about their last meeting. About this time last year, Jennifer had telephoned asking for some advice. Mr Rimmer had been unprepared for the changes that had taken place in Jennifer; the last time he had seen her she resembled plain Jane. Mr Rimmer can still picture her – dressed to kill - in her shortish black skirt, folded like a handkerchief; she wore black tights and a tight tee-shirt. Her breasts jiggled when she giggled – she was so desirable at nineteen. His mother used to say that when you're on a diet you can still look at the menu – nothing wrong in that.

Mr Rimmer decides he cannot call Jennifer before Monday evening. Monday evening and he will arrange a place and time to meet. Mr Rimmer's heart beats loudly against his chest; waiting games are the best – that is, as long as you're not the one waiting. It is a warm evening. Mr Rimmer takes another shower, all this excitement has caused him to perspire profusely - another shower and off to bed, to bed with the memories that keep him warm at night. Tonight it would not be Alice at the cinema; tonight it would be Jennifer at the cafe, Jennifer who needed his help.

18

WALTER WOKE HERMIONE Folkard up as planned; today they would enjoy a rare day out alone, a day without children. Sometimes it felt awkward, silly really; even after knowing one another for so long, being on their own could still draw a number of girlish giggles from the one who clearly wore the pants about the house.

Lyme Park Estate was not as grand as it had been projected on the screen for the latest adaptation of Pride and Prejudice, but still, it was breath-taking enough. Disappointingly the Edwardian mansion with deer park was closed. It proudly stood alone, the focal point of the enormous grounds that appeared sectioned, quartered and ornate. Established creepers and lilac laburnum flora drooped like bunches of grapes over the stony striking entrance: all very Downton Abbey.

Walking hand in hand, all was blissfully silent; trees stirred and gently swayed as described in the best books. The sun shone through every nook and cranny – warming their aging skin. They sat on an old bench and said nothing for a while. Walter sat upright, his chin balanced on the top of his wife's head. Secure, steadfast Walter kept her world afloat; at times like these the world seemed more rational – they needed more days like these.

The extensive grounds were divided into several different sections, each one as inviting as the next, every one offering the opportunity for a sit down or an embrace or both. Secluded from any draft at the orchard, they reminisced on the day they married - Comlongdon Castle, Boxing Day – Scotland - they loved Scotland. How nervous Hermione had been that day. In comparison, Walter was, as always, calm and steadfast - her rock.

About once a year they would return to reminisce the good old days; sometimes even for an entire weekend. How precious was their time together. On the last occasion the children had been with them – only a night but enough time to walk them through the memories of their wedding day. The last visit had been the most memorable of all.

The path that lead from the back of the castle to the small lake at the very bottom, was made up of inlaid square plaque stones that had replaced the original tiles in the path. The plaques bore the names of couples who had married at the castle over the last fifty years or so.

A short candlelit ceremony that evening took place, as well as the renewal of vows. A distinguished bearded piper with large hands and a dimpled chin to match who must have been at least six foot three, marched the small ensemble to the spot where the plaque stone was laid. The family had gathered about three-quarters of the way down the path. The girls were mesmerised with the whole scene; they stood holding hands whilst Harry watched from behind. They all giggled when their parents kissed shyly as the ceremony began.

In the rear view mirror, Lyme Park Estate looked much smaller now. It was time for some lunch. Walter held Hermione's hand as he drove – their shoulders leaning instinctively towards each other. They arrived to the Punchbowl, a country pub which stood adjacent to the village parish church, and found the place to be quite empty. Sat cosily by the fire, they began to habitually talk about the children.

Hermione relied heavily on Walter to keep her up-to-date with the small details the children chose to omit from their often brief conversations. They eventually concluded that the girls were doing well, and as usual, they had concerns over Harry's lack of effort at university, lack of part-time employment and lack of self-restraint when it came to the female kind.

It was easy to forget how one could veer from the path when out of sight from parents and conveniently away at university. Hermione Folkard, the eldest of two and with a strict Catholic upbringing, went a little wild in her first year away. Her ego, confidence and overdraft were in danger of getting out of hand. As

Harry had just replicated, she had failed one of her end of term examinations and would spend the summer vacation revising as little as possible.

Most conversations with Harry these days had to be tactile; they would usually take place over the Sunday roast. A typical student, Harry would return home when he was either broke, hungry or when his washing machine had supposedly broken down. Last month, mother and son had not spoken for three weeks in total. Sundays had been peaceful during this period of time but, as the girls often pointed out, life was not the same without Harry.

Smart, intelligent and very funny, Harry was wise beyond his years but like his mother, many moons ago, liked to break the rules, veer from the path, argue until he was blue in the face. Walter assured his wife that Harry's behaviour was the norm – that it would all come good in the wash. Now, nearly twenty, Harry thought he knew it all – like his mother, he'd have to learn the hard way.

19

MR RIMMER HAS given himself a headache. He has been so wound up about the phone call that now the time has come, he feels almost too sick with excitement to relish in the moment. Nevertheless, Mr Rimmer sits down. Mr Rimmer will tell Jennifer he has just got in after a busy day and apologise for not getting in touch sooner. No. Mr Rimmer's headache is getting worse.

Two Solpadine Plus and a cat nap in his chair and Mr Rimmer's mood has lightened. Jennifer is elated to hear the good news – Mr Rimmer insists on mentoring her for the agreed teaching practice – it's no trouble at all – they should probably meet soon to make arrangements for September. Jennifer accepts an invitation to visit St William's – Mr Rimmer will show her round. Mr Rimmer insists Jennifer call him by his first name. Bernard it is.

Mr Rimmer can hardly control his emotions. All week he has held off contacting Jennifer again, and as expected, because she needs him, she has texted to see if a visit to the school can be arranged. The Sunday evening before the final week of term, Mr

Rimmer has wound himself into a frenzy; Jennifer's visit is to take place this week. His feelings are only natural, she is after all no longer his student; in fact they are really equals, on a par. They are already friends.

At times like these, Mr Rimmer has a habit of neglecting his mother – he rarely gives her a second thought. In fact, he deliberately avoids eye contact with her – she can read him like a book.

Tonight, Mr Rimmer avoids snacking on his favourite crisps – bacon rashers; he has for the first time in a very long time, been successfully losing weight for ten days now. By nine-thirty Mr Rimmer cannot wait any longer; he forgets about watching his favourite programme - he is going straight to bed.

Mr Rimmer undresses and showers for a short while before he clambers quickly into his bed. Awake for at least two and a half hours, Mr Rimmer fantasises about the time they will spend together in the near future. At times Mr Rimmer decides that a particular bit in the story isn't quite right so he rewinds this bit and that bit before putting it right – he is going too fast. The build-up of excitement becomes too much too soon and Mr Rimmer has to make a huge effort to slow himself down, take his time, savour the fantasy. Disappointingly it all comes to a head when he deliberately thinks of Alice in wonderland.

The guilt doesn't last too long – Jennifer is clearly different. Jennifer is a different type of girl, educated.

She would not hurt him like Alice did. As soon as possible, Mr Rimmer will invite, no, insist Jennifer attends the Christmas staff night out on December the 20th. Jennifer and Bernard. Bernard and Jennifer. They both share an e, an r and an n in their names, that is why their names together look so good. He will take her, of course.

The next two days are mostly a blur; Mr Rimmer has been unwell, full of cold, and suffering from possibly a virus. A painful migraine drives Mr Rimmer to the doctors. Mr Rimmer rarely takes time off work. Mr Rimmer has had to take time off. On the Thursday, Mr Rimmer had been on his way home when his left arm began to ache, the back of his eyes irritated him, itching and aching at the same time.

By the time Mr Rimmer had arrived home, the headache had become a migraine again; Mr Rimmer has never really suffered with migraines but he knew this was one for sure. Mr Rimmer feels better when he vomits, then almost immediately after, his head begins to pound, pound like a pressure cooker until it is eventually alleviated by more sickness. This continues until late into the evening – his mother insists he visits the doctor again, first thing in the morning – he must take more time off and seek advice – it was foolish of him to ignore the pain in his right ear – she's told him many times about nipping things in the bud – but he never listens.

Mr Rimmer arrives to the doctors five minutes before his appointment; his usual doctor, Dr Merritown is not in today – Mr Rimmer likes to confide in Dr Merritown – he understands him. When Mr Rimmer's father died, Dr Merritown prescribed him some medication that helped him for many years; many years later, Mr Rimmer knows he can speak to him about most things. Dr Merritown comes from a long line of doctors, but his sisters are all teachers. Dr Merritown understands Mr Rimmer perfectly. Once, he briefly recalls, when he was too young to understand, he had accompanied his mother to the doctors – her old friend Rose came too.

Mr Rimmer understands now that his mother was very worried - she was getting throbbing pains in her right breast. Her old friend Rose had insisted they visit ASAP – that these things could not be left to fester – that they should be caught in the nick of time. Mr Rimmer remembers his mother and Rose discussing the importance of wearing a decent bra for such occasions, when in fact later, in Dr Merriman's room, she was asked to remove it behind the curtain before the examination. How they had laughed then. How they laughed later.

Mr Rimmer had sat uncomfortably on Rose's lap whilst Dr Merritown examined his mother's breasts. His mother must have been nervous; she giggled a lot – Mr Rimmer can understand that now. Dr Merritown still speaks of his mother to this day.

Dr Greenwood invites Mr Rimmer into Appointment Room 5 – pretty, slim, dark-haired, no breasts and far too young, Mr Rimmer explains the nature of this unusual migraine. The young doctor, with size 4 feet, looks into his right ear before his left and states she is unconcerned before closing the window blinds and turning out the lights.

In the near dark, Dr Greenwood asks Mr Rimmer to stare and remain focused on something on the back wall. Mr Rimmer catches sight of a fire extinguisher, appropriately above Dr Greenwood's left shoulder. Dr Greenwood switches on an instrument with a piercing light; it is hard to stay focused when her head makes the circular movements of an ostrich, her minute chest bobbing about, breaking his concentration.

Mr Rimmer is pleased to hear that the veins at the back of his eyes look healthy and that there are no visible shadows, no signs of fluid; she dismisses Mr Rimmer who refuses to budge. Eventually Dr Greenwood agrees that a course of antibiotics would be best to rid the right ear of any possible infection and therefore avoid a repeat migraine. Mr Rimmer is disappointed with her lack of confidence and wonders how long she has been qualified. The thoughtless thought prompts Mr Rimmer into reminding himself that we all have to train to gain experience in our field. Mr Rimmer will ensure Jennifer feels confident in her field – she will pass with flying colours.

Back at home, Mr Rimmer is tired; his eyes itch and any noise or light irritates him – he feels sick too. Mr Rimmer eats a slice of dry toast, settles down on his bed and falls asleep, unusually for five hours. When Mr Rimmer awakes it is six o'clock in the evening – he slurps some Scotch Broth, eats another slice of toast without butter and falls asleep for most of the night.

7:30 Friday morning, Mr Rimmer rings in sick – he still feels unwell. He explains to his line manager that he needs to have another day in bed – a chance to recover. he still feels weak and off-colour. On Monday he will return to work bright and breezy and ready to plan the next few weeks ahead – but for now, back to bed – as his mother would say.

Later that day, Mr Rimmer is sitting in his favourite armchair when he comes across Eva's thank you note; there is no real reason why he should not open it now – it probably just says *Thank You*. Mr Rimmer peels back the top of the envelope – For a moment or two he is mesmerised by the image of Eva licking the envelope to gum it down.

Mr Rimmer feels hot – angry – the note has clearly been written in her mother's handwriting. *Thanks for everything - Eva.* The envelope has probably been licked by her mother too. Licked by someone who cannot be bothered to teach her daughter how to say thank you to someone who has made a difference in her daughter's life. Mr Rimmer cannot believe he treasured such a pathetic gesture for so long, for nothing; he tosses the whole lot into the paper basket. Knowing it is there in plain sight infuriates him so much that he takes it out and puts it in the kitchen bin, in the bin where he doesn't have to look at it.

Unbelievably, quite unbelievably, Mr Rimmer is about to go for another nap when he thinks he sees the silhouette of Eva, of all people, outside his gate. For a short moment Mr Rimmer holds his breath. She is smiling. Mr Rimmer is not.

Despite the unarranged visit, Mr Rimmer is ready; he prepares his smile, relaxes his left hand and moves towards the front door. At the porch he takes in a deep breath – his mother is calling him but he ignores her closing the door behind him. Sunrays slice like ice through Eva's flaxen mop of brown hair. At the porch door Eva smiles confidently; she is full of life, vigour, youth. Mr Rimmer reconsiders before inviting her in; he looks up and down the road – no Conways at the window.

Eva says she cannot come in, no, she really can't – she's off into the village to buy a card for her mother – she'd forgotten it was her birthday and feels bad. Mr Rimmer insists she enters – he has a card that she may be able to give to her mother – a card he once picked up for his own mother – she might as well open her gift whilst he roots it out. Mr Rimmer closes the door firmly behind them both. His mother has grown silent – Eva does not notice he has locked the door. Once inside, Mr Rimmer invites Eva to sit in the back room, at the table, and to sit on the chair with the velvet seat – he will only be a moment – will just pop upstairs and be down in a jiffy. An unread Southport Visitor lays on the table; the headline does not catch her eye: **NEW LEAD SUGGESTSMARY-ELOISE KNEW HER KILLER**

Eva is fixing her tights when Mrs Rimmer unexpectedly runs into the room. Alarm spreads over Eva's face when Mrs Rimmer smiles, lipstick smeared onto two of her top teeth. Mrs Rimmer's long dark curly hair is flowing over both her shoulders; a brooch with tessellating patterns to the right breast decorates her peacock blue embroidered dress with chiffon long sleeves.

Eva's skull smashes like a coconut against the pillar that stands between two windows. Her blood speckles sideways onto the panes at either side, the granny house looming in the distance. Mrs Rimmer releases her grip and Eva's body slumps to the ground. Eva's head falls forward as Mrs Rimmer backs away. A sickening sight awaits Mr Rimmer when he returns, a sickening sight indeed.

Mrs Rimmer is now back in her room. She is rocking back and forth on her bed with her head held in both of her clammy hands. Her wailing is so loud and concerning, that Mrs Conway looks towards the upstairs window from the back of her garden, before entering indoors to consult with her son.

20

INSPECTOR FOLKARD LISTENED carefully to Ms Manning's words. As she spoke, small bubbles formed around one of the corners of her mouth – both hands shook. Her daughter Eva had been missing since yesterday, not long after school had ended. Eva had gone out without telling anyone where she was going. 'She said she was nipping out – wouldn't be long.'. Eva never came back.

Yesterday had been Rachel Manning's thirty-fifth birthday. She had cooked a special tea for them both; by seven she was beginning to feel angry; by eight she was beginning to worry. Rachel Manning rang the police at nine o'clock – she watched the clock, she watched the gate, she rang Eva's mobile but it just rang out. She rang her husband, Eva's father, they no longer lived together. 'But as usual, he didn't pick up.'. At nine o'clock, as agreed with herself, she dialled 999.

Police Constable Stanfield assured Rachel Manning that there would be a perfectly good explanation – that teenagers lost their mobiles all the time – that Eva was probably at a friends and would contact her at any moment. Ms Manning was not to panic – she was probably trying to contact her right now. But Eva never called and Eva never came home. Ms Manning had rang all the friends she knew of – no-one had seen her, not a soul.

Rachel Manning's mother and father arrived to the station to take their daughter home; they indicated to Sergeant Shakespeare that they would remain by their daughter's side until news arrived. Sergeant Cumming's statements revealed that neither of the grand-parents had either seen or heard from Eva since the weekend.

Her grandmother said that Eva was a thoughtful girl. 'Eva would not hurt a fly.'. Eventually, Mr Manning, estranged husband and father to Eva, returned Ms Manning's many phone calls. He had neither seen nor heard from Eva that day. In fact, he had neither seen nor heard from her for weeks.

21

JENNIFER'S TEXT GOES unanswered for a couple of days; finally, Mr Rimmer contacts her, apologising for his neglect - he has been under the weather – indisposed. Following a long discussion, it is all arranged - Jennifer is coming to St William's on Thursday for a tour and an informal discussion in order to arrange her teaching practice for the new term.

Elated after the receiver goes down, Mr Rimmer celebrates by walking to the take-away and buying a portion of fish, chips and mushy peas – lots of vinegar – lots of salt – even more vinegar. That evening, Mr Rimmer settles in his favourite chair, feeling a lot calmer than he has in a while. He is almost halfway through one of his favourite programmes when a young female character catches his eye – the spitting image of Mary-Eloise. 'Mary, Mary, quite contrary,' he whispers to himself. Looking over at the chair where Inspector Folkard had sat, Mr Rimmer remembered Mary-contrary sitting in the same chair, her sweet and innocent face – a scarf about her neck. Mary-contrary would sometimes sit in that chair following her lesson; from there she could watch out for her parents who had strictly forbidden her from walking home alone.

Mary-contrary had beautiful long brown hair and very long eyelashes; her freckles certainly enhanced her beauty – she was so polite, didn't have a bad word to say about anyone. Her goal in life was to achieve what her parents had, especially her mother, a family, a husband, a home. Mr Rimmer had done his best to reason with her, guide her – but that night, when she called in to pick up her reference, he felt so frustrated by his loss – her determination to not pursue English Literature at A' level any further – that he inadvertently began an unavoidable chain of events – something he would have never guessed could happen – something that should have never happened again.

Most students could be taught to understand a book, its characters, context and themes but Mary-Eloise instinctively knew how to explore the deeper concepts behind the writer's skill, their craft. Mary-Eloise was special, different from all the other girls – she was pure and uncorrupted in any way – she was like the daughter he had never had.

On the night Mary-Eloise had been taken away from him, she had not been sitting in her usual chair – she was not waiting for anyone – she had called in on impulse, on a whim – the reference, of course. Instead, Mary-Eloise, accepted an invitation to sit by Mr

Rimmer at the chair beside his own, it's back to the door.

Mr Rimmer had made polite conversation, made enquiries after her parents but still, he felt sick at the thought of not spending any more time with her. He felt he couldn't possibly let her go – he just couldn't. Mr Rimmer had made a big mistake that night; he was so wound up that he suddenly went upstairs on the pretence of fetching something in order to seek advice from his mother.

Shuddering now, Mr Rimmer recalls the events that followed. Furious, and before he knew what was happening, his mother came marching down the stairs and before Mary-Eloise could turn around she went completely mad and throttled the poor girl on the spot with the scarf about her neck. Mary-Eloise's eyes had risen upwardly as her hands grasped for the scarf about her neck – her feet rose momentarily before she urinated on the floor.

Mr Rimmer concluded that that was why he doesn't like telling his mother much about his private life. Since his father passed away she became unable to manage her emotions – sometimes they fall out on a daily basis.

Mr Rimmer is now dutifully washing his mother's peacock-blue embroidered dress – the pea soup stain won't shift. He holds his forehead in his right hand; it is difficult and very tiring cleaning up after his mother. Take the other day, Mr Rimmer had moaned to her in passing; he'd made an innocent remark about Eva because she'd not bothered to call in and collect her parting gift; once again, his mother took it upon herself to teach the ungrateful brat a lesson or two. Mr Rimmer isn't sure what to do about his mother; there is no-one he can turn to, no-one he trusts.

Determined now, Mr Rimmer resolves to not discuss Jennifer with his mother any more – his mother is clearly losing her mind and if discovered, he could be sent down for aiding and abetting a criminal – concealing the truth – holding back vital information. He must, from this day onwards, create an inevitable barrier between them, if he is ever to have a life of his own.

Mrs Rimmer had cried that night for hours. She explained to her only son that she still felt so bad about what had happened to him when he was young, that she had from that instance vowed to protect him no matter what – she could not allow anyone to ever hurt him again. Mr Rimmer understands perfectly. Mr Rimmer knows they are lucky to live reasonably far out, by marshland. Who knows what can be discovered if one digs deep enough?

22

BACK AT THE station, a call from Sergeant Shakespeare's mobile informed Inspector Folkard that coincidentally Eva Manning had, until very recently, been a private student of Mr Rimmer. For a few moments, Inspector Folkard was lost in thought – the one remaining year 11 student that Mr Rimmer had spoken of, was in fact Eva Manning. Inspector Folkard wrestled with the obvious coincidence. She was on her way.

In the far distance, Mr Rimmer's classic blue car could be seen travelling home towards the unmarked vehicle that awaited his arrival. A few moments earlier, Sergeant Shakespeare had Inspector Folkard's almost full attention as she recalled an incident in secondary school when she was caught criticising her teacher to another pupil for using the word *arson* in class.

A much younger Miss Shakespeare had suggested to her then best friend that her teacher had used 'foul language', only for the class to laugh out loud when Mrs Williams revealed the true meaning of the word. 'Arson!', Sergeant Shakespeare kept repeating, 'you know, like arsing around!'. In reality, Inspector Folkard was finding Sergeant Shakespeare more amusing than the story itself.

Sergeant Shakespeare had also detected a sudden change in speed as the car came into full view; it was a quick abrupt action, like an unnecessary change of gear. Mr Rimmer thanked Inspector Folkard for opening the gates, saving him from getting out of his car. The Conways, noted for their absence at their favourite window, were apparently having a short break in Prestatyn according to Mr Rimmer, who had instinctively noticed the two officers looking across the right wall.

Small chit chat over, Sergeant Shakespeare informed Mr Rimmer of the need for just a few further questions. Mr Rimmer seemed happy to oblige; he opened the porch door with a key from which a curious key ring hung - an animal of some sort, possibly a bull.

Once indoors, Mr Rimmer invited his guests to sit; Mr Rimmer sat once more in what seemed to be his customary armchair, offering them both a seat on the plush settee - no tea and biscuits today - a pair of binoculars on the coffee table. Sergeant Shakespeare, armed with a notebook, began to ask Mr Rimmer about the nature of his teaching. Inspector Folkard transfixed for a few moments by Mrs Rimmer's framed portrait, listened intently to Mr Rimmer's detailed and helpful response. Understandably Mr

Rimmer did not comprehend the reason behind their enquiries: he had told them all he knew during their last visit.

With intention, Inspector Folkard suddenly produced a recent photograph of Eva Manning; she placed it on the coffee table before Mr Rimmer, who seemed to deliberately move forward, leaned for a closer look. He remarked how much older students appear in their own attire before Sergeant Shakespeare enquired about his relationship with Eva Manning. Mr Rimmer asked for the reason behind their enquiry but before Sergeant Shakespeare could respond, Inspector Folkard asked Mr Rimmer to please answer the question.

As Mr Rimmer was about to answer, the din of a chime signalling the arrival of a message on Mr Rimmer's mobile sounded; Mr Rimmer apologised, glanced quickly at his mobile before turning it on silent. Mr Rimmer, enquired after Eva – was she ok? – what was the reason for their visit? Sergeant Shakespeare pursued her line of enquiry, asking once again about the nature of their relationship. Clearly irritated by the Sergeant's choice of phrase, Mr Rimmer asked for clarification to what the officers where suggesting. Sergeant Shakespeare, pleased to have extracted some reaction from him, changed her tone before rephrasing her question. 'How did you come to know Eva Manning?'.

Mr Rimmer looked again at the school photograph; all the while he spoke without looking away from it. He had taught Eva for approximately twelve months – on Mondays. Their tuition had recently ended. She was a capable student but not ambitious enough to achieve the top grades. He added that her mother was very pleasant, had recently brought round a bottle of wine to thank him for bringing her on so far in the subject of English – a lovely family – pity about the father. Eva had stated that he suddenly left the family home last year, that Eva had apparently been neglecting her work in school and had fallen behind.

Silence in the room, the three looked upon Eva's young face, a sweet and happy smile across it. Her dark hair was in pigtails; wisps of hair had been tucked behind her ears that stuck out like a sore thumb. Inspector Folkard then stated that Eva Manning had been missing from home for three days. Mr Rimmer, a look of shock upon his face, looked most concerned. 'Her poor mother. Was she the type to run away from home? She didn't seem to be that type – she spoke fondly of her family, seemed close to her grandparents. Could she be with her father?'

Ignoring Mr Rimmer's enquiries, Inspector Folkard asked about the last time he had seen her, the last time they had been in touch. Mr Rimmer looked up at the ceiling, as if deep in thought; he proceeded to inform that the last time must have been their last lesson – that he didn't even know it was to be their last lesson, not until he received a text from her mother afterwards - hadn't spoken to her since.

Sergeant Shakespeare stated that she'd feel let down, even frustrated by the chopping and changing involved tutoring on a one to one basis. Mr Rimmer nodded. He shared quite openly that some students could be thoughtless – that they didn't understand the preparation that took place for each and every student – the time involved – he wasn't even sure he would continue his tuition now – that most students attended because their parents wanted them to, not because they wanted it for themselves.

Sergeant Shakespeare nodded; she then explained that as a matter of routine she needed to ask anyone connected, in any way to Eva, for their whereabouts in the last seventy-two hours. Looking up once more at the ceiling, Mr Rimmer informed the officers he had been to school and back and nowhere else; he had recently been suffering from headaches and had been under the weather and so he hadn't ventured anywhere other than to work and back – oh, and to the doctors, of course – Churchtown Health Centre. Sergeant Shakespeare instinctively made a note to check CCTV in the area.

It was Mr Rimmer that remarked on the coincidence that a murdered and missing student had both been past students to himself – he understood perfectly their need for a further visit – he wished he could help further. 'Their poor parents.'. He added that he hoped this one would turn up safe and well. Suddenly, Mr Rimmer stood up whilst at the same time picking up the photograph of Eva to return.

Sensing a dead end, Sergeant Shakespeare thanked Mr Rimmer for his time. As Mr Rimmer held the front door open, Inspector Folkard enquired whether he had meant to exchange a parting gift with Eva – like a keepsake, a keepsake like a book or a gift card or even an item of jewellery? Mr Rimmer looked intently at Inspector Folkard – his hard, dark eyes transfixed momentarily on hers. 'Goodnight Inspector. Goodnight Sergeant. And no, I had not got round to thinking about a gift. Like I said, I've been very unwell - under the weather. I very rarely buy gifts for my students – inappropriate don't you think?'.

Sergeant Shakespeare commented as she exited from the porch door that seaside resorts like Prestatyn had offered the best of memories when it came to holidays – that the Conways were sure to be enjoying themselves, the weather being so agreeable. Mr Rimmer nodded, a small friendless smile fading over his stern face. Inspector Folkard remarked that, personally she preferred Blackpool for a day out, even a weekend – had Mr Rimmer ever been to such places?

Mr Rimmer hesitated for a moment. He then spoke as though he had rehearsed every word many times in the past – yes, hadn't everyone. 'I went there as a child and with both my parents. I've even been on the odd day out, but when, I could not say. It's been at least ten years since I last went there.'.

The porch and front door were now firmly closed behind them. Inspector Folkard asked Sergeant Shakespeare to inadvertedly ask the Conways sometime in the future about Mr Rimmer's days out, any holidays they were aware of in the last ten years. Sergeant Shakespeare nodded. Although neither spoke at the time, they were both thinking the same: if they could prove he had lied regarding his trips to Blackpool, if the trips had been more recent, they might just have enough to arrest Mr Rimmer and interview him further – such a lead could even secure that much needed warrant, so that they could search his property. Again, the term *a needle in a haystack* came to Inspector Folkard's mind.

23

ON THURSDAY MORNING Mr Rimmer rises from his bed half-an-hour early; he creeps about in order to avoid waking his mother. Already his suit has been hung, his favourite salmon pink shirt pressed and lucky socks selected. Despite another anxious sleep, today is the last day of term and the day when he will make all the necessary arrangements with Jennifer for the September placement.

Downstairs, Mr Rimmer helps himself to the now customary low sugar muesli; he gazes out from the kitchen back window across the garden before placing the bowl down and opening the back door. Mr Rimmer meanders down the right hand path that runs between the luscious garden on the left and the long greenhouse on the right, then left again at the bottom of the garden, along the narrow path to the Granny house. Mr Rimmer hums to himself whilst he retrieves a soiled shovel with an orange handle that stands against its side. He casually hums to himself a favourite tune as he heads back, past the long greenhouse on the left then places it in the garage which is situated almost adjacent to the bungalow.

Once indoors, Mr Rimmer retrieves his half-empty, half-full bowl and finishes the rest of his breakfast. A stroll into the front lounge, Mr Rimmer sits for about twenty minutes in his favourite armchair – he must not set off early. The excitement bubbling up inside him, Mr Rimmer pushes his spectacles back onto the bridge of his nose before he rehearses some polite conversation for Jennifer's benefit before setting off to work on time.

In the porch on the flaxen doormat a copy of the portrait of Eva Manning, identical to the one that was thrust thoughtlessly before him by the irritating officers hoping for the right reaction, looked up at him from the front page of the latest edition of the Southport Visitor – POPULAR TEENAGER GOES MISSING ON MOTHER'S BIRTHDAY. He purposefully steps aside from the midweek paper for the exit when suddenly one of the mother-in-law's tongues catches him across his right cheek. Mr Rimmer's reaction is to put his briefcase down and throw the dammed thing out to die in the garden – but Mr Rimmer cannot be late, his cheek is bleeding, he'll deal with her later.

As soon as the engine starts, BBC 3 executes a rendition of a soothing melody by Chopin; despite the composer's best efforts, Mr Rimmer is too upset to listen. He is by the large roundabout on Switch Island before he is able to calm down. At the lights, he lowers the mirror to investigate the painful scratch, too high to blame the razor – smaller than he thought though – it feels worse than it looks. The car behind sounds his horn for Mr Rimmer to hurry on. Raising his right hand, he signals an insincere apology: he needs to stay on the right side of the law.

Mr Rimmer is already by the school gates when he suddenly realises that he could have offered Jennifer a lift in. As soon as he gets an opportunity, he will insist on doing so, a lift to school and a lift home. Striding into school, his left arm now loosely swinging to and fro, Mr Rimmer looks about for his female friend but she is nowhere to be seen. He waits a further ten minutes, rehearsing the welcome until he gloomily heads upstairs for the English staff-room – no message on his mobile, nothing.

Through the vertical rectangular window, Mr Kennedy can be seen making a brew. Upon entering, to Mr Rimmer's surprise is Jennifer, seated and smiling. Jennifer quickly stands up and apologises profusely for not waiting in the foyer – Mr Kennedy had insisted on escorting her upstairs. Of course Mr Kennedy insisted; he's very insistent with the ladies.

Mr Rimmer forgets the earlier rehearsal in the bathroom - he welcomes Jennifer and states they have a busy day ahead; he is committed in supporting Jennifer so that this time she passes her final teaching practice. Mr Kennedy has already kindly introduced Jennifer to all of the English Faculty; he is happy for Jennifer to shadow him for the day or even part of the day. Mr Rimmer thinks not on your Nellie before whisking Jennifer away, mug of tea in hand and briefcase in the other, up, up to his humble, cheerless classroom: J21.

Jennifer understands the reasons behind Mr Rimmer's pep talk - Mr Kennedy is just the sort of distraction she should avoid like the plague - if she plays her cards right, there may even be a position in the future at St Williams - certainly Miss Ward is thinking of retiring by the end of the year. Jennifer nods; she leans back on a student's desk and reassures Mr Rimmer - sorry Bernard - that she is very grateful for everything he has done for her so far and that she will be guided only by him.

Jennifer removes her camel coloured raincoat and asks if she may put it on the back of Bernard's chair - of course, Mr Rimmer is happy to oblige. It is at this point that Mr Rimmer cannot help but notice how elegant Jennifer looks today; she is wearing a red pinafore that compliments her long dark hair. A crisp white blouse matches her pearl earrings- his mother always wore pearls, back in her hay day.

Yes, there is something about Jennifer today, he has never noticed this before - she very much reminds him of his mother. Two students almost fall through the door without the customary knock, and Mr Rimmer is back in the land of the living. Following registration, Mr Rimmer explains, he will be free to show Jennifer around and go through the schemes of work he has picked out in order to support her teaching classes next term. Jennifer smiles, she has a beautiful smile.

During the tour, Mr Rimmer proudly introduces Jennifer to a selection of colleagues about the school who are happy to take the time to make idle chit-chat. It is the last day of term and holidays are booked to hotter destinations than the north of England. Mr Rimmer repeats at each meeting point that he is hoping to get away for a week to the Lake District, near Ullswater - he is planning to take his binoculars and camera – he would like to take some photographs of the lake.

Finally, in the headteacher's office, Jennifer is welcomed and given the usual pep-talk before Mr Jessop compliments Mr Rimmer for taking on the mentoring responsibility, on top of all his other commitments. For once, Mr Rimmer leaves Mr Jessop's office feeling grateful; he wants to create the right impression – it is important to him – the last few days have been hell.

Mr Rimmer has been trying all morning to find a way of suggesting the idea of giving Jennifer a lift to and from work. When he eventually gets round to it, they are alone in his classroom – there really was no need for all the worry – Jennifer readily accepts and is extremely grateful for the offer. Times arranged for the pick-up, Mr Rimmer will drop Jennifer off tonight, on the way home from school.

At lunchtime, Bernard and Jennifer sit in the staffroom with their contrasting packed lunches; they exchange comments on the present state of examination boards and the marking process when Mr Kennedy saunters into the staffroom. Despite his best efforts, Mr Rimmer fails to keep Jennifer engaged and very soon they are chatting together about the weekend's shocking results on The X Factor's finale.

Lunchtime finally over, Mr Rimmer half-smiles before rising and finally leaving with Jennifer. For the next two hours Mr Rimmer introduces Miss Dwyer to her classes; the new academic timetable is always in place the half-term prior to the summer break. Students are eager to demonstrate what they can do; Jennifer has a knack with the more difficult ones. By the end of the day, Mr Rimmer is impressed with Jennifer's qualities. He is quite tired; he has been watching his *p's and q's* all day. In contrast, Jennifer is full of energy, eager to plan over the long break and determined to make this teaching practice a success. They pack up their bits and bobs and head for reception in order to sign Jennifer out.

Mama's and Papa's *California Dreaming* unexpectedly blasts forth from the stereo as the engine is turned on. Mr Rimmer, momentarily embarrassed, is consoled by Jennifer who exclaims how much she loves this song and together they head home, at times singing the odd bit out loud and laughing when Jennifer forgets the words.

Sitting on red at Maghull's main set of traffic lights, Mr Rimmer looks over to the right; a busy travel agents suddenly catches his eye. The sight suddenly makes him feels sad; it is the thought of not seeing Jennifer again for six weeks. He knows he cannot ask anything from her; he simply requests that she keep in touch to which she readily agrees. Mr Rimmer thinks to add that she may get in touch at any point over the break but quickly changes his mind – he has already achieved more than most.

At the next set of lights, he notices Jennifer's camel coloured coat has parted at her knees; sitting down has resulted in her red pinafore becoming a lot shorter and Mr Rimmer is suddenly aroused by such a sight.

Relieved to wave Jennifer off, Mr Rimmer heads quickly home; he needs a long shower and a peaceful night in order to gather his thoughts. Maybe Jennifer and him are not so unalike – he wasn't bad looking – but the age gap quickly brings him back down to earth and the reality fills him with melancholic thoughts. Mr Rimmer knows he must keep busy over the next six weeks; he will text Jennifer occasionally – he doesn't want to put her off. If he could talk to his mother he would. But he can't – not anymore. There is too much at stake.

Mr Rimmer thinks on what his mother might say. There was a ten year long age gap between his parents – the gap never caused any problems – they were happy. It was his father's death that broke his mother's heart. As if enlightened by these memories, Mr Rimmer takes to the stairs for bed – a stride in his step. As he removes his glasses, it suddenly dawns on him that a new pair of spectacles, or even contact lenses may give him the much needed boost to his low self-esteem. His mother was always saying that appearances mattered – that a small change could make all the difference.

In the early hours of the morning, Mr Rimmer wakes up pouring with sweat. In his dream Jennifer is at the cinema with him when suddenly he is no longer in the picture and he has been replaced by Marcos Kennedy. Ian had his right arm around Jennifer's shoulder. He was looking down at her breasts.

Frustrated by further thoughts that he might have passed his number to Jennifer on the sly, Mr Rimmer clambers out of bed to pace the floor and calm down. He now has a banging headache. Sadly, he has no-one to talk to, no-one who would understand; he knows he can no longer count on his mother. Mr Rimmer puts on his spectacles and goes downstairs; he makes himself a cup of tea. He cannot stomach the sight of biscuits – he can no longer take comfort from these. He thrusts a ripe banana into his mouth, the sweetness bringing him some comfort. Half an hour later, Mr Rimmer has calmed down – he places his mug into the empty sink deciding to take a short walk around the back garden. The warm, cool air restores his faith and the sounds coming from the summer's night raise his hopes once again for some type of a meaningful relationship.

Mr Rimmer is still a virgin. Only once has he ever lied in bed with a woman - at the time, a much older woman. She was kind, clean but ugly - a big gap between her teeth - bow legged. She was a bar-maid at the Catholic Club in Woolton, nearby to the camp where he carried out his university degree, before he began to train as a teacher. Despite all her efforts, Mr Rimmer could not rise to the occasion. Mr Rimmer is saving himself for someone special.

24

LYING WIDE AWAKE after midnight, on the right side of their spacious super king-sized bed, Hermione Folkard thought about Mr Rimmer's final words. What did the term *under the weather* exactly mean? Shortly after, Walter stirred; he turned over and shifted across the middle of the bed before putting his left arm around her curvy hips, or chunky chips, as he liked to call them.

It wouldn't be very long before the youngest of the family would disjoin them by landing at some point in the night – smack bang in the middle. It was just too irresistible for Zita, the choice of a comforting wing to nestle under, regardless of whatever side she slept on. Parenting was all so much easier now she was in school full-time; full of confidence – spoilt, a little maybe. Zita was an adorable, intelligent child. Walter had related earlier in the week that whilst helping Darcy with the spelling of the word distinctive, Zita had proclaimed that she had been learning all about distinctive that day – that dinosaurs were distinctive and that it meant that they had lived a long time ago and that they were all dead now.

Walter reminded a hysterical Darcy that when she was Zita's age she would often ask for a packet of opposites instead of a packet of Wotsits. Walter hadn't noticed that neither of the girls were laughing now, adding the story of when Darcy would at the age of two refer to a plug as a 'flug'. At that point Zita had begun to laugh. Darcy just upped and walked away.

A couple of hours later, Harry had called round; Walter wasn't laughing then – all he could repeat were the words, 'what is your mother going to say?' and 'how could you be so stupid?', over and over again. Wide awake now and unsure of whether it was a good time or not, Walter broke the news to his wife who simply said a four letter word beginning with 's' and ending in 't'.

Walter related how a past female friend of Harry's, dare he say – one night stand – had contacted Harry with the news that her son, Mark, now four months old was his likely son, since a DNA had revealed that her long-term partner was not. Hermione knew that these things happened; a voice within her provided the phrase – *news of a child should always be welcomed* – regardless.

Hermione nodded to herself, a little calmer now, before returning to the fact that the deed had resulted following a one night stand! How many times had they spoken to Harry about protection. On top of everything else he was still only twenty – he was at University – he could barely take care of himself, let alone a child – he still hadn't mastered how to hang on to a girlfriend for longer than five minutes!

Hermione Folkard was so busy thinking about how much she disliked the name Mark, god how ordinary, that she hadn't noticed Walter had slipped out to make her a much needed brew – not that this one would fix everything. She'd missed everything - the pregnancy, the scan, the birth, the clothes and toys, the photographs – all missing – and, and why hadn't Harry told her himself?

A longer conversation revealed her 'grandson's' full name: Mark Anthony Stirrup. Mark Anthony was a good name - a good solid name. Resisting the urge to call Harry at four in the morning, Hermione Folkard began to feel sorry for her eldest child – what a shock it must have been. Walter filled her in on what he knew – they were awaiting the results from a DNA test.

Following a chat that resulted in doing nothing until the results were in – they both decided on having breakfast in bed a tad earlier than usual. Before they cuddled up to sleep a further hour or so, just that little bit closer than usual, Hermione Folkard sent her son a text: 'I love you son – a baby is always good news.'.

25

THREE WEEKS PASS and Mr Rimmer almost grows used to the loneliness that engulfs him. Jennifer has, in fact, been the first to send a text about an idea on using John Boyne's text *The Boy in the Striped Pyjamas* for the second-half of the Autumn Term. The praise has worked and Mr Rimmer has often been on the other end of the telephone – that was until Jennifer went away to Spain, with her parents for the Summer.

Mid-August and the weather has been dire - a typical wash-out. Mr Rimmer has spent most of his time outdoors in the garden tidying this and that. Tickling the fuchsias with his grand-father's rabbit's paw has paid off; they are in full bloom and are jiggling about outside in different hanging baskets, both to the front and back garden. The window-boxes are a picture to behold. No amount of rain can take away the fact that Mr Rimmer's garden is a beauty; all the hard work has paid off, and now, now the garden is in full bloom, he can look proudly out from his dining come teaching room window in the knowledge that his mother is proud of him too.

Mr Rimmer has come to the conclusion that he no longer wishes to go away this summer to the Lake District; he is worried about the latest spates of burglaries in the area - he would rather stay at home and not risk a break in – his mother, for instance, would be devastated if the greenhouses or the granny house were broken into or damaged.

When Mr Rimmer was sixteen, he broke a window to the granny house – he threw a broken half brick used as a doorstopper to the shed before he booted the double doors repeatedly until they caved in. A week earlier he had tried to set the granny house on fire only to find his mother had returned from work early.

His mother had said very little about the incident; instead she held him for a long time on the flagged steps that lead from the kitchen window to the garden. She looked at the granny house and her broken son – she cried and apologised and apologised and said she loved him so much and that she was so very, very sorry.

A week later, Mr Rimmer returned home from school to find the granny house restored; window-boxes had been added to each side. Since then, it has remained locked – everything inside is in its place – a rug to the centre of the floor – the doll house figurines looking out from their bedroom own windows. The peaceful yet eerie atmosphere reminded Mr Rimmer of one of his favourite scenes in the black and white version of Great Expectations, the one where Pip revisits the mansion years later after he has been used and abused by those he loved and trusted. Pip made Miss Havisham aware of her errors – she apologised – she really meant it. Her wedding dress caught fire after he left.

26

AUGUST TWENTIETH. EVA was still missing; she had been missing for almost seven weeks. Already coverage in the media had slackened – CCTV revealed very little – nothing was certain. All they knew was that Eva had gone missing at some point after leaving her home. Numerous leads had grown cold; there had been many sightings, mostly in nearby towns, but some were even as far as Cumbria. Despite this, all leads had grown cold.

Inspector Folkard was almost sure Eva was dead. The minute Eva's body surfaced, vital clues would probably link her to the death of Mary-Eloise. As instructed by Superintendent Reid the cases were to be investigated separately. Despite this, Inspector Folkard knew the right evidence would most likely link them to the same killer – most likely, a serial killer.

In the knowledge that his leading Inspector was going on leave the following day, Superintendent Reid was not in the best of moods. He was not interested in suppositions or coincidences – he wanted hard evidence; it had been ten weeks since the first victim had been found – whatever their position it was time for a result – something must have been missed.

Inspector Folkard didn't think anything had been missed – she appreciated he had the Chief of Police breathing down his neck and all that – it was the parents of Mary-Eloise she had to answer to. Inspector Folkard knew she'd get her killer, all in good time.

In less than a fortnight, she would be taking her own child out for a family meal, her eldest, for his twenty-first birthday. DNA now matched, her grandson Mark would attend – he was five months old now. Only this weekend, they had met for the first time – he didn't really look that much like Harry – his chin was pointy – he was blonde, really blonde. All of her children had been dark. Her youngest daughter, Zita, had been born with across her entire back – even dark hair protruding from her ears. The words, 'I'm your grandmother.', just hadn't sounded right. In return, he withdrew into the arms of Harry – weary of her eagerness to please.

Back in the land of the living – Sergeant Shakespeare rapped on the window from the outside of the office before entering. Clearly frustrated, Sergeant Shakespeare shared her utmost desire to turn over the entire property of 260 Marshide Road. 'Suspicion was not proof.', repeated Inspector Folkard – sadly it was not. Any DNA would only be deemed as natural – they had after all both been to the property on several occasions. The key would surely lie in finding a link with another murder – a past one – one with similarities – one like the Alice Lau murder.

'Where had the bracelet been purchased from?'. Inspector Folkard thought for a short while before asking Sergeant Shakespeare to check every shop within five miles of Mr Rimmer's vicinity. Sergeant Shakespeare would ring Blackpool CIU – the bracelet needed to be forensically examined again and Mr Rimmer, a visit for a voluntary DNA sample she thought. 'To eliminate him from our enquiries, of course.'.

Just before midday, Sergeant Shakespeare informed Inspector Folkard that she had successfully contacted Mr Rimmer and that a further visit had been arranged in order to acquire a DNA sample. Mr Rimmer had politely stated to Sergeant Shakespeare that he was surprised they had not thought of doing so earlier. Very clever response thought Inspector Folkard.

Inspector Folkard was pleased they had a couple of hours to kill. She slung a book on greenhouses towards a bemused Sergeant Shakespeare before informing her that she *had always wanted* to purchase a greenhouse in order to grow something or other and to get reading. 'I want to get a good look in his back garden.'. Inspector Folkard informed her colleague that she too had been swatting - reading up on fuchsias – about one hundred varieties – named after a German botanist – Fuchs something or other –

loved for their teardrop shape and like willows, believed to be unlucky - bringers of sorrow. 'Apparently discovered first in the Caribbean in the Dominican Republic - still used in traditional funerals.'.

Sergeant Shakespeare yawned; she had another late night. Inspector Folkard knew when the time was right, her colleague of many years would introduce her, to her. Being gay in the police force was not easy - especially if you were a woman. A warm orangey beach scene on one of the text's front covers, an elongated rectangular photograph, reminded Inspector Folkard of the first time her husband and she had taken a last minute holiday together, not long after they had met. She was surprised looking back now how forward she had been; it had been her suggestion they travelled away in order to get to know each other more - they had worked together for two years, yet he had not noticed her once - she had noticed him.

Walter had worked in the ICT department as a consultant - everyone liked him and everyone knew her. In her earlier days, Hermione Folkard was very fond of a party or two. What she liked about Walter was what irritated her the most at the time - her rank had meant little to him - he was not easily impressed. He was unambitious and unpretentious - salt of the earth type. In the end, she just asked him out for a drink; it wasn't going to happen soon if he had been left to his own devices.

Walter had always reported to the children that he had been very much in love with their mother from the moment he had set eyes on her. The fact was he was not sure at all about P.C. Cummings, as she was known at the time, and if the truth be known he was more than a little scared of her.

The holiday in the Dominican Republic cemented both: they fell quickly in love. Many a night was spent swimming far out in the warm sea. Pink lightning forked across the evening sky and the warm rain fell at intervals. Despite spending a couple of days feeling under the weather, with what the locals referred to as the Puerto Plata Splatta virus – the holiday was magical. They drank a fair bit, they laughed a lot. Thinking back, Inspector Folkard could not recall seeing a single fuchsia plant in sight.

'It says here,' stated Sergeant Shakespeare 'that glasshouses go back to Roman times and that some French guy wanted cucumbers on his dining plate every day of the year - that in the end he managed to get one a day with his mini glass house invention. Blimey! – get this – in 1438 Koreans were growing mandarin trees in them.'. Inspector Folkard was now busy debating with herself the true meaning of the saying that people in glass houses shouldn't throw stones. 'Very clever really.', she'd remarked out loud, but Sergeant Shakespeare was far too engrossed in her book to respond.

Hermione Folkard had told Walter she could not return to a destination like the Dominican Republic again. On a scuba diving trip, the group was taken in an open jeep to their destination; as tourists, they were always asked for money whenever the vehicle pulled up at any lights. Neither of them grew used to the begging – especially from the children. It was hard to enjoy the island when others were going without. The untrained guide with orange skin unsuccessfully waved the beggars away. He kept shouting 'pissalo – pissalo' to the driver but the vehicle couldn't get away fast enough.

'Two o'clock. Time to set off and visit our man; Mr Rimmer will be expecting us and we must not disappoint.'. chorused Inspector Folkard. Books down, they waltzed purposefully out from the office bumping into P.C. Clark on the corridor in the nick of time. Blackpool CIU had telephoned – they were sending the bracelet over. 'Should be with you tomorrow.'. The following day was unfortunate, today would have been much better.

Tonight, Inspector Folkard would set off with her family to catch the early ferry from Calais to Dover: a shortened family break in France. The bracelet would be there when she returned. Mr Rimmer was sure to be going nowhere.

27

NOW THE MOTHER-IN-LAW'S tongue has been removed to the greenhouse, the porch seems brighter – more cheery. Mr Rimmer contemplates whether to move the young fuchsia back into the greenhouse too – she is withering – at night the porch can be as cold as a morgue. This particular type, the Vargaciana variety is of the miniature kind, less bulbous but longer with stamens that curl like eyelashes. Mr Rimmer's concern for his young plant engrosses him to the point where he does not notice the arrival of the unmarked vehicle.

Sergeant Shakespeare smiles directly at Mr Rimmer from the mustard gate whilst Inspector Folkard appears to be very interested only in his front garden. Such is her interest, that Mr Rimmer finds himself voluntarily exiting his porch to converse with the visiting party. It was indeed a fine day. Sergeant Shakespeare is glad to get out of the office – they had been immersed in paperwork all day. Soon, Mr Rimmer is sharing with Inspector Folkard the do's and must not's on the feeding of carp fish.' It is never a good idea to have any type of blossom near a pond –

poisons the fish – dirties the water – rots and chokes the pond life.'. Mr Rimmer is more than happy to advise Sergeant Shakespeare on the choice of a greenhouse. Fascinated by Sergeant Shakespeare's knowledge on the subject matter, Mr Rimmer pauses to enquire what it is she is thinking of growing.

Sergeant Shakespeare had no idea why she has said she likes to grow potatoes. A suspicious Mr Rimmer invites the chameleons in for tea. Custard creams plated and waiting, they enter the front room. When Sergeant Shakespeare steps forward to offer to make tea, Mr Rimmer declines politely, insisting he has matters in hand.

During Mr Rimmer's short absence, Sergeant Shakespeare can barely look at her Inspector who is glaring at her in disbelief. Potatoes indeed. It would be pointless to suddenly appear interested in fuchsias now that their game was obviously up.

Tea over, the DNA swab is quickly attained – a small painless scrape to the inside of Mr Rimmer's left wall within his mouth, bagged and sealed. Sergeant Shakespeare wonders if Mr Rimmer has acquired his numerous fillings from eating too many sweets and biscuits. She thanks Mr Rimmer for his time and her smile is reciprocated. Inspector Folkard then asks if she may wash her hands and is personally escorted by Mr Rimmer to the kitchen sink.

Inspector Folkard complements Mr Rimmer on his luscious back garden – a real haven. As the Inspector dries her hands on the tasteless seaside tea-towel, she notices the tall lonesome mother-in-law sitting on a ledge in the nearest greenhouse – she appears to be pointing across the garden. A real haven, contemplates Inspector Folkard.

Upon leaving the kitchen, Inspector Folkard enquires if Mr Rimmer has recently purchased any new plants – he'd obviously been very busy this summer in the garden. Mr Rimmer states that he has not, not recently – he would be returning to school next week and he has been making plans – busy – busy – it was important to be prepared for lesson. 'Teaching is after all a very demanding job and students can be quite challenging, if you're not prepared.'.

Inspector Folkard looks towards the granny house once more. How much she wished they had made it into the back garden and shrewdly obtained a sample of soil from the shovel with the orange handle that was leaning against the garage. It was probably nothing. One never knows. Polite conversation over, the inspectors leave Mr Rimmer's abode through the front porch and back out into the picturesque garden. The inspectors close the gate and look back towards the front porch, there is no sign of Mr Rimmer - although both detect a faint sound coming from somewhere behind the side gate – the sound of what seems to be something metallic scrapping against the paved floor.

28

THE FOLKARD SUMMER break to Pompadour in France would have to be cut short; although everyone was entitled to a break, this was just not the right time. Ferry arrangements changed, the Folkards trundled off for a much needed break and would return just in time to celebrate their eldest's 21st. This summer's vacation would be the first without their eldest child. Two end of summer resits and a strange child that needed a father, separated the closely-knit family unit. Hermione Folkard knew change was imminent and sadly unavoidable.

Despite Hermione Folkard's best efforts, it was impossible to leave Mr Rimmer behind. This was how it always was. Any suspect became part and parcel of her daily life; work never stayed at work – they travelled together, arm in arm, like criminals: resistance was futile. Either nothing or something would come about in her absence; Sergeant Shakespeare at the helm of the ship, would steer it steady through the murky waters until her certain return.

Like last year's trip, the girls were packed into the back of Walter's bright red convertible for their evening sleep and awoken in the early hours for the ferry from Dover. Approximately three hours following their arrival to Calais, they awoke in Paris for breakfast. Parking free on a weekend day, they secured the car down a busy street. They breakfasted at a corner café opposite the metro - sweet crepes for mother and eldest daughter, savoury ones for father and youngest – four Americanos and four colas later and they were ready for the day.

Walter held securely the hand of the youngest whilst the other two enjoyed sampling and sourcing what the street stalls had on offer. Police on bicycles were posted every eight stalls or so – none of them seemed relaxed. None of them smiled. Equally the frustration on the faces of the stall holders showed; they longed to succumb to the tradition of piling on the pressure. Despite the cultural differences present in the faces of each passer-by, each stall-holder too, they all intertwined gracefully as if they were actors on a stage conducting a dance, their purpose clear.

For a few seconds only, a tall, broad-necked and dark man selling knifes reminded Hermione Folkard of her dictator-like line manager, Superintendent Douglas Reid. He looked down upon Zita who gazed at a small knife – it's handle bejewelled with green beads and sparkling stones. When he spoke, the gentlest of voices emerged from between his lips. Zita smiled as her father led her away.

Regardless of having seen it all before, the sight of the Eiffel Tower, welcoming them back like old friends, drew gasps from all four Folkards. Once below, they looked up in unison, in all directions, at the beauty that grew upwards from the four corners surrounding them. Different sized chunks of light cut through various corners; the temptation to go up the tower soon disappeared as they recalled the time and exhaustion felt, when last year they attempted to go up via the stairs having taken the lift in previous years.

Three hours or so was spent walking about the surrounding area and its parks, taking in the buzz of the crowd and soaking up the sunshine that could be taken for granted in this part of Europe. Mid-afternoon, the Folkards were on their way to their final destination. Having passed several key cities on the A20 and all taking six of the longest of hours, they arrived at Walter's favourite town Mansac.

Fifteen minutes earlier they had passed Allsac but Mansac was definitely Walter's favourite. Hermione Folkard tried hard not to laugh but when on holiday everything was funny, even her husband's childish capers. The town of Leggett was soon upon them, small and very rural – one Postal, one Boulanger and no shops. The wide, towering church with its flat front, tall as a castle with the three big bells welcomed them back. Within seconds they had passed the entire town. They turned this way and that, down the rough track before they arrived to their cottage. With its small balcony, shutters and window-boxes, it stood cosily aligned to the owner's more impressively sized yet less charming abode. To the side and slightly behind the larger abode was the heavenly infinity-like swimming pool waiting on the edge of a small cliff.

They were welcomed first by Lara's dutiful barks, the owners' black Spaniel, then by Godfrey and Lisa who emerged with cold drinks for all. Soon, the dark set in and the stars emerged as they did every night after – the heat enveloped them and the crickets lulled them to sleep. Despite the bliss, Hermione Folkard was irritated by mosquitoes and midges and small fly. Whilst the family slept peacefully, Hermione Folkard lay thinking about her unsolved case and of course, Mr Rimmer.

The few days and many hours intermingled and at times Hermione Folkard forgot one or both. Drinking wine with an evening meal evolved into having a glass or two from early afternoon – relaxation was a welcomed friend. The girls went from swimming once in the morning and then later in the afternoon to swimming all day - the parents having to remove them in order to get anywhere at all. The button noses of both girls were peeling - fresh pink flesh contrasting against their newly acquired tan.

The night before they set off, Godfrey and Lisa invited them over for supper. At some point in the conversation they shared, what they referred to as, their madness in the re-building of their own abode.

With the money from each rental they would fix this and that. It was only in the last five years that the property had possessed a pool. They had dug it themselves – concreted it themselves – tiled it together. Their detailed account of the complexity and arduous work involving the building of the pool certainly changed Walter's mind about taking on such a project himself, to Hermione's relief. Still, the result of their efforts had been worth it, they added. The Folkards agreed.

Hermione Folkard was rocking the youngest in her arms, already asleep, when Lisa listed the rubbish they had managed to dispose of, by burying it under the pool. 'For sure if I was going to dispose of a body, look out Godfrey, there he would lie.'. Everyone was laughing at this point, bar the Inspector. Hermione Folkard rocked her young one more slowly now, her mind very much elsewhere, a picture of the shovel with the orange handle firmly at the forefront.

Sadly and necessarily, it was time for the drive home. Fortunately, the return seemed shorter and quicker. Once in Calais, there was really no point in keeping the hood down; already the dropping temperature could be felt from across the Chanel, Britannia bearing her cold shoulder for having deserted her for a warmer climate. In a couple of days, she would be back at work and away from home where the heart was. Hermione Folkard wondered what Mr Rimmer had been up to in her absence. She recalled the sound of what was surely the shovel being removed following their last visit and smiled.

29

'Remember, remember the first of September

the leaves are ready to fall

the wind will rise

and take them away

and the trees will stand naked and tall.'

MR RIMMER IS chanting a childhood poem to himself when Jennifer calls out of the blue. Jennifer apologises for not making more contact over the summer – she has enjoyed her break in Barcelona – she has a small gift for Mr Rimmer. Mr Rimmer too recounts some events during his busy Summer. 'Yes. I too often travel; usually to visit relatives in Wales.'.

Before allowing the conversation to end, Mr Rimmer arranges to pick Jennifer up, it's the least he can do. He reminds her that their first day will be an INSET day - this stands for IN-SErvice something or other Training and that basically they will spend half a day in the main hall being advised by someone or other who is probably a failed teacher in the first place and has ended up working as a local education trainer. They both laugh. Mr Rimmer states that in all likelihood, the afternoon will be handed over to departments in order to prepare for the return of the pupils the following day. Jennifer is not to worry – he will guide her. 'If you follow my advice then you will not go wrong.'.

Elated following their nineteen minute conversation, Mr Rimmer decides it is time to tackle the job he has been putting off. Mr Rimmer washes his favourite mug at the kitchen sink and stares intently out of the window towards the granny house.

Wearily, Mr Rimmer contemplates the job ahead. He delays things by tidying this and that about the house. Occasionally, he stares out towards the back of the garden. The granny house looks charming this late morning; sweet peas trail wearily at either side – it is time to dig them up. Yes, Mr Rimmer has decided to begin with the removal of the withering sweet peas. This task will help him to compose himself before he enters the old wooden enclosure; it is not warm today and it is dry – the conditions are almost perfect.

Mr Rimmer takes the key ring with the metallic bull on it out from his trouser pocket. It was his mother's key ring and holds the only key to the granny house. It doesn't take long to pull the sweet peas up; they are soon lying horizontally across the top of the compost heap at the back of the long greenhouse.

Standing on the open porch, Mr Rimmer opens with ease the right French door then the left; they are well-oiled. He hesitates for a few moments before entering. Once inside, Mr Rimmer closes the doors before habitually looking about the garden. From here, what can be seen of the back of the house looks quite quaint – framed by luscious foliage at either side, the weeping willow with the swing now to the right and the long established pond to the left.

Even farther left, divided by the long path, is the long greenhouse; the mother-in-law's tongue is pointing menacingly towards him from a shelf. Mr Rimmer contemplates leaving the granny house to fetch the damn thing and bury her with the others below him, but, now he is here, he will not allow himself to be distracted – he has a job to finish.

The rug rolled back now, Mr Rimmer composes himself before he lifts the wooden latch. The tomb is almost full. Despite holding his breath, Mr Rimmer is still unaccustomed to the foul smell. It hits him almost immediately.

Mr Rimmer gags before looking away. Moments later, he stares with disbelief at the mess his mother has made. Eventually, the diminishing roll of tarpaulin is removed with ease revealing a youthful corpse in its first stages of decomposition. Eva stares directly at Mr Rimmer – Mr Rimmer is taken aback; he was sure he had closed her eyelids – he always closes the eyelids. Mr Rimmer takes out his blue inhaler before removing his spectacles. None of the others looked at him like this. He wipes the grease that has gathered around the sides of his nose before taking two short puffs.

Eva's eyelids are ice-cold. Her thickened eyelashes catch his right open palm as he attempts to shut the lids closed. Eva's eyelids will not shut; she keeps staring at Mr Rimmer who is innocent of the deed. It is at least ten minutes before Mr Rimmer can successfully remove Eva's heavy corpse and wrap it in the last remaining piece of tarpaulin. With each roll-over comes a thud from the head, each roll-over quieter and quieter.

Silenced now, Eva has joined the others. Mr Rimmer decides that today is the day to bury the rug with all that is below – and his garden gloves – and his shoes and shirt and trousers before pulling the doll's house and his mother's rocking chair over the hatch with a latch.

Mr Rimmer is far too weary now to stand the wooden figurines back at their individual windows of the doll's house but the thought of leaving them there like that is all too much. As he has done since he was a child, Mr Rimmer sits almost cross-legged before pulling the double doors to the front of the house open. Mr Rimmer stands them all in their correct window, father is standing at the bedroom room window with mother-one, mother-two is standing at the second bedroom window with son. There was never any point pretending there was a sister.

Mr Rimmer hesitates before lifting the attic's wooden flap upwards. It began with a length of hair removed as a keepsake – a suggestion made a family liaison at the hospital morgue. a red ribbon in a bow securing the long lock of dark hair belonging to his mother. Mr Rimmer cannot resist touching the other bunches of hair, each tied with a different coloured ribbon. The fingers to his right hand fall upon each length and move downwards along the length – each one unique and very different . Over the last ten years, none of these have lost their lustre. Mr Rimmer cannot bring himself to place them down below, even though he knows he should. He will find somewhere indoors for them.

An hour has passed, having checked through the French doors twice, Mr Rimmer locks the doors before he uneasily gives it legs across the garden in his white y-front underpants and bottle green socks. He enters the house through the back door and stops to look back through the kitchen window. From inside everything is as it was. Mr Rimmer needs a cup of tea, with sugar today and a soak in the bath - he shakes his head; he would be having words with his mother later if she were not so ill.

30

HARRY FOLKARD'S TWENTY-FIRST birthday meal came and went. Although it was not really any different to any other birthday he had ever had – aside from his eighteenth, which was a great bash, something had very much changed. Hermione Folkard had hoped to bond a little more with her grandson but alas he was ill and could not attend; she now felt even more estranged from him. Her gut feeling had guided her most of her life but on this matter it directed her nowhere – maybe this time she would not be able to work out what was to be done – certainly, solving the murder of Mary-Eloise seemed more straight forward, more plausible – a matter of time.

Hermione Folkard spent the penultimate day of her summer break doing what most parents do during the last weekend in August, purchasing uniforms for the younger children. Darcy, about to begin her first year in secondary school, was more concerned with her small pot-belly and the small scar on her nose than making friends in a whole new environment. Zita was excited to say the least; she would soon begin Year

One and couldn't wait to re-join her old circle of friends from Reception – little phased her in life.

Confident and determined to get her own way, she had spent most of the holiday asserting her authority on others, almost always determined to have her own way. On the last day of their holiday, and to the horror of both her parents and the owners, she had sunk her two front teeth into Darcy's nose because her older sister wouldn't let her pass whilst playing at the Roman end of the outdoor pool.

A longer than anticipated conversation with Sergeant Shakespeare took place the evening before Hermione Folkard's return to work. The DNA swab belonging to Mr Rimmer had revealed nothing concrete – all plausible links so far could be easily dismissed in a court of law. In any case, it was on record; it could be matched to any other victim, past or present. And the charm bracelet? The bad news first. It could have been purchased from numerous catalogues as well as most high-street stores. The good news, interestingly, only two of the three charms were listed in the original report. One charm had gone unreported because it was later found to be missing. Inspector Folkard guessed correctly the first time. The unicorn. Pondering for a short while, Inspector Folkard enquired about the victim's shoes. Had Alice Lau's shoes been found? Mary-Eloise's hadn't.

Sergeant Shakespeare would check; she did however notice that in the report and during the original interviews with Alice Lau's parents, no list of charms had been made. Sergeant Shakespeare had telephoned the parents of Alice only last Thursday and enquired after the missing charm. It had been such a difficult time for them both that they could not recall exactly what they had and had not said in their interviews to the police. However, the Laus were certain that a charm of a unicorn had existed because she had showed it to them only the week before she died.

The forensic report also mentioned that chunks of hair were missing from the victim – could be something or nothing - natural under the circumstances – would have become tangled in this and that at the waste-ground tip. 'but still, some weirdo's collect this and that as a keepsake, bearing in mind we could be dealing with a serial killer.'. Inspector Folkard agreed. The unicorn charm could be anywhere.

Inspector Folkard thought about Mr Rimmer's merry-go-round – his present to Mary-Eloise. Yes, the unicorn charm could be significant . Inspector Folkard asked Sergeant Shakespeare to return to the forensic officer at the morgue; the pathology lab needed to check if Mary-Eloise had any hair missing. The saying needle in a haystack came to mind following the one about clutching straws.

After a short pause, an even longer and unpremeditated conversation took place about another unknown quantity, the new grandchild. Hermione Folkard had looked forward to being a grandmother one day – or a nanny – or whatever title she'd settle for eventually; she didn't much like any of the choices she had been provided with so far.

Catherine Shakespeare suggested that much like falling into a fast and choppy river, one could thrash about wildly as much as they wanted but the water would not run smoothly until it was meant to, until it reached the part in the river where it was meant to slow down – the peace and calm was sure to follow. The choice was simple. One could thrash about in the river, or lie in it and go with the flow.

Hermione Folkard slept soundly for most of that night before her return to work. She had decided upon the going with the flow method – not rushing matters – the bonding would surely follow – with time, and patience, and love. In the early hours, Hermione Folkard's dream became somehow embroiled with images that stemmed from a poem she had once studied at school. The youngest of chimney sweepers had had his head shaved by an older one, his blonde locks of hair lay on the ground - then suddenly they were all set free by angels holding large golden keys, after being locked up in small black coffins.

The chimney sweepers, then clean from the soot, sprang away like lambs, laughing and dancing and leaping away but from whom they were escaping, she did not know. Suddenly, a familiar face appeared at the window. He was waving at the children and he was smiling. But the angels were not. They turned and pointed at him with their golden keys for ever such a long time before the familiar man turned away and began to weep.

31

THIRTY MINUTES FOLLOWING Mr Rimmer's departure from Marshide Road and he has arrived to the small town of Maghull. Mr Rimmer has no problem remembering where Jennifer lives. He has unintentionally passed her parents abode on several occasions throughout the summer when toing and froing from Southport to Walton – a garden like Mr Rimmer's requires much attention.

Parked now, outside Jennifer's attractive semi-detached house, he is about to exit the comfort of his sky-blue car in order to personally call for Jennifer when disappointingly she spills out before the agreed time from the post-office red front door launching two large-sized canvas bags through the wide tunnel shaped porch doors.

Jennifer is now moving briskly along the newly-paved drive. An anxious yet larger than life smile spreads across Jennifer's face – yes, she is quite nervous – poor thing – understandable; she also looks very smart, wrapped in a light grey three-quarter length coat. Mr Rimmer approves too of Jennifer's choice of what must be size 6 patent-grey shoes, the heels about two and a half inches high.

Mr Rimmer proudly helps Jennifer into his deceptively medium-sized car, placing her colourful bags carefully into the back of his classic vehicle; all the while he is making small conversation regarding the fine weather. Seatbelts in place, Mr Rimmer is about to turn the key in the ignition when Jennifer passes him a medium-sized black plastic bag. Mr Rimmer makes a reference to the swirling yellow and red suns on either side of the bag before looking inside; he raises a rehearsed smile whilst fingering for the small item in the oversized carrier.

Predictably, it a key ring, but it is a key ring with a difference; it is a tasteful mini version of the Sagrada Familia in Barcelona. Jennifer educates Mr Rimmer along the way about some of the history behind this spectacular building. 'Did you know Gaudi died before he'd even completed a quarter of it?'.

This is what sets Jennifer apart from all the others – she is truly intelligent and Mr Rimmer is genuinely interested in almost everything Jennifer has to say. Jennifer's long legs are extremely tanned, thinner than usual and shaven. No, he did not know that – apparently, Gaudi never married because the one he loved didn't want to know, so he dedicated his entire life to the Catholic church!

Mr Rimmer tells Jennifer he will add the tasteful key ring to one he already has back home, from Spain, one of a fierce bull. No, he has never been to Spain – it was a gift from a friend of his mothers. Remarkably, and quite unexpectedly, a trip to Spain doesn't sound so bad after all – maybe a culture trip is needed – time to move on – time to exorcise the ghosts. Mr Rimmer decides he might take a look at Barcelona after all. He too possesses a solitary mind. Similarly he has dedicated his entire life to his profession. He too knows how it feels to be rejected – even feel unloved at times.

Jennifer is now speaking about her cat Missy. He looks unintentionally at the movements she is making with her hands and cannot help but notice the pressure the seatbelt is applying to Jennifer's bosom. Mr Rimmer distracts himself by observing the great outdoors – the September foliage remains fully intact on the yellowing branches– light greens, browns and oranges – the wind is picking up. Suddenly concerned, Jennifer tells of how she heard, whilst in Spain, of a girl in the area who had mysteriously disappeared – all over BBM. Mr Rimmer is about to contribute in order to correct some of this information but instead decides to divorce himself from the entire conversation. Mr Rimmer nods, umms and ahhs at the right intervals. When Jennifer finally pauses for breath, Mr Rimmer interjects by briefly recalling the structure of today's INSET day.

As if by magic, Jennifer quickly begins to share numerous ideas she has had over the last twenty-four hours – good ideas she hopes. Mr Rimmer laughs out loud before instinctively pushing his spectacles back onto the bridge of his nose. He suggests that she should try to not run before she can walk. A shy smile dawns on Jennifer's sweet and eager face as she tilts her head sideways before complementing Mr Rimmer on the new spectacles that he must have acquired over the summer. Mr Rimmer is feeling a little embarrassed; he nods coyly before looking away.

Now, about a quarter of a mile from their final destination, a few unfamiliar young faces, belonging to pupils of St William's, appear sparsely along the way. There are always pupils at the start of the Autumn term who turn up looking like this only to be suddenly rejected at the gates. Despite the written communication from school to home, they still come, looking weak and confused. Mr Rimmer feels slightly irritated by Jennifer's ignorant laughter.

Unintentionally, and quite suddenly, Mr Rimmer shares with Jennifer that he was often one of them too. Mr Rimmer cannot bring himself to say anymore. He has already said too much. Instinctively, Jennifer places her warm right hand over Mr Rimmer's. Mr Rimmer is shocked. The sense of touch is often underestimated – it heals, and comforts – that is, if it is welcomed.

Jennifer apologises as she now takes her hand away. Mr Rimmer shares how his mother was unwell following his father's death, when he was in year ten, and that for the next two years his mother had rarely opened any post. 'She used to even put the bills in the bin.'.

Mr Rimmer knows too that tomorrow, there will be many more feeling like this, mostly year seven starters. The vultures in upper school and their gangs of cling-ons will loiter the sweet-shops on the nearby corners sneering and laughing and breaking them in before they have even entered the school gates. Reality dawns on them both as they pass through the car park gates, but like a crutch, Jennifer and Mr Rimmer will have each other to lean on – not such a bad start to the term after all. In the main car park, familiar faces wave towards Mr Rimmer and Jennifer. Instinctively Jennifer waves back; one of them is Mr flaming Kennedy.

32

'KILLING TWO BIRDS with one stone is the best way of closing a case that has been especially difficult. You solve something whilst at the same time unintentionally solving something else - all the pieces fall into place, like a puzzle.', added Sergeant Shakespeare finishing her coffee.

'You're obviously firing your shotgun unloaded then.', interjected Chief Superintendent Reid, looming in the nearby doorway. 'A word in the Inspector's office if you wouldn't mind?'. Like a bolt of lightning, Sergeant Shakespeare ascended from her seat and headed across the room, Superintendent in tow – colleagues dispersed early from their Monday morning break.

Sergeant Bond was swivelling in his seat. He signalled to a nearby dumbfounded recruit before speaking. 'Watch. Regardless, the boss won't even flicker. I don't know how she does it. I can't stand him myself; he puts the willies up me. I'm really not sure the promotion and the minimal pay rise is worth all the agro when you've got a troll like Reid breathing down your neck.'.

Through the wide internal glass panes, the Inspector's pain-tightened lips could be seen speaking only when required. Sergeant Shakespeare interjected at one point, although from the look on her face, she probably wished she hadn't. The door was left wide open as Chief Superintendent Reid exited the Inspector's office – silence engulfed the incident room before Inspector Folkard stood up from behind her desk and calmly closed the door behind him.

Clearly frustrated, Sergeant Shakespeare stood up at once. For a short while Inspector Folkard said nothing; she just calmly paced the small floor space within her office, stopping from time to time to look out of the window. In the near distance, the Superintendent, in the comfort of the latest Lexus Challenge, could be seen exiting the car park.

Inspector Folkard listened as Sergeant Shakespeare proposed setting up all three investigations alongside each other – a whole new and fresh perspective, treating them as one case – exploring the possibility that all three where linked and that they may have been looking for the one killer all along – that there may even be other bodies, possibly undiscovered.

Inspector Folkard moved away from the window and sat down. Despite the impending consequences, should they be discovered, her gut feeling was driving her forward in the same direction. It was important that all work linked to this unorthodox investigation should take place outside office hours – everything had to be done by the book. It was one thing, disobeying a direct order but in their own time – plausible.

Sergeant Shakespeare nodded. Her partner Wendy probably wouldn't like it, but she added that she'd talk her round. Inspector Folkard enquired whether the word 'partner' suggested some form of commitment and did she mean Wendy as in a Wendy House? Sergeant Shakespeare reddened a little and with a look of disquiet joined her long-time friend at the window.

For a short while, neither spoke. Still looking out onto the busy car park, Sergeant Shakespeare shared with Hermione Folkard that she was praying Wendy wouldn't get herself arrested this weekend; she was a passionate gay activist and would be flying out this weekend in support of boycotting the Sochi Winter Olympics. As one of the main speakers, she was to lead protesters in a demonstration against the Russian President before the consulate in New York. Hermione Folkard's head lifted slightly as if her chin had commanded it so; at the same time her mouth made an 'ah' shape - she knew her colleague was generally private about her home life. Hermione Folkard suggested, as they moved away from the window towards the door, that if Wendy were to be arrested, it would more likely give her more time after hours in the office and less time at home in the doghouse. Smiling, they exited the office.

Although the Superintendent had seen red when he heard that Inspector Folkard had made applications to have the body of Alice Lau exhumed, on the whim, as he put it, that there may or may not have been hair removed from the victim, both colleagues were as determined as ever to find the link that would allow the murders to be investigated to be seen in a whole new light. More significantly, they needed the Alice Lau murder to be re-opened. Inspector Folkard hated to admit it, but they probably did need something more concrete before putting the victim's family through any further anguish - there was, after all, a fine line between doing what was morally acceptable and what simply needed to be done. Inspector Folkard had solved cases like this before. Sometimes, as Inspector Folkard's mother had often been reminded by her, a few eggs needed to be broken in order to make an omelette.

33

ON THE WAY home, Jennifer asks Mr Rimmer if he'd like to come in and have a cup of tea. Taken aback from the unexpected invitation, Mr Rimmer politely declines, unaccustomed to such a genuine request. A few seconds later, Jennifer repeats her request, this time with a humorous undercurrent, adding to the original offer that she also has coffee and some all butter shortbread in need of sampling. Mr Rimmer catches himself smiling whilst looking bashfully away into his wing mirror. Mr Rimmer has now found within himself the courage to accept – he can after all do his shopping later – nearby stores are open twenty-four hours.

Mr Rimmer takes Jennifer's heavy canvas bags out from the shutter-like back doors of his classic car and stands like a buffoon whilst she rummages for an uncomfortably short time in the smaller of the two bags. Eventually they enter her abode together. Mr Rimmer is suddenly alarmed by the thought of meeting Jennifer's parents again; it has been such a long time since her private tuition, that he cannot even remember what they looked like. He is not ready for this. None of this has been planned, or even considered. He normally takes them back to his. Or meets them there. Perspiring a little now, Mr Rimmer is directed from the fairly large entrance, with a plush wine - red carpet that travels as far as the eye can see up the stairs, into the front room of the house.

Jennifer gestures with her right hand towards a comfortable armchair for Mr Rimmer to sit in. She informs him that her parents will not be back for a couple of hours. 'Don't know if you remember, they're both hairdressers – still have the shop in Ormskirk – they're lucky if they get home before six.'. Mr Rimmer removes his jacket before habitually pushing back his spectacles; despite their absence he is still feeling a little anxious. In contrast, Jennifer is more at ease; she nips in and out of the room asking questions about tea and sugar, all the while ensuring Mr Rimmer is feeling right at home.

The cream-like room is pleasing to the eye. Like Mr Rimmer's front room it has a small rectangular window to the left and a large bay ahead – to the right a dark oak upright piano. Above the piano stand many different sized frames with photographs of unfamiliar faces – cream candles at either end. In the bay window an array of books and five pots with plants that look like African violets. Above the majestic fireplace, more photographs – one of these is a fine family portrait.

Mr Rimmer is trying to figure out how old Jennifer was, when the picture was taken - maybe six or seven – she could have even been ten – what matters? It is one of those common portraits that can be seen in most households, the focal point of most fireplaces. For a few moments Mr Rimmer is trying to think if one of these ever existed back at home – maybe his father died before one could be taken.

Mr Rimmer observes closely the interlocked hands belonging to her parents. They sit close together with Jennifer at their feet - it is as though they are presenting the single most important thing in their life. Jennifer's father appears to be much older than her mother.

Jennifer has been standing behind Mr Rimmer for a few seconds before he notices her; she informs him that she very much dislikes the portrait for she has two front teeth missing – Mr Rimmer had not really noticed – they laugh before they sit. Moments later they are chatting like old friends. Jennifer asks Mr Rimmer about his school days. Sensing his discomfort, Jennifer explains she too was bullied at school and that she had sensed earlier in the day that he too had suffered at the hand of bullies. Mr Rimmer only ever talked to his mother about the bullies – right now he has no idea what to say.

'Moving school was the only option left for my parents.', explains Jennifer, 'It was only then, when life became normal that I realised there really was nothing wrong with me – that *their* behaviour said more about them than it said about me.'. Jennifer adds that she wasted so much time trying to fit in, trying to be accepted.

Mr Rimmer has been listening intently; the smallest of shortbread crumbs have gathered in both corners of his mouth. His mother loved shortbread – especially slightly salted, like this variety. Mr Rimmer is now sharing with Jennifer the time when on the playground he was fisted in the face and his glasses were broken. Feeling a little vulnerable now, he goes on to falsely inform that he too found peace, once the bully was eventually expelled. Mr Rimmer is now standing – he would be most grateful if Jennifer could point out the little boy's room.

The winding stairs take Mr Rimmer to the first floor where the bathroom can be seen at the end of the corridor, after passing some of the other rooms. Mr Rimmer is thinking about Jennifer suffering at the hands of bullies when he catches sight of an array of clothing tossed upon a three-quarter bed in the final bedroom to his left, and just before the bathroom. The room has a yellow glow about it; there are many shoes scattered about the floor. It is Jennifer's bedroom.

Upon reaching the bathroom Mr Rimmer closes the door behind him. He wipes the beads of sweat that have gathered about his brow. Mr Rimmer's hands are clammy; he is washing his hands in the sink below the bathroom window when he catches sight of a young mother pushing wearily a pram with a smaller child in toe. Mr Rimmer thinks of his mother and the hardship she must have endured bringing him up alone following his father's sudden death. Mr Rimmer sighs. He had never really thought of his mother as a single parent before.

Although he has so far ignored the burning desire to enter Jennifer's room, Mr Rimmer's need to take anything, anything at all, anything belonging to her becomes too much for him to ignore. He glances around the bathroom - he looks inside a small cabinet, then fidgets with some cosmetics on a shelf - his eyes fall upon the white wicker laundry basket.

Upon his re-entry to the front room, Mr Rimmer speaks of an oval painting at the top of the stairs that caught his eye on way to the bathroom. Jennifer has no idea where the painting came from - her mother bought it at a car boot sale. It had caught her eye because the elderly lady spinning the wheel looked like she was telling the children such an enthralling story, for they are all sat around her, looking at her, as if hanging onto her every word.

Moments later, Mr Rimmer thanks Jennifer for her kind hospitality. He compliments her efforts on her first day, her elegant attire. 'I very much liked the pearl earrings you had worn on the last occasion - you suit your hair tied back.'. He puts on his jacket and begins to head for the post-office red front door which is painted cream on the inside. Jennifer assists the exit from the difficult-to-open porch doors only to find Jennifer's cat, Missy is waiting outside. Mr Rimmer is about to bend down when the cat sprints off; he half smiles at Jennifer before awkwardly walking away along the paved path towards the fine gates.

Feeling a lot more in control, Mr Rimmer enters the comfort of his old and maybe not so interesting classic car, anxious to leave before Jennifer's parents get home. Mr Rimmer waves a little longer than usual before pulling away and heading quickly home. At the lights, at the first opportunity, he removes from his back pocket the stolen item of clothing.

Back home, Mr Rimmer has been in the shower an unusually long time. Eventually he exits the shower and, with some determination in his stride, heads towards his mother's bedroom with only a large mint green towel wrapped about his waist. Mr Rimmer hesitates before touching the handle – he takes a deep breath and enters.

Everything now packed, Mr Rimmer feels more confident than ever. The house is silent, almost peaceful. It is now time to move forward. Like his mother, it has taken a while for Mr Rimmer to come to terms with his mother's departure – but it is time. Mr Rimmer takes the two suitcases of clothing and other significant items before placing them in the boot of his car. Upon closing the shutter-like doors, Albert

Conway suddenly exits the side gate in order to start up a conversation with Mr Rimmer. Albert Conway did not realise he was planning to take a trip. He believed the new term had only just begun.

Mr Rimmer is happy to relate that he is sending these two cases to a local charity shop – some old suits that he has outgrown – he has after all lost over a stone in weight recently. Albert Conway looks Mr Rimmer up and down and agrees that Mr Rimmer is looking better that he has done in a long time; he even remarks positively on his choice of new spectacles.

Mr Rimmer begins to walk away when Albert Conway remarks that his mother too always liked to look her best. 'Mrs Rimmer had a fine figure.'. Mr Rimmer has now stopped dead in his tracks. He is about to give Albert Conway a piece of his mind but he has escaped indoors in the nick of time.

Still irritated by Albert Conway's earlier remark, Mr Rimmer sits down for a light evening meal – his hand in the shape of a fist. He enjoys a light egg salad and a glass of wine before he decides to end the evening by watching a recording of his favourite programme. Mr Rimmer rarely records anything on television. Now days, he is not really fussed whether he is watching it before nine or not. The past behind him, Mr Rimmer is committed to moving forward – a new chapter in his life – no more girls to the house – no more tuition – he will concentrate on Jennifer and Jennifer alone.

Mr Rimmer has avoided so far texting Jennifer this evening. It is late now, time for bed. However, after he has made his customary cup of cocoa, Mr Rimmer sends a quick text thanking Jennifer for the tea and shortbread which is reciprocated almost immediately with a smile icon and a phrase that means so much more than was intended.

Lying in bed, Mr Rimmer fingers for the stolen item that is now stored safely inside the case of his feather pillow. Many wet September leaves have gathered on the windowsill – some are stuck flat onto the pane. Mr Rimmer turns the floral bedside lamp off before turning onto his stomach in the missionary position. Mr Rimmer's left arm is secure under the pillow, his hand immersed in the lace; he falls sound asleep, that is, until the rest of them start complaining.

Alice is pointing at him – they are all pointing at him – moments later he is pulling Eva of Jennifer, she has scratched her face – Jennifer is bleeding. None of them will listen – none of them – he is unable to stop them. Then suddenly they all look behind him. Mr Rimmer turns to see Mrs Rimmer in her pale blue peacock dress; she is looking at him disapprovingly – she is holding Jennifer's lace patterned tights in her right hand and is tutting, shaking her head from side to side. Mr Rimmer pleads with his mother. He is pleading with her over and over again but she will not listen. The other girls are writhing like snakes and laughing like the bullies. She owes him. You owe me. Remember Javier. Javier the spaniard. Please mother.

I beg you. Mrs Rimmer has stopped dead in her tracks; she is thinking about her son's last words when he suddenly wakes drenched in his own sweat.

Unable to stop shaking, even to move for a short while, Mr Rimmer begins to cry like a baby.

34

MIDWEEK AND THE whiteboard on the far wall of Inspector Folkard's office, to the left of her door and opposite to the desk, was taking shape. The photographs of the three females were aligned, side by side with their details listed below. How beautiful all three were – they had so much in common, young, innocent, intelligent, all with promising futures. With the exception of Alice, they lived close enough to one another; despite thorough and extensive interviews, it appeared they had never met at any given point, not once. They were all pretty, similar in age; they were all only children.

As separate cases, only one victim could be linked to Mr Rimmer; there was no proof that Eva had not ran away. Like the rest of the cases reported and unsolved on their database, Inspector Folkard reminded Sergeant Shakespeare that 250.000 U.K. citizens went missing every year – 100.000 were below the age of 18. In a recent report, The Runaway Helpline stated that a teenager went missing in the UK every five minutes – 3000 of them were in care. Sergeant

Shakespeare stated she was glad she was not a parent –the job had certainly put her off.

There was no evidence that Eva Manning was unhappy; if she were missing, she would fall into the category of 7000 teenagers missing a year. Her mother was adamant she had not ran away, that they were close, very close, and that Eva would have never left her, let alone not contact her. Eva would know her mother would be frantic with worry – Eva didn't have a cruel bone in her body.

Similarly, the Chambers had stated that they knew Mary-Eloise would never run away – that they knew she was either in trouble or dead, almost straight away. That seed of doubt, that neither parents believed their daughters to have ran away, was gnawing away at the back of Inspector Folkard's mind.

At times like these, against the judgement of most, her gut feeling was all she had to go on. Neither Inspector Folkard nor Sergeant Shakespeare believed Eva had ran away. It was time to look for a body. If Mr Rimmer were the killer, where would he have disposed of her? Why had Mary-Eloises' been found and not hidden like Eva's? Could there be others?

The key link between the bodies of Alice and Mary-Eloise was that they had been found within three miles of their home. The likelihood was that, Eva Manning was hidden somewhere closer to home maybe right under their nose.

A Southport map was blue-tacked to the wall by Sergeant Shakespeare; a pin pierced through the place where the Mannings resided: 23A Botanic Road, Churchtown. A five, four and three mile radius was circled and identified. If the killer was the same as the other two then anywhere outside the area of Crossens and Banks could be discounted. Mr Rimmer lived 1.9 miles from the Manning abode and 2.3 miles from Mary-Eloise's.

That afternoon, Inspector Folkard and Sergeant Shakespeare drove to Blackpool to explain the reasons behind the exhumation of Alice Lau's body. In theory, the drive to Blackpool should have taken twenty minutes according to Sergeant Shakespeare but the quick-sand and protected marshes had prevented a road from being built on two occasions in the last thirty years. Instead, the drive would take a cumbersome hour and ten minutes – the views were not as scenic as those presented in the media. Inspector Folkard was not really listening. She was wondering how the Laus would react – how she would react if she were in their shoes.

Mrs Lau opened the front door of the B & B. She half-smiled before inviting them into the back room of the household. Inspector Folkard thanked Mrs Lau for her time before sitting down – Sergeant Shakespeare chose to stand. Mrs Lau's narrow eyes widened when Inspector Folkard explained the reasons behind their decision to exhume Alice. Quickly and unexpectedly, Mrs Lau stood up and walked briskly towards the door by-passing Sergeant Shakespeare as if she were not there. She began to yell upwards for her husband to join them – she repeated her request until he marched anxiously down the stairs.

Mr Lau calmed his wife as best he could. Ten minutes passed and Mrs Lau did not speak again. Consent gained, Inspector Folkard and Sergeant Shakespeare thanked the Laus for their time and apologised once more, for what could have only been an unwelcome intrusion. Upon their exit from the back room, Inspector Folkard assured Mr and Mrs Lau that Alice would be returned to them in no time at all. Inspector Folkard knew her words were of little comfort to them.

Inspector Folkard looked back at the aging Bed and Breakfast – the coral paint peeling back from all the windows, the ones to the left of the property worst off. An arm suddenly appeared in the left hand bottom window; the VACANCIES sign was removed and quickly replaced with its opposite. Everyone knew that businesses such as these were suffering greatly following the recession and that the resort had hit an all-time low. But Inspector Folkard and Sergeant Shakespeare understood money could not by happiness and that only time would heal those open wounds.

35

LOOKING BACK UPON the first week as a whole, Jennifer's chances of passing her teaching practice are looking very promising. Her organisation and delivery of lessons reveal she is a natural; her lesson plans put Mr Rimmer's to shame. Next week she will be observed by Ms Lofthouse, her supervisor at Ormskirk University. In ten weeks time she will complete the final part of her teaching practice and may qualify as a Teach First undergraduate which will enable her to stay on at St William's for the rest of the year.

As soon as possible, Mr Rimmer will invite, no, insist Jennifer attends the Christmas staff night out on December the 20th. Jennifer and Bernard. Bernard and Jennifer. They both share an e, an r and an n in their names, that is why their names together look good. He will take her, of course.

On the first Sunday of each month, Southport hosts a World Market Day which runs along the main road of the town: Lord Street. Mr Rimmer has not been to one of these in a while, the gardens having taken priority in the recent past. Mr Rimmer rises earlier than usual today; downstairs he eats a small bowl of muesli before putting on a light green raincoat with a gathered hood.

For a short while Mr Rimmer looks out of the front room window; he realises that over the years he has changed very little in the front garden – no new plants – no hanging baskets. Mr Rimmer has spent too much time trying to preserve the past – picture perfect really. A dog walker passes the house; for a moment the sausage-like dog pauses at the second post of the mustard gate – the one furthest away.

Mr Rimmer is now considering re-painting the whole front of the house – the gates – the lot, and why not? Only a couple of years ago Mr Rimmer took a shine to a sea-side town-house in Blackpool. From what he now recalls to mind, exterior features were glossed over in darker greens – duck egg greens and cornflower blues or was it that mid-blue that is often used to paint sea-side huts? Mr Rimmer unintentionally begins to recall a few more memories before he suddenly and by choice ejects and rejects that video from his mind. He will ponder on this possible change over the next few days and may even pay a visit to the hardware store during the week – there is one past Maghull on the Aintree Estate.

Upon parking his much loved matchbox shaped car at the fire-station end of Lord Street, Mr Rimmer is about to check the parking time allowance plus charges when a familiar face comes into view at what seems to be the Paella tent on the opposite side of the street. Curiosity ignited, yet apprehensive from the onset, Mr Rimmer resorts to continue with his plans for the day. Sundays: free parking for all. Mr Rimmer locks the vehicle and upon looking up and down the street decides to cross over and mingle with the nearest crowd, close to where the market ends.

It makes such a difference sampling this and that on a fine September day - few clouds in sight, the temperature is most agreeable and the breeze is pleasant. It is half-past eleven in the morning yet the crowds are hungry already; colours excite the palate and unfamiliar spices tempt passers-by who depart from tent upon tent with plain polystyrene bags having spent obscene amounts of cash. An attractive dark woman in the not too far distance invites a stranger inside her tent. She is already looking intently at Mr Rimmer before she turns her back and disappears with a middle-aged woman looking worse for wear.

Mr Rimmer has already bought a jar of lemon curd and three varieties of cheese – he is considering the purchase of a large sweet crepe when he catches sight again of Inspector Folkard. How humane she looks with her hair down, tied neatly to her right side - sunglasses. Mr Rimmer scoffed once at the claim by Dune FM Station that wearing sunglasses made one look 20% more pleasing to the eye – it was certainly worth considering – without a doubt smiling certainly improved *her* appearance. Her husband followed; on occasion he would seek out her arm or hand before children – two, possibly three – no, two – both girls – separated them with their inaudible laughter, questions, examinations.

Like a drug, the temptation to mingle within that perfect circle becomes too much. Mr Rimmer has often thought about their meetings – although she has given little away so far, she's the one who clearly thinks she has the upper hand. Just yards away, and the youngest of the two, maybe five years of age, dark like her father, insists upon the rest the need to move elsewhere; she points across the busy street. Unable to resist, Mr Rimmer decides upon casually stroking, with his left hand, the hair tips belonging to the last person to cross the road.

Unaware, the eldest, the older girl with the thick hair with blonde highlights, freckled face and clear blue eyes, hesitates just in time for the contact to be made, that is, until a large arm intercedes and the big woman with the dark face and deep eyes insists upon a reading. Intent on refusing, Mr Rimmer swallows hard and is perturbed momentarily by her hard gaze and determined eyes. Walking away, Mr Rimmer resists looking back over towards the Folkard clan. He does not want to see the dark woman with the all-knowing eyes. He decides he will turn right at the bottom of the street and take a walk along the promenade before heading home.

Despite the promises he has made to both himself and his mother, the desire to crush is still there. Mr Rimmer is feeling a little anxious – his left arm is aching. Passing a vintage bookshop brings Mr Rimmer back down to earth – the window brimming with Study Guides for the various Key Stages. Jennifer certainly has a way of keeping Mr Rimmer on the straight and narrow.

The long walk back diminishes Mr Rimmer's frustration with this and that. He decides upon calling in at the hardware store. Desperate now to make contact with Jennifer, Mr Rimmer settles for sending a text about having to pick her up ten minutes earlier as he has a meeting with a parent first thing. Mr Rimmer adds that he hopes she has enjoyed her weekend so far – he has been to the World Market Day in Southport and is now in Aintree trying to choose paint colour for the exterior of his house.

Unbelievably, and within ten minutes of sending the text, Jennifer has replied that she is, at that moment in time, at the World Market Day too. Her parents are buying sweet crepes whilst she stands in a queue for some clairvoyant who insists upon reading Jennifer's palm. Mr Rimmer stares at his mobile for a long while before replying. His remark about his own personal reading from the clairvoyant has the desired effect; Jennifer will save her pennies for something else then – that they will catch up tomorrow in school. Mr Rimmer feels relieved – at what, he is not quite sure.

Mr Rimmer doesn't believe in any of that malarkey – a load of nonsense, his father would say.

36

MOST OF THE Folkard family were looking forward to September's World Market Day. Their Sunday would end the same as it did each time they went. They would spend too much money – they would eat too much food – they would always come home with a bundle of French soap!

Having conveniently parked at the station – handy working at one end of Southport's main road, smack bang in the centre of the town – the Folkard party headed almost instinctively to the Paella tent on the opposite side of the street. It is like this every time - food first – then shopping – then usually crepes – then everyone is so tired that they head off home. Hermione Folkard could have quite happily skipped the whole event – she had more pressing matters on her mind. Having finished off the far too small portion of paella, Darcy insisted on the urgent need for a drink – cries and pleas ensued from the youngest and so the clan moved towards a drinks tent. Walter was busy handling the buying of beverages when an attractive dark woman touched Hermione Folkard gently on the inside of her left arm before inviting her inside her tent. Politely, Hermione refused; her determined gaze hard to break – how convincing these characters could be? Smiling politely Hermione moved away in the direction of her small family – Walter waiting, his hand held out, beckoning her.

Hermione and Zita began to laugh out loud; they could see a Punch and Judy show in the near distance. Both Hermione and Walter detested them but the girls were insistent and excitable; they beckoned their parents to cross the road.

At their point of arrival, Judy, who looked much like Punch was smacking him over the head with what looked like a baseball bat. The girls immediately started laughing. To officers like Hermione, domestic violence was no laughing matter. Hermione turned to make a comment but Walter was deep in conversation with an elderly Italianish looking man. To Hermione's surprise she was quite fascinated to learn that the show originated from Italy and that the original Punch - Pulcinella (a clown then) dated back to the sixteenth century. It was in the eighteen hundreds that Mr Punch gained a wife and was to travel about Europe often bestowing some political message or other to the adult crowd. The transformation from adult morality play to the colourful 'knock about' Punch and Judy show was complete by the end of the nineteenth century. Show ended, it was time for an ice-cream!

The weather now almost overcast, Hermione and Walter sat quietly once they were back home, hand in hand. The girls had settled for a movie about a pig in their bedroom – the evening was temporarily theirs. It wasn't often Hermione's attention span could be expected to commit itself to an entire episode on television but the Breaking Bad Season was irresistible to them both. The good teacher gone bad had been so convincingly portrayed, so cleverly executed that anything appeared plausible, even understandable under the circumstances.

Girls bathed and bedded, Hermione set to work. A list of possible places where a burial or body could have been disposed of needed to be made – this time with Mr Rimmer in mind. The marshland was still close enough to the Manning household. Tomorrow she would organise a team to search for Eva's body, that was, after they had visited the Manning household to warn them.

Sergeant Shakespeare had commented humorously, only that Friday, that Mr Rimmer had probably hidden Eva's body somewhere at his home, right under their noses – that they could have been interviewing him at the time whilst she was right there, somewhere – either dead or even still alive. Inspector Folkard recalled the conversation by the pool that summer with Lisa and Godfrey, about what they had managed to bury under the swimming pool. Deep in thought, she made a list; pond; greenhouse; garage; upstairs; granny House; St Williams.

37

ON TUESDAY AFTERNOON Mr Rimmer is approaching home when suddenly he sees an array of vehicles on both sides of the marshland, at the very end of Marshide Road. Mr Rimmer has now stopped whistling. He has been in such a good mood all day. The scent of Jennifer's perfume still lingers in the air – for obvious reasons, Mr Rimmer wishes it did not. He opens the windows but this makes no difference.

Once indoors, Mr Rimmer makes a nice cup of tea. They are searching for Eva. They must think her dead – killed by the same person as Mary-Eloise – otherwise, why look in the same area? What connection could have been made other than to himself. Mr Rimmer is sweating now. He sits down. He cannot think straight. Mr Rimmer thinks upon visiting his mother but he does not want to worry her. What should he do? What would she advise?

Forty minutes or so have passed and Mr Rimmer is feeling better. He puts his binoculars away – the pain in his left arm eases. He is now sure that Inspector Folkard and her side kick are clutching at straws – any proof would have resulted in a warrant to search his home – yes, clutching at straws, that must be it. His mother would advise that he either remain indoors out of the way or do as other neighbours do – go and have a nosey. Mr Rimmer decides on the latter – they were after all students of his – his absence might look suspicious – guilty even.

Ten minutes later, and Mr Rimmer is watching a busy team at work on his side of the road when he hears Albert Conway speak to one of the team on the other side. The onlooker, probably the foreman, is explaining to Mr Conway that it is all in a day's work. 'In the last fortnight alone we have been hard at work in two of the region's lakes, several canals, one river and even scoured an entire coastline.'. Mr Rimmer looks at Albert Conway's face – he is genuinely transfixed. The speaker adds that they not only search for missing people but weapons, stolen goods and even submerged vehicles. Mr Conway's mouth is now slightly open – his right arm is now on his hip and his left palm is open – he looks like a tea-pot. It is obvious to all that he has numerous questions to ask.

Mr Rimmer joins Albert Conway on the other side. Mr Conway nods towards Mr Rimmer before he points to the lettering on the navy van: North West Regional Underwater Search and Marine Unit. He goes on to add that there are in total twelve divers in the team and that they are all going to be working here, right by their homes.

The speaker introduces himself: Sergeant Barnes. His superior, an Inspector, with several of his constables are in the water – his technician is in the van. He will remain there for the duration. Mr Conway leans forward. Sergeant Barnes adds that he will analyse shots taken under the water, test various water samples and study the sound waves emitted.

Mr Rimmer nods before asking about how far and wide they intend to work. The Sergeant explains that in marshland things rarely move from where they are deposited – half a mile either side should do it. Mr Rimmer remarks on his poor eyesight. He pushes the rim of his glasses back onto the bridge of his nose before he shares that he would struggle to work under such conditions. Sergeant Barnes states that each typical dive involves little or nil visibility so night time is no problem for the unit as they are fully equipped with lighting, sonar technology and generators.

Mr Rimmer and Albert Conway survey the impressive scene. As they do, two 4x4 off road vehicles arrive towing, what must be, at least, a forty foot launch boat, a survey vessel and six smaller inflatable boats. The Sergeant politely excuses himself, giving orders for the closest divers on the team to clear the area and communicate with the local police regarding the closure of the road at either end.

Walking back, Mr Rimmer and Albert Conway exchange polite conversation about what the dive might discover. Mr Rimmer is surprised Albert Conway had not mentioned it earlier: 'That Eva Manning girl? She was a student of yours too, wasn't she?'. Mr Rimmer is ready; he looks solemnly at Albert Conway before stating that it is all a horrid business – that she will probably turn up safe and sound but who knows – that he often communicates with her family and that they are devastated – that they believe she is still alive – but where and why, they do not know. Albert Conway nods then he makes a detrimental remark about teenagers. At the mustard gate, Mr Rimmer waves to Mrs Conway nodding in the bay window, who in return waves back.

Mr Rimmer walks around his classic sky-blue car and is about to enter the back garden via the side wooden gate, adjacent to the house and opposite to the mustard gate, when Albert Conway remarks that his mother was concerned a few weeks ago because she thought she had heard the sound of loud crying coming from his house, possibly upstairs. He adds that she came into the house to fetch him but by the time he'd got out of the bath and dressed he could hear nothing.

Mr Rimmer looks at Albert Conway with a vacant look on his face. He has no idea what he is referring to – it must have been a cat or even someone next door, on the other side – he didn't hear anything himself – maybe the television? Mr Rimmer looks solemn now; he adds that he hasn't had a good cry since his mother passed away and with that both men nod politely before entering their homes in silence – the sound of voices growing louder in the distance.

38

IN THE DISTANCE, an array of vehicles had gathered closely together; canary yellow inflatables were being lifted from their roof racks – one very large boat had been towed to the site. Sergeant Shakespeare shook her shoulders as she shared her dislike for the cold and damp – she'd never thought to ever ask any of her colleagues on the Cheshire team if they'd become immune to catching colds – the flu – the weather conditions they worked in 24/7 – 365 days a year – she couldn't do it. Mind, they'd probably say the same about her job.

Seconds later, their unmarked vehicle arrived outside the Conways household. Inspector Folkard was unsurprised to see Albert Conway in the front garden. He was communicating with his nodding mother who sat at a table on the other side of the downstairs window. Obvious to all, Albert Conway's excitement was uncontainable. Delighted to be of any help whatsoever, he offered a warm handshake to the officers, referring to them respectfully by their full titles.

Although only next door, the semi-detached abode was a stark contrast to Mr Rimmer's. Certainly less orderly, Albert Conway seemed to pay more attention to the front garden than to anywhere else on the property. Tea and jammy dodgers served, and the three sat cosily around an oval green marble coffee table with brass gilt edging and block lighter to match whilst his mother remained at the window – her body turned towards them – her orange stockings wrinkled – her purple slippers on the wrong feet.

Mrs Conway thanked her son for the tea; on occasion, she'd lift her left arm upwards to wipe her wet lips with a crumpled up and almost invisible tissue. For a few moments the three seemed involuntarily transfixed by her. Inspector Folkard thanked them both for their time. Seeming a little less confident now, Albert Conway fidgeted with a small stack of magazines apologising for the untidiness, adding that taking care of his mother took up most of his time. The officers smiled before Sergeant Shakespeare took out her pad. She was about to ask her first question when Albert Conway made a remark about the team of divers down the road. Inspector Folkard was quite taken aback by how much he had learned from Sergeant Barnes – his irrepressible excitement clear for all to see.

Albert Conway leaned forward at the point when he casually dropped into the conversation that Mr Rimmer had been with him all along. He reported that Mr Rimmer had been quiet for most of the time.

Inspector Folkard hastened to ask any further details. Albert Conway seemed like he was about to fall off the edge of the settee. He volunteered the full details of their brief conversation – that Mr Rimmer was sure the missing girl would be found alive – that he spoke often to her relatives. Albert Conway had assured Mr Rimmer he'd not meant to offend him when he stated the obvious coincidence between the deceased student and the one they were obviously looking for.

Sergeant Shakespeare was about to intervene when Albert Conway made a grand gesture, his right hand outstretched, almost like an apology. He added that he fully understood they could not confirm anything to an outsider like himself – indeed one could only speculate what seemed obvious by the force's return to the marsh so soon after the last murder. 'I was only yesterday speaking to my mother about the poor girl found in the marshes – what had become of it all – when lo and behold, there they were, this morning, at the very same spot.'. Mrs Conway nodded her affirmation – crumbs now gathered in the corners of her smile.

Inspector Folkard had waited patiently for Albert Conway to stop talking. Briefly and carefully she reminded him that himself was as much a suspect as the dog-walker that had found the corpse on the morning of her discovery. It was important that the investigation continued based on facts and facts alone – although anything he had to share with them, about anyone at all would be most appreciated.

Inspector Folkard handed their business card over to Albert Conway who in turn showed it to his mother. Inspector Fokard complimented him on his obvious commitment to his community through the neighbourhood scheme – he was clearly a valuable asset to the area. Could he see much from his upstairs windows – burglary, for instance, had decreased in the area by 26% in the last two years, thanks to the work of people such as himself. Without hesitation, Albert Conway offered to take the Inspector upstairs.

Albert Conway's face was now pressed sideways against the left pane of the front bedroom window of the house - he related that in this position, he could see six houses from either side of his own, thanks to the type of bay window frame. Inspector Folkard nodded approvingly, the faint smell of urine lingering, in what was obviously his mother's room. It reminded her of the nursing home she worked at whilst studying her A' levels. It seemed impossible to rid the home of that familiar smell. The overqualified sister always blamed it on the carpets.

Looking about, it was a room filled with memories – photographs of her son everywhere on the beige canvas wall, from birth into adulthood. Albert Conway was recognisable in every shot. He hadn't changed much – his hair loss recorded in every frame – in each photograph he was smiling. Directly across the dark hallway were two more bedrooms. Albert Conway lead Inspector Folkard into the one to the left – the one with the best view to Mr Rimmer's garden.

Albert Conway explained that from the back, he could see umpteen gardens, 'even the two allotments belonging to number ten from the road around the corner'. The view from the back windows was certainly more interesting. Although a large willow tree shaded the centre of the garden, almost all of the long, impressive greenhouse could be seen – various fuchsias still in bloom - the elegant cactus static on the shelf.

Inspector Folkard casually praised Mr Rimmer's skill as a gardener whilst looking out of the window and in the opposite direction; she made a reference to the different ponds in the front garden and like a fish Albert Conway took the bait. Yes, Mr Rimmer was a skilled gardener, much like his father and his father before him. There was a large pond to the back too, although not visible from any window, the large willow sheltering the view. Mr Rimmer could spend hours in the garden, even in the late hours he could spend time moving this and that in and out of the greenhouse or the garage or even the wooden house at the end of the garden.

It had been difficult to supress the question any longer. Inspector Folkard asked how often a pond needed to be emptied or repaired or could they simply be left to their own devices. Albert Conway was quick to answer. The smile on his face belonged to someone who had been taken aside to share a dark secret. As far as he knew, the ponds in both the front and back gardens had been there before Mr Rimmer was born.

Albert Conway's voice was almost a loud whisper; he had not seen nor heard Mr Rimmer working on them for a while – he was sure he would have noticed. The two fell into a short and awkward silence. Albert Conway pointed to the wooden house at the back; he paused before he spoke. He related that many moons ago and mostly over one long hot summer, not long after Mr Rimmer senior had passed away, Mrs Rimmer had entertained the odd guest or two, back there. Inspector Folkard looked at Albert Conway who seemed to avoid her curious gaze. 'Mostly during the day', he added 'but on occasion after Bernard had gone to bed. He once caught her at it one night in the late hours; soon After he tried to set the little house on fire.'. Albert Conway sighed as he stepped back from the window. 'No more visitors after that incident.'.

Inspector Folkard then asked about the relationship between mother and son. Albert Conway only spoke a word. 'Close.'. He added that she had died suddenly one Christmas – unexpected. 'must be over ten years now. Bernard had come home and found her dead – dead in her bed following an overdose. Pills. Apparently lots of pills.'. Inspector Folkard was taken aback by the emotion present in Albert Conway's face. Beyond that detail, he knew little else. For a while, Mr Rimmer shut himself off from everyone. 'He loved his mother – loved her dearly.'.

39

TUESDAY EVENING AND Mr Rimmer is feeling more than a little anxious. Although several neighbours have been interviewed in the area, the presence of Inspector Folkard and her colleague make him feel uneasy, even fearful. Tonight, Mr Rimmer has received at least two messages from Jennifer. Despite their welcome intrusion, they do nothing to alleviate his nervous state – pains working their way down his left arm – the index finger tingling.

The last time Mr Rimmer felt this unsure about the future was when his mother died. Although many years have passed, Mr Rimmer can recall events as if they were yesterday. The term *a dog's life* has now come to mind. Mr Rimmer takes off his spectacles before shaking his head from side to side. In the last few years leading up to his mother's death, he had certainly given her one of them. His poor mother. He knew he'd tortured her – made her life unbearable - the guilt eating away at her and him making matters worse.

Two weeks before her death Mr Rimmer had come home from work, on a fine December morning, to find his mother asleep in her bed. He had called her name several times; he had thought her to be out at the shops. He had somehow sensed that something was not right. When he eventually entered her bedroom he found her to be fast asleep, her back to the door, the curtains half-open.

Affectionately, he pulled the covers right up, just how she liked them and was about to tuck them beneath her chin when he saw that her eyes were wide open – like they were frozen in time – lifeless almost. Mr Rimmer then noticed the blood oozing outwards beneath the sheet. To this day, he can still see it all.

Mrs Rimmer had begged her son not to sign any papers – she would not even agree to be voluntarily sectioned – no. Crisis team assigned and medication administered, Mrs Rimmer was sent home from hospital after only a couple of days; she seemed to be making a slow but steady recovery. As agreed, Mr Rimmer would stay at home with his mother, at least until after the Christmas break. Really, he should have known better.

Christmas came and all seemed to be going well. Both had exchanged small gifts – the love between mother and son unmatchable. It was whilst they were eating their Christmas dinner, in front of the television, that it all began to go wrong. How they had laughed at the latest Christmas rendition of *Only Fools and Horses.* But then the adverts came on.

It's difficult to enjoy one's Christmas dinner when the N.S.P.C.C. reminds you of the cruelty subjected to the innocent and naïve – their young sterile faces staring out from behind the glass, reaching out – impossible to ignore.

Mr Rimmer had seen red. It was hard to remember how it all happened, it happened so quickly. Somehow he had physically shaken his mother quite badly that afternoon. He did so whilst tears rolled down her sunken pale face – gravy stains smeared onto her new beige cotton dress. He knew he shouldn't have – he would have killed anyone else if they had treated her in this way.

Mr Rimmer was not a heavy drinker but that evening he drank half a bottle of whisky – a present from a fellow colleague. At about twelve the following day, Boxing Day, Mr Rimmer had risen and was about to go downstairs to speak to his mother, apologise even, when he noticed her bedroom door was closed. Fearing the worst, he opened it slowly. Although Mrs Rimmer was on her back, her head was slightly tilted to one side, looking towards him. Her face was paler now, almost grey. She somehow looked peaceful – her lips almost blue; her breathing was quiet yet erratic. On the floor, sheets of tablets were strewn in many directions – an empty bottle of red wine on the left bedside table. Frozen and still framed in her doorway, Mr Rimmer looked about her room; after a few moments he suddenly closed the door behind him and moved downstairs. There he sat, in his favourite armchair, for hours. Mr Rimmer is still not entirely sure why he did not call an ambulance – why he did not cry out for help. What Mr Rimmer knows is, that he still deeply regrets not sitting with his mother when she drew her last breath. No one should die alone. The thought of that alone causes him to cry profusely – tiny bubbles forming around his mouth.

Mr Rimmer stands to go upstairs. His head is banging - he needs to lie down. The pains have now subsided in his left arm. Mr Rimmer is nearly at the top of the stairs when suddenly he remembers the unmarked vehicle outside, the divers by the marshes - he stops. He is about to turn around to descend the stairs when he decides he really doesn't care whether any of them have left the area by now. Besides, he knows there is nothing there for them to find, and as for the Conways, there is nothing they know, nothing they have seen, nothing to reveal – Albert Conway would have let him know somehow. Suspicion – that's all it could be.

Mr Rimmer ascends the last two steps before pausing momentarily by his mother's door. He places his right palm upon the door – the desire to enter and spend the night sleeping in her bed is strong – if only he could turn back time. He moves wearily away from the door and gloomily heads to his own room.

40

FRIDAY MORNING AND the full report on the marsh had revealed nothing – nothing at all. Moments later, a phone call from Superintendent Reid summarised precisely the cost of the work carried out on the marshland earlier that week. Inspector Folkard had taken a deep breath before looking out of her window onto the busy car park; she stood there for almost five minutes before Sergeant Shakespeare walked in with the inquest report on Mrs Rimmer's death in her hands.

Sergeant Shakespeare related that during late spring in 2003, the Coroner had returned an open verdict - not unusual when the deceased had not left a note – kinder on the family. The toxicology report showed a large quantity of Paracetamol substances in her system. Mrs Rimmer had died on December the 26th 2002, of Acute Paracetamol Toxicity and Coronary Artery Atheroma. Paramedics pronounced her death before her son. Mr Bernard Rimmer formally identified her corpse. The Statement of Facts had concluded that Merseyside Police were not treating the death as suspicious and did not believe that there had been any third party involvement.

It was Sergeant Shakespeare who pointed out that in the local doctor's report, addressed to the coroner, it had been recorded that a failed attempt at taking her own life, a couple of weeks earlier, had resulted in Mrs Rimmer being cared for solely by Mr Rimmer prior to her death that Christmas. Her medical records revealed a diagnosis for severe depression and chronic anxiety. She had been assessed by the psychiatrist at the time as being 'high risk' in terms of suicidal intent. How ridiculous then that the hospital had discharged her so quickly.

A police interview with Mr Rimmer, much later that evening on Boxing Day, had revealed that he had thought her to be asleep, when he looked in on her earlier that day. They had had a few drinks the previous night: Christmas Day. Both had gone to bed late. Mr Rimmer had gone to Southport Town Centre to spend a voucher he had received from his mother for Christmas – had gone to the sales. The discovery was made soon after his return that evening. Mr Rimmer had called for an ambulance at 18:08.

It was commonly known that the highest percentage of fatalities occurred around the Christmas and New Year period. The most recent analysis of mortality rates, and over a twenty-five year period, identified an excess of 42,325 deaths in total, fatalities above and beyond the normal seasonal winter. This rise was mostly attributed to suicides, patients in hospital settings, tree fires and alcohol consumption related incidents. It was also true that during the season of goodwill, domestic violence and murder and manslaughter rose by 20%.

Inspector Folkard looked downwards and tutted like a typewriter to herself; she then opened her middle draw and took out her list: pond; greenhouse; garage; upstairs; granny house; St Williams.

It was time to pay a visit to Mr Rimmer - time to look in his back garden. Although there was no warrant – there was no reason why he should refuse them a look – it was certainly worth a try. As Sergeant Shakespeare pointed out, they were desperate and desperate times sometimes called for desperate measures.

Mr Rimmer's classic blue car could be seen in the not too far distance. It was difficult to see him, the bright sun blocking their view. Smiles adopted, the two exited their plain maroon vehicle and stood by the gate waiting. As Mr Rimmer turned right onto his drive, the two followed, shutting the mustard gate behind them. A polite nod was issued by Inspector Folkard towards the Conway bay window – the acknowledgement returned. Mr Rimmer appeared calm, as though he had been expecting them. Despite this, he seemed tired, unhappy even.

Once indoors, Mr Rimmer began by letting them know he had noticed their car outside the Conway household. Mr Rimmer paused as if expecting some sort of an explanation. Sergeant Shakespeare was prepared; she was about to share their necessity to interview anyone in the area that might have had any contact at all with Eva Manning, when Mr Rimmer asked quite calmly if he was a suspect.

Inspector Folkard returned in a nonchalant manner that anyone and everyone who could possibly be connected to either of the girls were naturally possible suspects – that in reality, they were now in the process of ruling suspects out, hence their visit today. Mr Rimmer nodded.

Tea stirred and bourbon creams issued, Sergeant Shakespeare began to speak of the many years the Conways and Rimmers must have known each other. Inspector Folkard leaned forward and took a bourbon cream from the patterned plate. Mr Rimmer smiled; it was as if some secret victory had been gained – the discovery of a weakness. Inspector Folkard smiled in return; she volunteered her liking for the biscuits adding that shortbread was most definitely her favourite biscuit. 'The saltier the shortbread, the better it tastes.'.

Mr Rimmer seemed taken aback; he volunteered that his mother loved shortbread. 'It was her favourite too.'. Mr Rimmer added that his father had never liked shortbread and that his mother had always kept a special tin for both herself and himself on the top shelf in the kitchen – 'still there now.'. He smiled. Inspector Folkard smiled back. Sergeant Shakespeare was about to share her love for ginger biscuits when Inspector Folkard asked if he had been in contact with the Manning family recently. Mr Rimmer stated he had not. He added that he was going to send a card sometime in the next few days, that he thought about them very often, that he still believed Eva to be alive and well – yet, she did not seem the type to run away. Had they managed to find her father?

Sergeant Shakespeare confirmed that they had. He had not heard from Eva for a fortnight before she had disappeared. Mr Rimmer shook his head from side to side. The sooner Eva was found the better. The Inspector and Sergeant nodded. Inspector Folkard chose her words carefully. They were conducting voluntary searches in several areas of the neighbourhood – they had conducted one yesterday, at the Conway household – tomorrow they would try next door. 'Do you mind us looking about your property? There is no need to open any draws or search through the home, just a look around.'.

Inspector Folkard added that he did not have to agree of course – he would be well within his rights. Mr Rimmer hesitated before he nodded. 'Yes. You can look around. Where would you like to start?'. Inspector Folkard took one last glance at Mrs Rimmer's portrait on top of the television set before stating that upstairs would be fine. 'I'm looking forward to the view of the back garden from upstairs – it had looked impressive from next door.'.

Together they ascended the stairs. The place certainly smelled as though it had recently been cleaned. In Mr Rimmer's own tidy bedroom there was no clothing or footwear about – a small bin empty. The apple green theme ran through the entire bedroom although the en-suite was a vibrant peach. The three quarter bed with electric blanket, had a floral cover that matched the only bedside lamp. In truth, there were few personal items about; it was as though they had been deliberately put away – it didn't seem right that after living his entire life at this address, that his personal area should be so sterile and unrevealing.

On two of the bedroom walls there was a single, predictable Constable print, framed in a dark oak but on the third wall, directly opposite to his bed, was a large portrait of his mother, a much larger version of the one downstairs, the one on the television set. Inspector Folkard spent more than a few seconds admiring it – her features more prominent, more lively, more beautiful. It somehow engulfed the room, really the only bright colour in it. Inspector Folkard thought of Mr Rimmer going to bed each night, him looking at her portrait, she watching over him asleep. It seemed to have taken the place where others would have placed a cross or something just as significant.

Sergeant Shakespeare complimented Mr Rimmer on his tidiness remarking that her own bedroom bared no resemblance to his own. Mr Rimmer said nothing. He was leading the officers to the second of the two bedrooms when Inspector Folkard noticed as she was about to close Mr Rimmer's bedroom door behind her, a reflection in the wardrobe mirror, just to the left of a Constable and opposite to the door. A peach dressing gown hung on the back of the bedroom door – and on the floor, a pair of matching slippers. Inspector Folkard closed quickly the door and continued to compliment Mr Rimmer's choice of décor.

Mr Rimmer paused before he opened the second bedroom. He explained that this was his mother's room. It had been his parents' room since before he was born – that he hadn't changed much in the room since his mother had died – there had never been the need. Immediately to the right, a three quarter bed with a white wrought iron headboard could be seen – pale blue flowers adorned the white bedding like confetti. The walls were painted a similar colour, much like the colour of Mr Rimmer's classic car. From her bed, to the right, an open window, an antique oak dresser and another open window.

Long, white muslin curtains carelessly waved in the pleasant breeze. Despite the peaceful atmosphere, the room seemed solemn – possibly the circumstances behind her death affecting those who stood on the very spot. It was hard to imagine the woman opposite

Mr Rimmer's bed lying and dying years later. It seemed almost impossible.

Opposite her bed, stood a large looming wardrobe that matched the expensive dresser; it had a key in the lock - a purple fabric heart hanging from it. Inspector Folkard wanted to look in the wardrobe – she really did. Behind the door, nothing. The view from the window was so different to the one from the Conway's. It presented the garden in an altogether enhanced picture. It looked like one of those pages from a gardener's manual – perfectly structured, divided accordingly – every spot seemed to have a purpose. No longer did the yellowing willow tree shadow the large pond to the right of the lawn; it folded over it protectively – the sun piercing between its many limbs - a Constable to be sure. Certainly from the window, there seemed to be little evidence of any new additions or changes. Everything in the garden appeared established, trimmed or manicured.

The swing hanging from the silver birch tree on the left, half way down, moved of its own accord – such a perfect and tranquil scene. To the very right, and in the long greenhouse, many fuchsias were still in bloom. On the shelf, the large and soaring mother-in-law pointed menacingly across the garden.

At the end of it all stood the granny house. Bathed in sunshine, it seemed the ideal haven for any escape and the perfect way of viewing the garden from an alternative angle. Yes, the shovel with the orange handle was gone now – possibly in the garage. For a few moments no-one spoke – the breath-taking view taking them all elsewhere.

Mr Rimmer began to lead the party downstairs when Sergeant Shakespeare picked up a hairbrush belonging to an antique set from the top of the dressing table. She remarked that she too had had one of these sets as a child – that they were worth a small fortune now. As Inspector Folkard closed the door, she pictured his mother lying on the bed looking right and outwards of the nearest window. She was in no doubt their relationship had been very close.

Downstairs, the front room to the left of the porch revealed another sitting room but smaller. It certainly seemed untouched. No personal items could really be seen at first glance. In the corner stood a tall wooden coat hanger; an array of coats sagging from it – a distinctive light green mac with a gathered hood closest to them. A brown leather jacket hung from there too. It was difficult to picture Mr Rimmer in a leather jacket – not at all him. At the top, wooden curls coming from the hangers moved inwards in order to form a bowl-like shape. In the middle of this, a few hats, gloves. Mr Rimmer explained he did not use the room at all – no need, living on his own – the house was a little big for him and the garden required quite a lot of maintenance. The thought of moving though, was inconceivable – the house had originally belonged to his grandfather. Out and left to the kitchen with the downstairs bathroom to the very right - the small dining area ahead. Mr Rimmer pointed out the table with the house shaped biscuit container to the officers, stating that it was here he did his private tuition. From the red velvet seats inspector Folkard could see which of the two had been most frequently used. Inspector Folkard was curious to know what variety of biscuits Mr Rimmer kept in his impressive jar. Mr Rimmer stated that the jar was now empty but that custard creams had often been the most common choice.

Sergeant Shakespeare made a complimentary reference about the view from the window adjacent to the table before they were led outwards onto a small open porch, down some concrete stairs to the right and left down a path that parted the lawn and the pond, with the long greenhouse that ran from the back of the garage to nearly the bottom of the garden.

At the top of the path and immediately to the right, the concrete garage with the wooden exterior had been painted thematically in mustard brown. Behind them was a spacious yard where the bins stood, and a tall wooden partition with a gate that led to the drive at the front of the house was now behind them. As Mr Rimmer led them down the garden path, Inspector Folkard noticed some white marks on the grey pavement by the outside wall; she also glanced through the garage window once they began to descend the path, quickly locating the spade with the orange handle. It stood beside some rubber footwear and a wheelbarrow. In the dark, it was hard to see anything else.

Mr Rimmer invited the officers into the long Victorian greenhouse. Eloquently maintained, the glass house boasted many varieties of fuchsia; some adorned the busy shelves – others hung like fancy chandeliers from above. How striking they were as a collection. Mr Rimmer was most definitely impressed with Inspector Folkard's knowledge of the species. 'About one hundred varieties – named after a German botanist - Fuchs something or other.'. Mr Rimmer began to nod approvingly at the point when she said that they were obviously loved for their teardrop shape, much like the awesome willow adjacent to his impressive greenhouse. 'Although believed to be unlucky – a bringer of sorrow.'.

When Inspector Folkard added that apparently they had been discovered first in the Caribbean, in the Dominican Republic, and that they were still used in traditional funerals, Mr Rimmer stepped forward. He pointed to a much smaller one on a shelf and added that they were not as resilient as most think. 'The one I hold now has been in the front porch, for instance, for a few weeks. As soon as the temperature fell, she had begun to wither.'. He added that she was of the Vargaciana variety, of the miniature kind, less bulbous but with a longer bell – 'stamens that curl like eyelashes.'. For a few moments all three seemed entranced by her beauty – a look of concern on all their faces.

Sergeant Shakespeare nodded towards the large cacti in the corner, having noted that Mr Rimmer had also moved the mother-in-law from the front porch too. She noted that she too was probably getting a little too large to remain there. Mr Rimmer nodded in return; he shared that the cacti had belonged to his mother and that she had liked it very much – himself, he didn't care much for her although she rarely needing watering. His father had given it to his mother a long time ago – he couldn't remember a time when the cacti had not been there.

He continued to add that, when his mother was alive, it lived in the front room windowsill; his mother used to affectionally jest about her own mother-in-law whilst cleaning it. 'She wouldn't let anyone dust her long prickly leaves, lest they cut themselves in the process.'.

Mr Rimmer asked Sergeant Shakespeare if she had got round to purchasing her greenhouse. It was difficult for both the Inspector and Mr Rimmer not to grin. Sergeant Shakespeare shook her head – she had decided against it – felt she didn't have the time right now but was looking to possibly purchase one before the spring. Silence fell amongst them; the heat warming them like a long lost friend.

Having walked to the end of the greenhouse, the three moved towards the exit. Mr Rimmer turned to close the sliding door and caught Inspector Folkard looking at the rusty garden chair in the corner, a large straw-brimmed hat stood on its side parallel to the back of the chair. 'My mother's.', he commented before sliding the door shut behind them.

The walking party progressed along the narrow path, across the bottom of the garden towards the granny house, and left onto the lawn. There they meandered about a hundred feet away from the back of the house. To the left, the majestic willow weeping over the large pond and to the right the large silver birch with its curry coloured mistletoe protruding about ten feet up from the ground. The swing hung without the slightest movement from the birch's longest and thickest branch. It beckoned the women to sway both to and fro. Had their visit not been as formal, for sure, one would have pushed the other.

Both officers looked about the garden skimming and scanning the site as a whole. Sergeant Shakespeare considered Mrs Rimmer's bedroom from the outside, the muslin curtains still swaying in the breeze. Inspector Folkard was trying to ignore Albert Conway's gaze from his own bedroom window. Mr Rimmer simply stared onward; his hands held with some composure behind his back. Keen to view the pond, Inspector Folkard moved in a casual manner towards it, crossing the weed-free lawn with care.

Evening rays sliced through the willow branches and stabbed at the water's edge. Coy carp surged to the surface sensing the shadows forming overhead – greedily they shoved about below the stark surface.

The water sparkled and for a second or two Inspector Folkard closed her eyes – the autumn calmness too beautiful to describe in words. Almost disappointed by the established nature of the area, Inspector Folkard looked nearby, her appetite unsatisfied, her determination to uncover something still strong.

Moving along the lawn, Mr Rimmer was happy to pause on several occasions by this and that – only a few new and small additions to the opulent garden – some lilac dahlias, pink nerines, a few varieties of cyclamen and the brightest of yellow winter aconites. Little difference did they seem to make, yet looking at the garden as a whole, it was evident that every little bit of flora added something to the whole picture. What an artist Mr Rimmer was.

The sound of birdsong was now in the early evening air. Foreign imposters like starlings, siskins and thrushes had stopped by for food, water and shelter. Here they would find plenty. This perfect habitat would allow them to hunker down before the oncoming winter when the moist ground would be sure to turn frosty. Having approached the top of the garden, Inspector Folkard looked back upon the breath-taking scene – she agreed with herself that if this was her garden, she'd probably spend more time outdoors. She'd probably have a bench here or over there; certainly she'd have a couple of chairs on the wooden porch of the Granny house. She'd plant the window-boxes with herbs so that she could look upon the splendour of her creation whilst taking in scents from various plants, mint, rosemary, even lavenders. Had Mr Rimmer two such chairs on the porch then they would have probably sat there and considered the beauty to behold. But there were no such chairs.

In fact, Mr Rimmer hadn't even mentioned the granny house to them, one of the focal points from the back windows and in the garden itself. Inspector Folkard wondered if Mr Rimmer had been deliberately obliging whilst inspecting the recent additions to the flora with the sole purpose of distracting them and moving them deliberately forward, away from the small lodging. Maybe. Maybe not.

Inspector Folkard began to raise her right arm in order to point out the wooden enclosure when Sergeant Shakespeare asked about the little house herself. Her mother had one just like it – how they missed it. Their mother had bought it as a retreat for herself but as children they had used it more than she had. Sergeant Shakespeare stated that she had noticed a wooden doll house inside the enclosure and asked if it had belonged to his mother.

Mr Rimmer replied that it had – that his mother had hoped for a daughter one day in order to pass the doll house on to her. Really he should have sold it; it was quite old, maybe an antique. Mr Rimmer then stated that maybe he should donate it to a local hospital, or a nursery.

Inspector Folkard apologised before she mentioned that she had observed that Mr Rimmer had retained about the place numerous articles belonging to his mother – that the two had obviously been very close. Mr Rimmer nodded solemnly. He added that, although she had passed away only ten years ago, her passing felt like it had happened only yesterday. He then looked like a man that was about to add something else, then stopped, thinking better of it.

The sky was darkening now. Mr Rimmer began to move forward towards the concrete steps that lead indoors. Inspector Folkard was sure Mr Rimmer's demeanour had changed in the meantime. She regretted not looking behind the granny house although it was firmly adjacent to the garden's back wall. Having reached a dead end, the three made their way into the kitchen, past the stairs on the right, through the front left lounge and out through the porch into the lavish front garden.

Inspector Folkard was leaning over a large pot of hostas and was about to ask Mr Rimmer for some advice on keeping the slugs away when Sergeant Shakespeare enquired, as agreed beforehand, about the whereabouts of his mother's grave – asking if she had been buried with his father, in the cemetery on Southport Road.

It was obvious that Mr Rimmer had been unprepared for such an enquiry. Mr Rimmer shook his head from side to side before pushing his spectacles back onto his nose. He shared with them that is mother had been cremated and that her ashes had been spread on Ullswater in the Lake District – where his parents had spent their honeymoon.

Inspector Folkard turned as Mr Rimmer closed the rectangular gate behind them. She looked directly at him when she enquired after the student he had mentioned previously to them – the one who was on the verge of passing her P.G.C.E. Mr Rimmer appeared suddenly more uptight, maybe by the request, maybe because the whole experience had been too taxing. He also seemed to hesitate before handing over her name: Miss Jennifer Dwyer. His demeanour unchanged, he added that she was on a placement at St William's High School – about a third of the way through her placement and that she had been a promising student from the onset.

Inspector Folkard smiled as did the Sergeant. They thanked him once again for his time and for voluntarily allowing them to look about his charming home and gardens. Within seconds they had folded into their unmarked vehicle, and with that, they made their way back to police headquarters, a faint light pouring out from the street lamps as the sun had begun to set in the west.

41

IT HAS BEEN raining all day. Mr Rimmer woke up a little later than usual following a restless night's sleep. Literally dot on three in the morning, he was awoken by what seemed to be loud cries coming from outside his bedroom window. By the time he reached the garden, all was quiet and calm – a dream, most likely a bad dream. Outside, the dark had enveloped almost everything. Some outlines were visible to the right of the back garden where a little moonlight existed. Mr Rimmer opened his window ever so slightly. As a child he had always been afraid of the dark and what lived in it and what could come from it. Despite all the years that had passed, he still felt uncomfortable sleeping with the window open – even on a hot summer's night.

A light breakfast of toast, butter and marmalade is enjoyed more than anticipated. No marmalade can compare to the one his mother used to make, the rind thick and the golden juice like syrup. Mr Rimmer observes the rain falling sideways; there he meditates from his teaching table, a pot of tea before him. He knows the rain is necessary for the garden's growth but how miserable the scene is – the sky permeating its bleakest grey across the garden, spreading its misery everywhere.

His mother used to say that days like these were days when the depressed took to their beds, when in fact they should be doing the very opposite. Mr Rimmer knows she was right. He too has, in the past, spent days in his bed growing more afraid by the hour, less predictable by the day.

Sundays always have a way of getting Mr Rimmer down. His mother died on a Sunday. Each Sunday he'd recount to himself the total of weeks passed since his mother had passed away. It went on until he began to confuse the total amount of weeks; for a while Mr Rimmer had to get a calendar out and count backwards. Eventually, he lost count - the guilt began to eat away at him – the grief unbearable.

As a child, he'd been made to go to church on Sundays. His father refused to swap the dreaded event to a Saturday night – traditional to the end. He detested the priest with the hard glare and the cold hands. When his father died, they stopped going to church all together. His mother had vowed to never set foot in a church again. When his mother died, it was a relief that Father Hickey was no longer alive to conduct the service.

An hour later and Mr Rimmer is still sitting at the table looking outside. The grass is now spongy and the rain is falling heavily downwards. Condensation is gathering in the window. Mr Rimmer has grown cold all over – his hands are ice-cold. For the last half-hour he has been going through each conversation held with the Inspector and her Sergeant, room by room, question by question. Mr Rimmer concludes there is nothing more to be done just as the sound from a text startles him. It is Jennifer. If he is passing at any point today, would he mind dropping off the book he had suggested to her for her top set in year ten – the William Trevor one – she couldn't remember the name. Mr Rimmer smiles a little.

An hour has now passed and Mr Rimmer is sporting his favourite light green raincoat; the rain is still falling but less aggressively. He knows that once he is outdoors he will begin to feel better – the dark clouds will shift and problems may be replaced by solutions.

Mr Rimmer is reversing his classic sky-blue car out of the drive when he notices the same maroon unmarked vehicle that was used by the officers, parked two doors down to the left of his house. Mr Rimmer feels better already. He didn't really expect to see any further voluntary searches being carried out in the neighbourhood. For a few moments he hesitates, wondering if Inspector Folkard is leading the search herself when two unfamiliar police constables suddenly exit from the front of the semi-detached house.

Mr Rimmer ponders for a short while on the significance behind the search being conducted by two different, lower-ranking officers before concluding that he is getting himself all worked up for no reason – no reason at all.

On the way to Jennifer's, Mr Rimmer drops off more of his mother's items to two separate charity banks, one in the Asda car park and another outside Tesco's: most of these items are shoes. Most of the items have been disposed of with the exception of one carrier bag. Various dark wigs are visible through the plastic. For a short while, Mr Rimmer holds on affectionally to the bag, before tying a firm double knot with the two handles.

Mr Rimmer approaches the rusting green metal container. Across the middle, the fading familiar logo for the charity that helps children catches his eye; he touches the face of one of these children – the youngest who appears to be crying. He drops the bag into its rectangular mouth. At the point of tipping the horizontal handle forward, Mr Rimmer pauses as if he is about to retrieve the bag. It is only because the sound of a vehicle approaching that he lets go. Mr Rimmer quickly folds closed the shutter-like back doors before getting into his car.

Tears well up in Mr Rimmer's eyes when he momentarily thinks of the day his mother lay dying in his bed – most candles still alight from the night before. Had he called an ambulance earlier that morning, she would have surely survived. When he looked in on her half an hour later, she had moved slightly over across the bed; two of the candles had expired – the air filled with the scent of her favourite candle *Freshly Cut Roses.* Next to her bedside table, the photographs of his father and himself stood alighted by the largest of these candles. Underneath the frame that held a photograph of Mr Rimmer on his first day at secondary school was a folded piece of writing paper.

The rain has ceased and the sky is less cloudy. Mr Rimmer sits outside Jennifer's house for a short while, his left hand resting on the book Jennifer had asked for. From the car he can see the African violets in the front room bay window; the Siamese cat is slinking in and out between this and that until it settles in the nearest corner looking out onto the garden. It is nearly three o'clock now; Jennifer's parents are in, there are two green cars in the driveway. One of them, the humped back one, has a light blue butterfly hanging from the rear-view mirror – probably one of those scented car fresheners; the other has one of a large red rose.

Mr Rimmer remembers that Jennifer's parents are both hairdressers; he has never, to his recollection, met a married couple that are both hairdressers – teachers yes, doctors yes but not hairdressers. Despite the desire to meet her parents, Mr Rimmer decides upon texting Jennifer and asking her to come and collect the book from him as he is on his way to a garden centre which shuts within the hour.

Almost instantaneously, Jennifer comes to the bay window and waves before running out from the porch. Jennifer's feet are bare. She is wearing nothing but a pair of white shorts and a white tee-shirt with a large imprint of the Eiffel Tower on the front of it; her long dark hair is tied in a pigtail to the right side of her head, the tail of it almost curled around her right breast. Before he knows it, she is leaning through the passengers car window. Her wide smile is bewitching.

Jennifer's parents have gone to London for the weekend. Having taken the train, they are likely to return about ten that night. Jennifer is hoping to ask him a few questions about the text; she has done a fair bit of research on it and the writer too but is still unsure about the crafting and central themes. Mr Rimmer smiles broadly before stating that the garden centre can wait, he probably didn't have enough time anyway for what he had planned.

Missy exits the porch as they walk up the path, disappearing between the cars. Mr Rimmer Is eyeing attentively Jennifer's feet from behind – it is such a pleasant sight – no apparent blisters or rough skin, a bright red nail polish to the toes making each one look like a glace cherry. His mother had size 6 feet too.

Three quarters of an hour has passed since his arrival. Jennifer thanks Mr Rimmer for his time before offering him a cup of tea. Mr Rimmer is feeling quite relaxed. The day has improved already; the waves of anxiety have disappeared. Missy is now sitting on his lap and he is stroking her affectionately – as a child he never really had any pets. Mr Rimmer involuntarily shakes his head from side to side when he recalls his mother's face as she yelled at him having found a pencil sticking out from his pet hamster. That came before he set the granny house on fire.

Mr Rimmer stands suddenly. He calls to Jennifer in the kitchen asking if he may use the lavatory – the smell of tea-cakes lingering. Outside Jennifer's bright yellow bedroom, Mr Rimmer pauses looking around the tidy room; he is about to go to the bathroom when he spots on the windowsill of the furthest window an ornament he gave to her the last Christmas before she finished her A' level tuition – a snow globe depicting a scene from her favourite childhood story: Beauty and the Beast.

For a few moments Mr Rimmer thinks on how at the time he had not even met Alice Lau. She had looked a little like an Alice – she seemed good and kind like Alice herself. He fleetingly recalled the afternoon he had met her – the sun brightly piercing her long blonde hair. Then the memories of her not wanting him, rejecting him - the lie she had told: those feelings he encountered at the time were worse than anything he had felt in a long-time – at the time unbearable.

Mr Rimmer pushes his spectacles back onto the bridge of his nose; he continues his journey to the bathroom. He wants to splash his face with cold water; he is feeling weary again. Inside he retrieves his purple inhaler from his front pocket. He is now thinking about the dangers of growing too attached to anyone, well specifically to Jennifer, when she calls out that tea is served.

Mr Rimmer exits the bathroom only to find Jennifer waiting for him at the top of the stairs. She motions politely with her right hand downstairs before using the bathroom herself. Somewhat started by their meeting upstairs, Mr Rimmer hastily descends the plush wine coloured carpet before sitting back down in the front room. Tea has been poured and tea-cakes await him. Mr Rimmer cannot resist skimming the golden spread with his right middle finger before closing his eyes: best butter, he thinks to himself – there's nothing like it. It is almost half-past-five before Mr Rimmer leaves.

Back home and with a cup of tea in hand, Mr Rimmer is pondering once again on the Inspector's visit and her enquiry regarding his mother's burial. When Albert asked about his mother's funeral, he accepted, without question, that due to the nature of her death and because of the seasonal delays, the funeral had taken place as soon as it could be arranged and that only a small circle of close family and friends had attended. He had when asked, been very much put on the spot; from the top of his head, he shared that his mother's ashes had been scattered in the Lakes, her favourite place in the world, the best of memories – her honeymoon. In reality, Mr Rimmer could not decide where his mother should *Rest In Peace*.

His mother had requested to be buried with his father. When his father had died, she had often visited his grave, with him in toe. For the first month or so she would lie on her front, regardless of the weather, as if she were lying right above him, her arms outstretched across the entire grave, always sobbing. She'd said over and over again, so that he should not forget, that she wanted to be with him, when the time came. But Bernard Rimmer could not bear the thought of his mother being so far down, cold, wet and far away. He wanted her close by. He wanted her closer to him.

One day in January, he returned home with her ashes. He had decided he would keep her at home, in her room, but after a few sleepless nights he decided upon burying her under the willow tree. Mr Rimmer was digging a rectangular hole by the weeping willow; the ground had frosted over and it was difficult to dig quickly unnoticed. On top of things, he could not stop crying. Every time he stabbed downwards, he became distracted by the sight of the granny house. He kept digging and looking back at it – each time growing angrier and angrier. Almost spontaneously, he decided he'd bury her with the Spaniard; he'd already helped his mother dig the hole after cutting through the wooden floor; he'd already helped drag his carcass across the lawn late that night. Their lives had then been changed forever –

because of his mother and her inability to grieve like any decent wife.

It had been so much easier than he'd originally thought. The doll house removed and the rug rolled aside, the wood lifted with ease, the stench more like a strong musty odour. Before he knew it, his mother had joined him – they were both there, where they belonged – at the time he felt justified. By morning he knew what he had done was wrong – very wrong.

Night after night Mr Rimmer had looked out from his bedroom window regretting his every action. Had he not poured her ashes into the tomb, he could have retrieved them easily but no, her ashes had spread everywhere and there she remained crying out to him, reaching out, night after night, begging him to forgive her, asking for him to bring her back home at least, bury her with her one true love.

Mr Rimmer has never forgiven himself for putting her in there, with the Spaniard. He knew his mother had never forgiven herself since the day she learned of the abuse he had suffered. Wearing her peacock-blue embroidered long-sleeved dress, her face made up, her curly wig on for going out, she invited the Spaniard in before they were to go out for the night. She drew the curtains before she smiled. She kissed him on his right cheek when he asked her to, then thanked him for the bottle of cheap Italian wine before she offered him a cup of coffee. Mr Rimmer sat opposite him, as quiet as a mouse. Javier downed his coffee in three gulps. He winked at Bernard Rimmer. Mr Rimmer just stared blankly back.

As arranged earlier on in the day, his mother called him into the kitchen. But Bernard Rimmer refused to budge. She called her son once more. He was not going to move. He was stopping. Determined not to miss her chance, his mother entered the front room with a hammer in her hand and swung it whilst he looked on. The less blunt end had stuck into his forehead just as he had turned around, the horror imprinted on his face – his mouth wide open.

Before Mrs Rimmer was finally cremated, Bernard Rimmer had sat in the allocated room at the funeral directors every day. A candle burned brightly on a table that stood by an unread Bible. Different items were added daily; at first it was unintentional, a couple of photographs and some of her favourite keepsakes. The following day, as suggested by one of the staff, he took in some make-up with a set of brushes. He kept her make-up simple. Despite the embalmment, patches of darkness were appearing about her chin and on one of her cheekbones. The Christmas season had meant more days than usual at the morgue with his mother, the cremation delayed. As time passed, Mr Rimmer found himself adding this and that – even painting her pink nails on the last occasion.

By the time his mother was taken away, she looked like a queen about to be burned and offered to the gods, much like a scene in one of those medieval movies where the solemn music plays as the loved one is set alight on a bed of wood and straw, placed upon the water and sent respectfully on their journey to what was believed to be their final resting place.

It was a difficult decision to have his mother cremated. Never again would he be able to hold her, see her; cremation seemed so final, so clinical. Mr Rimmer brought a pair of nail scissors with him on the second to last visit. They were small enough to quickly take out and put away. Holding the scissors to the side of her head, he took a thick length of hair from her cold scalp. Once back home, he tied it with a red ribbon at the top of it, all before wrapping it carefully in some white tissue paper. He placed the curled length neatly in a nylon sack-like bag before placing it under his pillow.

In the last few days, Mr Rimmer has taken this yellowing see-through sack out several times. It has travelled to and fro over the years between the attic in the doll's house and his bedroom. Mr Rimmer has often slept with it under his pillow. Having undone the ribbon that tightens only at the top, Mr Rimmer has taken out the bunch of different hair lengths, each with a different ribbon, and fingered them nervously, in the knowledge that their disposal is imminent.

Mr Rimmer pictures the suicide note that was left by his mother by his portrait in her bedroom. Mr Rimmer can no longer remember all that was shared in the note that said it all; he deeply regrets disposing of it – many times have passed when he dearly wishes he could re-read the note again. Mr Rimmer's eyes are full of tears now. The room has grown dark. How long he has been there, he is not quite sure. Involuntarily he recalls the words out loud; the words sound like a whisper. Mrs Rimmer is saying: *'Since the day you were born I have always loved you. I have always loved you more than any other.'*.

42

DESPITE THE SEVERAL 'voluntary' searches, two conducted by the Inspector and Sergeant Shakespeare and all of the rest by their diminishing team of officers, little information had come to light - none of it significant enough to apply for a warrant. The neighbours on the other side of Mr Rimmer's household had kept themselves to themselves since they had moved in eighteen years ago and were unbelievably unaware of what most neighbours were deeply concerned about: that a teenage girl had been missing in the area, for now fourteen weeks, following the death of another.

Navy raincoat in hand, Inspector Folkard signalled Sergeant Shakespeare for the off. It was almost one in the afternoon now; they had arranged a visit with Liam Manning, Eva's father. According to the last interview conducted, Mr Manning had not seen Eva in the last two months prior to her having gone missing. Solid alibi for the twenty-four hours surrounding her disappearance, he seemed an unlikely suspect for the type of crime Inspector Folkard had in mind. Despite this, Inspector Folkard had not carried out any of the interviews herself and wanted to speak to him face to face – she also knew no questions regarding Mr Rimmer would have been asked at the time. Inspector Folkard knew every detail mattered when connecting one crime with another.

Ten minutes later and they had arrived to their destination: 92 Scarisbrick New Road. Mr Manning had lived there since he had separated from his wife, just over a year ago. The house was almost as large as the impressive abode of the Chambers. Sadly, like a few homes down Cambridge Road, this house had too been converted. It had been divided into many bedsits and on all three floors. No gate to the wide entrance, the front garden had been changed into a large parking space that could easily house eight cars. The arched porch with its large white wooden door had a post-box with plenty of junk mail protruding from its rectangular mouth.

Inspector Folkard pondered for a short while on the appearance of the door before stepping back and looking objectively at the large and wide windows. In the region where they had holidayed in France, almost every building possessed some painted door, window, shutter or the like that presented a 'stressed' appearance - one that presented one or all of these features with the paint wearing wearily away and for some unknown reason, the dwelling would look even more appealing – its characteristics enhanced by the passing of time.

It seemed impossible to recreate such an appearance back home in the UK. No amount of flaking paint seemed to ever look good on an English residence – especially not on a house as large as this. It was as if neatness and order were important ingredients to the typical image of an English abode. Even a cottage couldn't afford to venture much towards the natural and wild approach when presenting itself. Inspector Folkard was thinking of a farm in Cornwall when Sergeant Shakespeare pushed a button above the handwritten and cellotaped rectangular card that read: L.MANNING – FLAT 6.

Moments later, a medium built male, no taller than six foot, bearing a true resemblance to his daughter opened the neglected entrance door. He half-smiled; like most, he merely glanced at the I.D. badges before inviting them in. Inspector Folkard had walked into many hallways like these. Supermarket leaflets were strewn in a corner on an old carpeted floor. Mr Manning looked embarrassed and apologised as he picked a pile up and attempted to bring some order to the untidy stack of paper in his hand. Having placed the mound that refused to be tidied on a circular glass and white wrought iron table, he lead them upstairs to the first floor where they passed half-way a stunning colourful window. The size seemed unusual, it was as large as some that could be found in most churches. Its elongation depicted the four seasons. For a moment, Inspector Folkard paused to admire the detail to each sector as Sergeant Shakespeare followed Mr Manning to a room in the far left corner.

Mr Manning knew there had been no new developments; Sergeant Shakespeare had spoken of this during their short conversation the previous day. They both knew an unexpected visit from the police could either raise the hopes of family members or even fill them with unnecessary dread. Mr Manning offered them a drink. He moved diagonally across the wide space to the 'kitchen' and put the kettle on before they had had a chance to reply.

Sergeant Shakespeare looked upwards to the top of a large antique double wardrobe stacked with cardboard boxes; there were another two at the far side of it, adjacent to the left side of the large bay window. Mr Manning nodded and half-heartedly laughed as he stated that he had intended to unpack them within the fortnight he had moved in but had failed in doing so, thinking that there might have been a reconciliation of some sort. Nodding, the Sergeant thanked him for the mug of tea before he passed the other to the Inspector.

Pointing to a small wooden table in front of the bay window, with a chair at either side, he invited them to sit. He added that he had made another attempt to unpack a fortnight ago; he hadn't been sleeping well since his daughter's disappearance and had decided to unpack to keep busy. The first item he came across was a tie that Eva had bought for him. He wasn't sure for what occasion. For a short while he seemed bothered by his own remark. He then added that he soon realised, that most of what he had unpacked had either been bought by Rachel, his wife or Eva.

Mr Manning moved across the room, about twenty feet, then sat on the end of single bed holding his head in both hands. Both the Inspector and Sergeant Shakespeare knew the quiet sobs indicated some deep regret or another. Resisting the temptation to console they watched every reaction – the Inspector filming with her eyes for the inevitable playback and analysis that would follow their departure.

A few moments later, Mr Manning spoke as though the last three months had revealed something he hadn't considered before. He spoke of how he couldn't even remember what all the squabbling, as he called it, had been about, back when he lived at home. In the last fifteen minutes or so, Mr Manning seemed to have aged, although not beyond recognition. Deep lines aligned his forehead. Although his file had stated that he was thirty-two years of age, right then, at that moment in time, he could have passed for forty, maybe even fifty.

Sergeant Shakespeare deliberately apologised for the question she was about to ask. Why had he not seen Eva in the last two months? Following a short silence she added that the report had stated he had been busy working - that they had spoken on the telephone on occasion. Mr Manning simply nodded.

For a while he appeared to be holding his breath. It was evident to anyone that he was in much need of a hair-cut, his ears stuck out slightly from beneath his dark thick mop of hair, much like Eva's. His dark eyes filled once again. He continued to nod before he spoke once more.

He couldn't explain. Yes, he had always worked long hours - worked at a petrol station, sometimes nights. He couldn't and wouldn't excuse his absence from his daughter's life. 'I thought she'd always be there. I invited her for her tea on a few occasions - she cancelled on me twice.'. He'd decided to stand back, to make a point of some sort – she'd taken her mother's side during the separation.

Speaking in a lower tone he added that he hadn't even paid his wife any maintenance – a sort of pointless protest because he hadn't seen Eva. Looking up, his eyes almost frantic now, he stated that since his daughter's disappearance, he had roamed the streets often at night, especially during the first month. Mr Manning's gaze moved from the officers faces to above and beyond their silhouettes. He looked out of the solitary bay window for a short while then as his gaze moved from one officer to the other he stated: 'I know she is dead.'.

Inspector Folkard had already noted that he had been speaking of Eva in the past tense. A few moments later, he added: 'Eva would never run away. If by any remote chance she would have done so, she would have contacted her grand-parents, Rachel's parents. They adored her. She adored them. They would have helped her with anything, you name it, anything at all. They always did.'.

The Inspector and her Sergeant nodded sympathetically. They both believed he was telling the truth. Something in the noise that followed, something dark and desperate reminded Inspector Folkard of the sorrow articulated by Mrs Lau during their last visit. Their reconciliation had at least offered some support to the grieving parents. They had each other.

Inspector Folkard could not help feel sorry for Liam Manning. Something instinctively told her that he would not be that lucky. The least they could do for the Manning family was to provide them with some much needed answers – some closure to the situation. The inspectors had both met over the years too many parents struggling with closure – it seemed cruel to say the least, that all too often these families of missing persons, parents seeking daughters, sons, children seeking parents, grandparents, never gained the like and were left dangling as such, grieving, lost.

Sergeant Shakespeare reminded Mr Manning that the search for his daughter was on-going and that there was still hope that she would be found. Mr Manning stated politely that the first and second officer that had interviewed him, P.C. Clark and some other he could not recall, had said that should Eva have been abducted, outside the first forty-eight hours, the chances of her being found alive would diminish by the hour. The police officer that had driven him home tried to make him feel better; she said that Eva, being an older teenager, meant that the chances of her having ran away were much higher – he was not to give up hope.

Mr Manning repeated that he believed his 'little girl' was dead - that it was a matter of time before she would be found - he was sure of it. Inspector Folkard knew her children well – likewise did the Chambers – and likely the Mannings. They knew that their children would not have run away, had not been detained by anything usual by the time they had anxiously rang the police. Likewise, Inspector Folkard understood their instinct – and like them, trusted it.

Mr Manning unexpectedly stood up and appeared immediately more composed. He turned and asked quite openly, as if the thought had never entered his mind beforehand, if there was a link between his daughter's disappearance and the death of the other teenager a few months earlier?

Sergeant Shakespeare immediately applied the familiar tone expected in order to answer such a pertinent yet intuitive question. Inspector Folkard did not fully hear what she had said to Mr Manning. Something secretly inside her rejoiced at what had been suggested. His words had breathed her very thoughts and had made what was a possible connection between the two girls, what was a gut feeling, a real possibility.

Sergeant Shakespeare, having put such thoughts to bed, reassured Mr Manning that they would continue to do everything they could to find his daughter. At that, they both stood up. Inspector Folkard handed their mugs to him and thanked him for his time. She began to head for the bedsit door that would lead to the first floor hallway when, as rehearsed many times in the last fifteen years or so, she made a last minute enquiry as though the question had been a sudden afterthought. Inspector Folkard asked about Eva's private tutor, Mr Rimmer. Did he know anything about him?

Unfortunately, Mr Manning was not even aware that she had been receiving extra lessons in English. His wife had mentioned something about extra tuition, a month or so after they had separated, following a row about maintenance. As if disgusted by the revelation, the reminder of how much he had failed his daughter in the last year, Mr Manning followed in silence to the door before closing it, the sound of a profound sobbing throbbing through his bedsit door.

43

'Schoolbag in hand, she leaves home in the early morning, waving goodbye with an absent-minded smile. I watch her go with a surge of that well known sadness, and I have to sit down for a while.

The feeling that I'm losing her forever, and without really entering her world. I'm glad whenever I can share her laughter. that funny little girl.

Slipping through my fingers all the time, I try to capture every minute, the feeling in it. Slipping through my fingers all the time. Do I really see what's in her mind. Each time I think I'm close to knowing, she keeps on growing. Slipping through my fingers all the time.

Sleep in our eyes, her and me at the breakfast table, barely awake, I let precious time go by. Then when she's gone, there's that odd melancholy feeling, and a sense of guilt I can't deny.

What happened to the wonderful adventures? The places I had planned for us to go? Well, some of that we did, but most we didn't, and why, I just don't know.

Slipping through my fingers all the time, I try to capture every minute, the feeling in it. Slipping through my fingers all the time.'

MR RIMMER HAS been an Abba fan for as long as he knows. He has been playing one of his mother's favourite albums on his record player. On the *A side* he has been listening to a particular song that his mother made reference to, the Christmas before she died. His mother suddenly spoke out on the evening of Christmas Day, following a furious row, that she knew, since the revelation of what Javier had done to him, that she had slowly been losing him, losing his affection despite all of her efforts. At the time, Mr Rimmer was taken back, aghast. He had not expected her to speak of what had happened in such detail. She still didn't fully understand him, all of it, everything. Despite this, he still loved her as much then as he had always.

In the past, his mother had gingerly spoken to him about 'the incident' – had even suggested they attended counselling together. But the anger refused to budge. He felt, as he has done almost all of his life, that the surging anger within him was normal, acceptable, under the circumstances. At times he would even find himself losing time – find himself somewhere in the house he had not originally started out in – sometimes sobbing. The thought of speaking of it, even thinking on it, was an impossibility. It still was and it always would be like this. Although he knew it had happened, for sure, it all seemed like a dream – as if it had all been fabricated. But it had not. He knew it had not. Some days he felt so confused, lost track of time. Some days he just wasn't himself.

On that day when his mother allowed Javier to 'babysit' him, the day she had gone out for a new outfit and had brought back a striking pale peacock blue dress, the one with the embroidery and the long sleeves, Javier had lured him into the garden, almost straight away, and into the granny house under the pretence that he had a gift hidden there for his mother, one that required his approval.

Bernard Rimmer had every intention of never telling. He didn't want to ever speak of it. At his age, as Javier had stated with a cigarette in his left hand, who would believe him? He was after all big enough to fight him off – and he hadn't, Javier kept repeating. He was already a recluse at school – had barely any friends. If anyone found out, he would become a 'leper', an untouchable.

But something scratched quietly away on the inside of him, all over. Soon small worms felt like they were wriggling inside him and literally overnight they seemed to grow and move about in the pit of his stomach. The skin right below his chest would spasmodically move at night, just in the middle – the air was getting harder to breathe. The lack of sleep and too many dark nights meant that he could not reason with reason. He knew himself to be an animal by then. After a short while, he slept comfortably enough on the floor of his bedroom, right in the corner, with his back against the wall, where he belonged.

Once in P.E., when he had forgotten his kit and had been sent to the changing room to get into a spare from the *you're not getting out of P.E. basket,* he squatted down in the empty room and without really knowing why, he emptied his bowels onto the tiled floor. He did it a few times after that. It felt good. He didn't know why, but he felt more in control of the whole situation – he even slept better at night. When his mother found out what Javier had done, he stopped. It seemed wrong to continue – although he continued to sleep in the corner, on the floor for a while, his mother by his side, her arm firmly around him.

Mr Rimmer has been sitting in his favourite armchair for a long while now; the sky has darkened and the room has grown silently cold. Despite this, and as if in a trance, Mr Rimmer stands up in order to turn the *Visitors* album over onto the B side. Unlike the other seats in the front room that have remained mostly unoccupied for years, the seat cushion from his armchair has a familiar resemblance to those that have been worn out to such an extent that when one stands, the cushion remains deflated, shaped by its faithful occupier. Mr Rimmer sits slowly down and looks again towards his mother's framed portrait. The quality of light in the room is poor yet he continues to stare at her portrait, as if lost in a moment in time, in a time that has long since passed.

Yes, many years have passed since his mother's death – ten to be precise – then Alice pushed him back into that dark lonesome corner once again. He had felt such contentment before her demise that summer in 2011. Mr Rimmer had made huge efforts to help Alice, Alice in Wonderland, as he liked to call her. She had such big dreams; she wanted to be a star of some sort, but how she'd achieve this dream, she was not sure.

Now Alice and the memories of Alice seem almost a dream to Mr Rimmer. Really, he knew she had 'used him' as they call it – but from the onset, this was not obvious to him, not obvious at all. That was the big problem really, like most things that had affected him greatly in his life, he had not seen them coming

Mr Rimmer has his eyes closed now. He had met Alice Lau on a bright winter's day when he was walking along the fairground end of the long promenade in Southport. It was unusually warm for January. It was one of those days when, if one avoids the cold breeze and the long shadows and manages to stay in the sun's glare, then the day could be mistaken for a Spring day. To this day, Mr Rimmer can still picture Alice when he first met her, the sunrays lighting her whole dark blonde head as if it were on fire at the very moment when she approached him to ask for the time.

Somehow, they ended up talking for a significant while and in that time he had learned that she was from Blackpool. She'd let it slip that she was unhappily living at home with parents that spoke often of separation and seemed to listen very little to the feelings of the only child they had. In return, she had briefly learned that he was a teacher – that he lived alone in Southport and that he too had experienced similar problems when his parents had rowed over the years.

Alice had finished their conversation by asking in an embarrassed manner for some small change, change that she would return, of course, as soon as she could. She cocked her head, pigeon-like to the side and leaned forward before speaking in a conspiring manner. She said that she had left herself short and did not have enough for the fare home. Immediately and without question nor answer, Mr Rimmer had produced a hand-full of change from his trouser pocket. His hand gestured that she should take what was needed – he did so by moving his hand twice forward, staccato fashion. He did not want to ask how and when he would receive the money back. How much she had taken, he was not sure. Fascinated, he had watched her pick a handful of coins, like a squirrel that feeds quickly from a hand full of nuts.

It was Alice who asked for his email address. She promised to return the money owed as soon as she could. He thought it best not to offer his – it seemed inappropriate, she was after all much younger than himself. There was something very special about Alice, though she never knew it herself, no matter how many times he had told her in the time they had known each other. Her confidence, in reality, was almost non-existent yet she knew how to survive. Her crescent dark eyes where nothing short of dynamic; somehow, and quite unusually, her mop of golden hair did complement her exotic appearance.

Mr Rimmer still thinks of Alice's hands. He used to watch them with fascination. It wasn't just that they were the most elegant hands he had ever seen. It was because of the manner in which they moved, like waves; when she spoke, she moved her hands every time. Her elbows would stay neatly by her side and her hands would move like a conductor's, caressing the air, undulating, waving. Her bones seemed as perfectly constructed as those belonging to the hands of any skilled seamstress. Her nails were always kept short, although he often noticed she had a habit of biting her right thumb nail, something he would caringly reproach her for. At the time he remembers, he couldn't wait to see her feet. He was sure they would be dainty – perfectly constructed: from her red sneakers, she was a size three or four.

It was later that month that he had financed her move from her parents' home to her new flat. She had, within the next six months, grown in confidence, pretty much as her independence from the adults, that had let her down, had evolved. She had begun a full-time job at an ice-cream parlour not far from where she lived and, although Mr Rimmer could not visit her much in the day time – he would still take a weekly trip to Blackpool to eat with Alice on a Sunday night.

Their Sunday's spent together where the very best he had encountered in his entire lifetime so far. It was Alice who got him interested in the genre of crime and together they watched the scheduled episodes before he would leave empty-handed and head back to his solitary home. At first, Alice would ask him to stay longer – they could spend hours painting this and that, talking, him putting her new furniture together.

Her mother had taken up with a guy who was eventually jailed for G.B.H. although Alice had hinted that he had attempted to seduce her on many an occasion. Alice had also suggested that she was also scared of him. Mr Rimmer could not let her return home under such circumstances. He would not allow her to suffer in the way he had done. Although in her early twenties, Alice was slight in stature – she could have only been over five feet tall. Her mother's boyfriend could easily have taken advantage of her. This was not something he was prepared to risk.

Recalling as though it was yesterday, Mr Rimmer thought about the first time Alice removed her shoes. She was sitting on the orange settee she had picked out in the catalogue, whilst he was putting together a coffee table. She did it so quickly, and before he knew it, she had folded her legs sideways onto the settee, hiding them under her. There was nothing about her feet that he had not already pictured in his mind, that was, with the exception of her toes. Her toes where slightly longer than he had imagined. They were painted too. Each toe looked like a small black cherry. Beautiful. Truly beautiful.

It was during the early summer months of that year when Alice began to cancel, always last minute on a Sunday afternoon. At first she would call. A few weeks later she began to text. Mr Rimmer was genuinely concerned for her health at first but in time he began to feel a bit of a fool. He noticed she never cancelled before she received her monthly cash allowance, an allowance that would pay for the rent and bills. It was always after.

When he was there, she seemed as though she wanted to be elsewhere. On that August evening, he had gone down despite her protests. He had arrived early and had waited for the Mediterranean looking male to reach the bottom of the road before he had knocked on her door. Alice stood rooted in the entrance. She was wearing a very small pair of denim shorts and a graceful blue and green top that had bat-wings for sleeves. She hesitated before she invited him in, then almost immediately after, she stated that she wanted him to stop calling – that she no longer needed his money – him - that she needed space.

Dazed from the quickness of it all, he asked if he could sit down. He shared how much she meant to him. When he saw the frustration in her face, he pleaded with her to continue their Sunday evenings, even changing them to just once a month – that he would still pay her allowance – no strings attached. At first, she seemed gentle and thoughtful with every response but with every word he spoke she seemed to grow smaller and smaller and move further and further away. When he unexpectedly began to cry and speak of all that they had in common, she seemed agitated, even angry. Her hands began to move in Tsunami waves and before long the elbows had risen upwards like a bird's wing – she strutted about like an aggressive peacock.

When she stated that she had not meant to use him – he felt a little angry. He began to feel as if he were no longer there – floating, unable to handle the pain any longer. When she suggested that he was like some sort of pervert, a stalker, though she soon apologised, he began to cry once more. He couldn't believe it. It was when he spoke up for himself that Mr Rimmer's demeanour began to change. He stated a little more confidently that he was nothing like her mother's partner – that he had never asked anything of her – never made any demands. At that point he knew he was right in what he had said. Had he not treated her with dignity? Had he not provided her with all that she asked?

Mr Rimmer is uncomfortable recalling what happened next. At the time he had never seen her laugh out loud like that before. Her face was contorted as she spoke, and for a split second he wondered how someone so beautiful could look suddenly so very ugly and menacing. Alice had delivered her words quite abruptly. Michael, her mother's partner had been good to her. He had never attempted to molest her – it had all been a lie. He had in fact turned her down on account of her age. Alice paused. She looked thoughtful, even regretful. Mr Rimmer was dumbfounded. Moments later she began to insist that Mr Rimmer leave and never return.

Mr Rimmer suddenly stood up. He asked her to explain what she had said. He'd never doubted her fears, her version, not once. How could she have lied about something like that? How could anyone lie about such things? How could she mock him, hurt him, reject him – like this! His mother would be turning in her grave, if she could. He had blamed her for so many years, despite her relentless quest to make him happy once more and it was only now that he realised how constant and loyal she had been to him over the many years.

Alice was about to shout something or other at him whilst reaching for the bedsit door. But instead Mr Rimmer got there first. He reached over and moved quickly behind her. He cupped his right hand over her mouth whilst holding the back of her head with his left. He then calmly lifted her up a little from the floor before he dragged her backwards into the bedroom, closing the door behind him.

44

SERGEANT SHAKESPEARE HAD been making notes on the incident board, adding the words 'peach dressing gown' and 'matching slippers' below the name of Mr Rimmer. Was there a chance that Mr Rimmer had a partner, or a girlfriend, a lover that he had not told them about? Not likely they agreed. Albert Conway would have let them know.

Inspector Folkard stood up and joined Sergeant Shakespeare. She tapped on the board staccato fashion whilst stating that something instinctively was telling her that these two items had once belonged to his mother. Sergeant Shakespeare added that many a bereaved family had held onto the items of their loved ones for years, even indefinitely. It could be true - but often these items were stored away – not on display as if they were still in usage.

Inspector Folkard pursued the nagging notion that there was something very different about these particular items. If the items had been in Mrs Rimmer's room, on the back of *her* bedroom door, then she could have almost ignored the questions that had bothered her late into the last night. She had after all, only seen the items as she had closed Mr Rimmer's bedroom door, a reflection in the wardrobe mirror.

Sergeant Shakespeare added that it was as if everything had been tidied ahead of their visit; that the two items had probably gone unnoticed because they were behind the door, unnoticed. 'Possibly forgotten.'. Sergeant Shakespeare then proposed that maybe Mr Rimmer wore the items, maybe for comfort, then laughed nervously as she pictured him momentarily in the dressing gown and slippers. Inspector Folkard did not laugh and the two stood in silence. They considered the notion that Mr Rimmer, for whatever reason, was playing a role of some sort. It would have been fascinating to have looked in his wardrobe, rummaged through his drawers. Something wasn't right. They were sure he was no cross-dresser but whom could be sure?

Sergeant Shakespeare tapped her whiteboard pen to the left of Albert Conway's name. She was still concerned with the reason behind Mr Rimmer's lie, when he allegedly stated to Albert Conway that he had been in touch with the Mannings on a regular basis. Some would say that he said so out of guilt. After all, he could have lied because he knew that he should have been in touch, at least once, hence the lie. 'Maybe he had wanted to divorce himself from the whole incident.'. Coincidentally, Mr Rimmer had not once been in touch with either the Chambers or the Mannings. Sergeant Shakespeare then added, 'Some folk don't know how to handle tragedy or show concern. When my own father died, some people, some whom I'd known for many years, behaved most peculiarly – some avoided me.'. A good friend had even crossed over the road in order to avoid talking to her.

Inspector Folkard was only just listening. She kept playing back in her mind details of their recent visit to Mr Rimmer's cosy home. Consequently, she wrote below the two items on the board the words: 'large straw brimmed hat'. He had admitted in the greenhouse, even volunteered that it had belonged to his mother. Yes, Sergeant Shakespeare was probably right - keepsakes.

It was then that Sergeant Shakespeare smiled wryly. Whilst she had been admiring the antique hairbrush set, she had noticed some thick dark hair in the hairbrush. At the time she thought little of it. She then concluded that either he did have a lover, or even an accomplice, or that the hair belonged to a wig – part and parcel of the dressing up scenario they had discussed earlier. Inspector Folkard tried to picture Mr Rimmer in a woman's dark haired wig wearing his mother's peach dressing gown and sheepskin slippers. It was not a pretty sight.

Inspector Folkard spoke quite slowly as if thought and word were working together and being delivered all at once. Over the years, more cases, usually involving schizophrenia, were on the up – these involved a serial killer who had acted because either someone had told him to or because they were able to switch between different personalities – one could be passive, the other aggressive – a split personality disorder. What seemed unlikely could go unnoticed by most, certainly if this person was a hermit, a loner or a mentally unstable individual with often a background of abuse.

The Hesketh Centre's report containing Mrs Rimmer's file caught Sergeant Cumming's eye. She then rang the number listed at the top of the report, asking for a Dr Michael, the named psychiatrist who had signed the medical statement based on Mrs Rimmer's mental health state following her first suicidal attempt. Yes, Dr Michael was still working at the centre, and was on site, but was with patients all day.

She would be finished by five and could possibly see them at the end of the day. Inspector Folkard had looked at her watch. It was four o'clock. If they set off now, they could call in on Jennifer Dwyer, Mr Rimmer's ex-student, who was now, as Mr Rimmer put it, on the verge of passing her P.G.C.E.. Inspector Folkard picked up her navy raincoat – Sergeant Shakespeare followed closely behind.

Luckily, Miss Jennifer Dwyer was home when Inspector Folkard and Sergeant Shakespeare rang the doorbell, to the left of an impressive red door. They did not wait for long in the porch. A voice could be heard speaking as the door opened; it suddenly became apparent to the officers that she had been talking to a cat - she continued to do so, even when the skinny individual slinkered past them both, passing into the front garden. Although still smiling, she wore the facial expression of most when receiving a police officer unexpectedly at their door. Before she spoke any further, Sergeant Shakespeare reassured her that she had nothing to worry about – that they were simply making enquiries in the area. Smiling once more, Sergeant Shakespeare asked Jennifer Dwyer if she could spare them both a small amount of time to help them with their enquiries.

When Jennifer smiled again, her dark eyes widened. Sergeant Shakespeare could not help but wonder if she was in any possible danger. She was so polite and pretty; her long dark hair was tied in a low pony tail, the length of it neatly curled forward onto her right shoulder. Certainly she did not appear streetwise; her formal choice of clothing, and yes, red really suited her, with the addition of pearl earrings made her appear much older than she was. Sergeant Shakespeare found herself mentally comparing her with the three young women pinned onto their incident board back at the station. Inspector Folkard was busy recalling the portrait of Mrs Rimmer on the top of the television.

Inspector Folkard was first to sit down in the agreeable cream front lounge. She looked opposite and out of the large bay window before enquiring after the cat, whilst Sergeant Shakespeare looked closely at the family portrait before lightly running her three middle fingers along the keys of the upright piano. In the meantime, Jennifer informed the Inspector that the cat was called Missy – it was a lilac point Siamese; her parents had come home with it after they had visited a pet rescue centre. 'At the time I pestered them and pestered them until they agreed to get him.'. Jennifer sat down in a nearby chair by the door before adding that Missy, waited for her every day until she would arrived home. Once she had arrived, she'd take off, 'job done, I suppose.', she added. Jennifer then fell silent, curiously regarding the reason for their visit.

Sergeant Shakespeare asked Jennifer to confirm a few details before enquiring if she was still at that moment in time in the middle of a teaching practice at St Williams School for Girls in Walton. Jennifer nodded before correcting the Sergeant. She was now close to the end of her teaching practice. For some reason, this detail concerned the Inspector. A concerned look returned to Jennifer's face. Sergeant Shakespeare repeated again that their enquiries where nothing other than a means of gathering information, checking alibis and that sort of thing. Inspector Folkard wished her colleague would just move onto the agreed line of questioning. She was sure the longer they spent time with Jennifer, the more suspicious she would become.

Jennifer repeated that she was on the verge of completing her P.G.C.E. and without any prompting of any sort, volunteered some information regarding her mentor: Mr Bernard Rimmer. She spoke favourably of him, painting a picture of a selfless man whom she had known for a significant period in time – about seven years. He had tutored her in the subjects of English and English Literature for both her G.C.S.E.'s and A' Level. 'I contacted him earlier on in the year, the last academic year, following an unsuccessful placement in a previous school.'. Mr Rimmer couldn't do enough for her. He presently picked her up and dropped her off daily. She owed much to him over the years. Inspector Folkard nodded along leaning forward as Jennifer then spoke of the possibility of being kept on at St William's – although at first it would be on a temporary basis with a contract for the remaining academic year.

Sergeant Shakespeare interrupted before apologising. She enquired if she may use the toilet hoping to be pointed in the direction of upstairs. Thanking Jennifer, she headed to the first floor as Jennifer returned back to the front room. It was obvious Jennifer was curious now. She had been courteous so far. Curiosity ignited, she asked Inspector Folkard what the officers exactly wanted to know. Inspector Folkard stood up and thanked Jennifer for her time. She had given them all the information they needed. They had taken up enough of her time – they would be on their way – they had an appointment with another family at five o'clock. Inspector Folkard then added that she had a son at

Ormskirk University. 'Harry Folkard? Has also began a P.G.C.E., in Mathematics – do you know him?'.

Sergeant Shakespeare joined Inspector Folkard and Jennifer at the bottom of the wine carpeted stairs. Jennifer thought carefully before shaking her head from side to side. They thanked her once more for her time and exited via the front porch onto the newly paved area. Jennifer called after them just before they reached the gate. They both turned around at the point when she asked how she was, if at all connected with their enquiries. Sergeant Shakespeare looked back at Jennifer, concern written across her face. Before Inspector Folkard could speak, Sergeant Shakespeare related that a young woman murdered earlier in the year and more recently a missing person, had both been previous students of Mr Rimmer.

It was left to Inspector Folkard to add that they were speaking to many other people connected in any possible way to these women, adding that Mr Rimmer was not a suspect. But something in the way Sergeant Shakespeare had looked at Jennifer clearly suggested otherwise. Jennifer's sweet smile disappeared before she returned indoors, her cat snaking through the porch doors just in time before she closed the porch and front door, locking them both behind her.

As soon as their car doors closed, Sergeant Shakespeare apologised; she shared her frustration at not being able to warn Jennifer of their suspicions.

Inspector Folkard breathed deeply before placing her right palm on her colleague's left arm. 'If Mr Rimmer finds out about our visit – he may do something, sooner rather than later. His anxiety could lead him, if indeed he has multiple disorders, to behave irrationally.'. Sergeant Shakespeare nodded. 'On the other hand, Jennifer may not share details of our visit with him. She was a pleasant individual but was clearly intelligent too. You may even have done her a favour. Jennifer might behave more cautiously – think upon what you said and avoid, say, being alone with him, for instance.'. Sergeant Shakespeare was feeling better now. Jennifer could be safer now, if indeed Mr Rimmer, as they both suspected, was their man.

Sergeant Shakespeare started the engine as Inspector Folkard asked her if she had forgotten something. Back in the land of the living, Sergeant Shakespeare listed the possible 'gift-like' items she had observed in the, what could only be described as, sunshine yellow bedroom that obviously belonged to Jennifer. The five that caught their interest were: a paper weight with a red butterfly imprinted at the bottom, a glazed and plain miniature house/cottage, a statue of two girls wearing straw hats and holding hands with baskets, a medium sized porcelain Siamese cat and a snow globe depicting the dance scene from the film Beauty and the Beast. Despite the debate, neither could agree on the item they favoured, if at all it were connected in any way to Mr Rimmer.

The Hesketh Centre was a five minute drive from the station. Over the years they had visited the large semi-detached building on several occasions. There was something about the whole place that oozed misery from every brick - the prison that housed involuntarily the sectioned part of society that were often victims of the abuse of others.

Last year, Inspector Folkard had sat for longer than anticipated with a member of a popular band going back to the 1970's. At first she thought he was making it all up; then he brought out his photograph albums. By the other patients' faces, he had brought these out many times before. Like most, the patients looked harmless enough – harmless to others, a nurse had stated at the time, but not harmless to themselves.

As they were directed upstairs, Sergeant Shakespeare shared her distaste for the décor. Indeed she was stating the obvious – surely any idiot could see the bleak uniformity of the place with its startling white walls and practical furniture could only make them feel worse – the place was not mood enhancing – it was depressing to say the least. Ushered into the visitor's room, the officers waited a few minutes before an elegant woman in colourful clothing and trendy blue knee-high boots welcomed them. She had a short, dark brown bob; her green eyes smiled at the same time as her thin mouth. She immediately invited them into her office. She directed them away from the empty visitors room, along the corridor and into her pale green office, showing them a couple of seats behind what seemed to be her desk – all paperwork sorted in neat piles.

Inspector Folkard passed Doctor Michael the report she had written about Mrs Rimmer. Without much explanation, she immediately rose to look through her filing cabinet - a few seconds later she had retrieved a file. Although she couldn't picture the patient nor remember many details behind her visit to Mrs Rimmer at Southport General – it was almost ten years ago and she had only met her once – she could see from the notes that Mrs Rimmer had been suffering from anxiety and depression and had been on and off alcoholic for several years.

Following Inspector Folkard's question on mental health disorders she confirmed that there were no such concerns identified in her notes. There were a few handwritten notes on the reasons identified by Mrs Rimmer herself, reasons behind her suicide attempt. Dr Bond paused for a few moments before speaking. She could remember now.

Mrs Rimmer had stated that her son had been sexually abused by a past partner, as a teenager. The suicide had been attributed to feelings of guilt and neglect. Mrs Rimmer had stated that she could not live with the guilt and the affect she knew the abuse had had on him ever since. Mrs Rimmer had agreed to undertake counselling and had been placed on two different types of medication, Fluoxetine for the depression and Monodosphne to help her with her feelings of anxiety. Dr Bond apologised for she could not enlighten them any further – there were no more notes – she had not been admitted.

Inspector Folkard thanked Dr Michael who then placed the file back into her cabinet. She moved to and from her desk with such grace – and so quietly. Sergeant Shakespeare requested the spelling of both medications before Inspector Folkard asked if she could pick her brains on a particular topic. She was curious about the medical traits of a serial killer – a male serial killer.

Dr Michael sat back and put her hands together before she looked to the back wall. She shared that unlike the characters portrayed on television, serial killers were rarely geniuses, that they were often opportunists. To Sergeant Shakespeare's question on depression and split personalities she responded that disorders with people grappling with mental health issues where more common these days and could mostly be categorised into three, bipolar – also known as manic depression, schizophrenia and multiple personality disorder – clinically known as dissociative identity disorder.

To Inspector Folkard's question she paused a short while before answering. Case studies had shown consistently throughout a significant period of time, in fact the last study had been conducted over a period of twenty years, that males dealt with sexual abuse by another male far worse than if abused by a woman. A frightening amount went on to abuse others, although not necessarily other boys – a significant amount – approximately 82% of victims, ended up divorced. Of these many had received medication for the symptoms of depression at some point in their lifetime.

'A person with schizophrenia will be prone to hallucinations or delusions. Such patients continue to believe in their delusion, even when presented with the evidence that the delusion is irrational. Schizophrenics, for example, generally find it hard to hold down a job because they struggle to socialise. In contrast, Dissociative Identity Disorder is quite different to the other two disorders because Another person or persons often existed within them; they could have more than one identity.'

Dr Michael leaned forward taking turns at looking at them both. 'These identities can talk to the person suffering with the disorder and the identity can talk back to them. One identity can control the other. For instance, an identity can engage in behaviours that the core personality would not otherwise engage in. People with this disorder often lead 'normal' lives, as one identity can compensate for the other. For example, if the core personality struggled to speak in a meeting with their boss, because they were shy or afraid, then the other personality could take over and behave assertively. This could take place without anyone even knowing it.'.

Silence had enveloped the room. Inspector Folkard leaned forward before asking if a trauma caused by abuse, sexual abuse in particular, could trigger a multiple personality disorder. Dr Michael's unusually thin nostrils flared a little, possibly as a result of not having referred to the disorder by its proper name. She summarised that Dissociative Identity Disorder was often the result of childhood trauma, usually following repetitive sexual or emotional abuse. 'Highly trained experts have openly admitted that this disorder is the most difficult to diagnose. Often psychotherapy fails; there is no real medication to help individuals. Most patients I have treated over the last twenty five years or so, have been men, men who have been sexually abused as a child.'.

To answer Inspector Folkard's final question she stated that symptoms would often include, memory loss (seconds or hours), sleep problems, eating disorders, compulsions or rituals, anxiety attacks, asthma, depression and mood swings. Inspector Folkard looked to Sergeant Shakespeare who was taking down notes. Together they stood in unison and thanked Dr Michael for her time. They left quietly out of the room, both deep in thought.

As they escaped the dreary enclosure, Inspector Folkard stated that her gut instinct had initially been attracted to item number five: the snow globe. For a few moments Sergeant Shakespeare was not entirely sure what her colleague had been making reference to. She then added that if indeed Mr Rimmer had a dissociative disorder, then she was sure it was the same personality buying the gifts, and gifts were usually chosen with thought and care. If Jennifer was the 'Beauty' then she dreaded to think about the profile of a personality who had chosen such a gift – one who was possibly the 'Beast'?

45

USUALLY ON A Friday, Mr Rimmer can be counted upon being a little more cheerful than normal. Today the November school day will end at 12:30. It is always like this on a Friday. Most staff at St. Williams feel like this – most children do too. But Mr Rimmer's morning did not get off to a good start. Once again, he had not slept very well; he tossed and turned for most of the night.

Yesterday, he had bought some new paint from a local DIY shop, not too far from Jennifer's home. He spent a long while that afternoon choosing the right colour; he eventually settled on a terracotta-like shade. It was not too different from the present shade of mustard. His mother would have approved, it was warm and peachy yet not too bright. Just right. A nice autumn colour.

Mr Rimmer was eager to get started with the painting. He decided upon painting the front first. He thought he might get the first coat on the gate painted that early evening but alas, upon leaving the busy store the weather had taken a sudden change and it had begun to rain. Mr Rimmer felt frustrated all night.

The rain had prevented him from starting something he desperately wanted to do – a change had been long overdue - out with the old and in with the new. A counsellor once told his mother that, 'he who rejected change was the architect of decay.'. For as long as he could think back he had always resisted change – didn't like it – couldn't adjust – didn't want to adjust.

Today Mr Rimmer has woken up to more rain. Although the garden needs it, Mr Rimmer does not. The thought of picking Jennifer up cheers him on his way. He has left the house equipped. When he arrives to Jennifer's house he will take the wide umbrella with him up to the porch and make sure she does not get wet – Jennifer is likely to have a couple of bags with her too. Also today, first period, Mr Rimmer has a meeting with Jennifer's course supervisor, Mrs Lofthouse; that is before Jennifer is observed teaching a bottom set period 2. Mr Rimmer has no doubt that the lesson with go according to plan although Jennifer's frequent conversations and texts over the last few days could make one think otherwise. As always, Jennifer is keen to do well; she knows there is a chance of a temporary job at St Williams.

The traffic on the coastal road is a little busier than usual. Visibility is poor; because of the pouring rain, the traffic is moving a little slower. Mr Rimmer arrives to Jennifer's house five minutes late; he has managed to make up most of the time lost, on the dual carriageway. He is about to exit his recently cleaned classic car when she spills out of the porch, spotty red and white umbrella in hand. Mr Rimmer manages to quickly open the rear shutter-like doors whilst holding on to his large navy umbrella. From the anxious look on Jennifer's face one would think her life depended on her supervisor's visit. Engine started, they set off.

It is obvious from the dark circles underneath Jennifer's eyes that she too has not slept well. However, when Mr Rimmer asks after her, she replies that she is well and slept soundly all night. Jennifer seems a little quiet. Mr Rimmer apologises again for arriving late before explaining the chaos he endured along the way. He goes on to assure Jennifer that she has nothing to worry about, that she is a natural, will do just fine. At that, Jennifer smiles and thanks him. She seems a little more relaxed.

Despite the earlier set-backs, they arrive almost on time. Jennifer does not have time for the customary cup of tea in the English staffroom –she wants to check things over before she carries out some last minute photocopying. It is just after half-twelve before Mr Rimmer sees Jennifer again. At break she did not come into the staffroom – she was probably chatting with Mrs Lofthouse following her lesson observation. From the moment Jennifer enters his more cheerful classroom, he notices a look of absent-mindedness – or concern on her face – which, he is not quite sure. Mr Rimmer is wondering if some student or other has played up during her lesson and caused her to not do as well as she had hoped, when she begins a conversation about how well it all went – *good with outstanding features*. Her supervisor had spoken of the conversation Mr Rimmer had had earlier on with her. Jennifer thanks Mr Rimmer for his support and dedication in getting her through her final observation, as well as for the kind things he had related to Mrs Lofthouse. 'I am now eligible to take up the offer of a Teach First graduate programme for the remaining two terms of the year at St Williams.'.

Jennifer's more relaxed demeanour and wide smile disappears again when Mr Rimmer places his hand over hers whilst congratulating her. Mr Rimmer is surprised and asks what is wrong. It is a few moments before Jennifer speaks. She apologises for her aloofness on such a special day. Twice she begins to speak before stopping. Eventually she speaks out.

Mr Rimmer is not prepared for the conversation that he must now have with Jennifer. He is sure not to be too defensive. He is supportive of the officers' actions, after all, they are only doing their job. Jennifer smiles. She understands this. Jennifer is a little surprised he had not spoken to her about recent events. The murder of one of the girls had been in the last year, as well as the disappearance of another. Jennifer pauses before stating that she thought they were friends – that they could confide in each other.

Looking back, when Jennifer had handed to him the tasteful key ring of The Sagrada Familia from Barcelona, he should have taken the opportunity to speak of it then – she had heard about it from her parents and he had not responded. Mr Rimmer is anxious to stand but knows he must remain seated and calm. For a few moments he feels unable to respond to Jennifer's statement. Mr Rimmer states that he assumed she knew, most people knew. 'I did not speak of it because it is so gruesome and living alone, I am not used to speculating on such sad matters. I have often thought of Mary-Eloise since it all happened, well, more of her parents actually – I have called in on them a couple of times – dropped in flowers and a card – the usual. The funeral was difficult, heart-breaking.'.

Mr Rimmer explains that maybe it is because he is a man or because of his generation but he does not usually discuss such gloomy matters – not since his mother died. He had thought of speaking of it that time when she handed to him the lovely key ring – a key ring that he has since used for the spare key to his home – but that he thought better of it not wanting to spoil things just as she had returned from holiday. 'You were so happy and relaxed.'.

As to Eva, he had also spoken to both her mother and father who are now sadly separated. Despite newspaper reports, they believe her to be alive and well and have not ruled out the possibility of her having ran away with a boyfriend that was much older, one that they both clearly disapproved of. It is obvious from Mr Rimmer's face that he is clearly upset. Mr Rimmer has adopted the look of a wounded animal.

It is Jennifer who is apologising now. Both her left and right hand are now on top of Mr Rimmer's right hand, like a short tower. Three fingers from his left hand are holding his left brow in place. Jennifer is quite annoyed with the officers because they were unclear about the reasons behind their visit. They had not stated that there were any suspects but she did feel uneasy by the little they had revealed.

Mr Rimmer insists Jennifer call him anytime she feels the need to talk. 'You should know by now that you can ask me anything.'. He knows now that she has been unduly worried about telling him of their visit and he does not want her to ever feel so upset. In fact, after he drops her off home, he has every intention of calling the station and speaking to the officers himself – really, they need to be clear when communicating the reasons behind door to door enquiries.

'Did you know that both a neighbour and a close friend of mine had also and very recently complained about their methodology following a so-called routine visit? Even poor Mary-Eloise's father confided in me about a visit sometime in May when he was taken in for questioning. He was both shaken and appalled, and at a time when he was clearly grieving for his only child.'.

46

IT WAS RAINING heavily outside; it had been raining heavily all night. Despite the early dart, the traffic had been a hellish. Walter had since texted to say the girls had arrived late for school. As of late on a Friday morning, Inspector Folkard's small team gathered for an unofficial meeting in her square-ish office that looked out onto the station's busy car park. The four stood around the whiteboard, coffee in hand; they had begun to re-analyse all the facts and information gathered in the last twenty four hours – a list of possible motives needed to be compiled.

It was whilst looking at the three females aligned side by side with their details listed below, that Sergeant Shakespeare proposed the first possible motive. She suggested with some certainty in her voice that a motive to be explored should be the motive of rejection. 'Alice may have rejected Mr Rimmer – he could have become too attached to her, pestered her. Mary-Eloise had changed her mind about doing her Advanced Level in English – Mr Rimmer could have felt she had rejected him in some way. Eva was also due to finish her classes with Mr

Rimmer – had cancelled their last lesson – this could have enraged him – triggered something.'. P.C. Clark proposed that maybe Mr Rimmer's trigger was not rejection – maybe it was loss. She added that maybe it was also linked with the loss of his mother, her death. 'Clearly from the information they had, she was a significant person in his life – and still was.'.

Inspector Folkard added that if Mr Rimmer had a Dissociative Identity Disorder then he could have felt distressed following any such rejection or loss. 'As the anguish turned to anger, another identity could have possibly taken over - be responsible for the attacks on the three young women.'. They knew now that he had suffered a childhood trauma, one of sexual abuse. They also knew now that his mother's depression had been attributed to this event and that it was likely that Mr Rimmer had not married or formed a lasting relationship with another person because of this. It was obvious he had been close to his mother. Who knew the extent of anger felt by Mr Rimmer following the assault by a past partner of his mother's?

None of the girls had met, as far as they knew; despite thorough and extensive interviews, it appeared they had never met at any given point, not once. Only Alice had moved away from her parents. There was no proof that the others were unhappy at home.

P. C. McKenna pointed to the pictures below Alice and Mary-Eloise – the one's that depicted the crime scenes. He stated that having looked at the missing persons list – a radius of fifty miles – there appeared to be no missing persons that were linked in any way to their suspect. 'The likelihood of there being other victims seems low. Mr Rimmer fits the profile of a killer who responds emotionally to an event – be it rejection, loss, change but he did not fit the typical profile of a serial killer.'. Neither of the girls had been molested – the motive behind their deaths was too unclear for such a killer – no real pattern other than the way both girls had been strangled and the possibility of missing hair.

Inspector Folkard reminded the team that the bodies of Alice and Mary-Eloise had been found within three miles of their home. The likelihood was that, if Eva Manning was dead, then it was likely that she had been buried somewhere closer to home. Their suspect, according to the time frame, had been one of the last people to have seen both Mary-Eloise and Eva alive before their disappearance. Then there were the possible keepsakes and coincidences.

Sergeant Shakespeare pointed to a photo of Mary-Eloise's charm bracelet, and then to one of the crime scene. 'Mary-Eloise had been found face down in the marsh fully clothed but with no shoes. Alice Lau's shoes had also not been found on the dump site and yes, both had some hair missing. Mary-Eloise's hair had been cut with a sharp implement - scissors. The exhumed body belonging to Alice revealed that her hair had not been cut by scissors, the tear-like cut had not been made at the root.' A jury could be persuaded that her hair had been damaged/torn by anything or anyone sometime between the time of her death in the flat and the time of discovery at the dumpsite – inconclusive. 'The fact is, both shoes and hair is missing from both victims; together they add some weight to our angle of investigation.'.

Inspector Folkard referred once more to the dressing gown and matching slippers – the large hat, the way the bedroom had remained unaltered, the photographs, the portrait opposite his bed. 'I have to agree that Mr Rimmer does not appear to have moved on much in the last ten years, since his mother had died.'. She had considered that maybe the dark hair in the hairbrush might still belong to his mother – that he had deliberately kept it so for all of these years. The thought of the hair belonging to a wig seemed unlikely – although possible. 'Maybe if we get another chance in the future, we could take a sample of hair from the brush.'.

P.C. McKenna asked what had been learned following the visit to Jennifer Dwyer. Sergeant Shakespeare was about to speak when she paused for a brief moment. She stated that not a lot had been learned. 'Jennifer spoke highly of Mr Rimmer. She did not appear vulnerable nor in any direct danger although Mr Rimmer did take her daily to and from the school they both worked in.'.

Inspector Folkard sat down. She enquired after the time when P.C. McKenna and P.C. Clark would carry out their follow up visit with Vicky Manning. P.C. Clark confirmed it was to take place that morning and that as requested both grandparents would be present to help them with their enquiries. Inspector Folkard reminded them to be very subtle when asking about her extra tuition. It was important they gained as much information about Mr Rimmer without raising any suspicion. Sergeant Shakespeare nodded in agreement before opening the office door.

It was later in the afternoon that Sergeant Shakespeare entered the toilets in hot pursuit of Inspector Folkard who was adjusting some smudged eyeliner on her right eyelid. From the pace of her colleague, she knew something had happened – what it was she could not ascertain but from the smirk on her face – it was something positive.

P.C. Clark had just telephoned. About half way through the interview, Eva's grandparents had involuntarily spoken of Mr Rimmer, sharing how much Eva had improved in her English studies since she had been having private tuition. The grandfather happened to mention that Eva had spoken recently with Mr Rimmer about a school trip to Blackpool. Eva had been excited because she was going on an end of term trip with her year at school and had related that Mr Rimmer had spoken of not liking fairgrounds – apparently his grandfather had worked on the one in Southport just like Eva's grandfather had. He was sure that Eva had said that, once upon a time he used to visit the seaside town – that he used to have a friend that lived there. Eva's mother also recalled the conversation. At this point she had begun to cry. Her daughter never made it on that trip – the coach had left without her.

For a moment, Inspector Folkard was speechless – such valuable information –and from a routine visit. For a moment, they felt elated. They quickly exited the toilets and headed for the office – she needed to hear it all again from the officers herself. Sergeant Shakespeare related that they were due to arrive back within the next half-hour.

47

MR RIMMER'S JOURNEY home went almost unnoticed. He was passing the Chambers property down Cambridge Road when he realised that being on automatic pilot meant just that. He couldn't even recall passing any of the traffic lights along the way. Mr Rimmer thinks back for a moment or two; the last thing he can remember is passing a garden centre in Maghull, not shortly after he dropped Jennifer home.

His classic blue car is third in line from the Churchtown traffic lights now; Mr Rimmer glances to the dashboard quickly before turning left down Marshide Road. It is a quarter to three. For a moment he wonders where he has been since passing the garden centre, but after a minute or so his left arm starts to bother him – he has been here before, countless times, for as long as he can remember – it is so frustrating. Time flies, but where?

Determined to make a call of some sort to the station – ideally to the interfering Inspector's line manager, Mr Rimmer begins to rehearse a few choice words as he gets out of his car to open his metallic mustard gate. 'I'd like to register a complaint.', he mutters to himself. Mr Rimmer is about to rehearse a few other choice words when he sees Albert and his mother Julia sitting at their customary table in their front bay window. Braving a smile, he goes as far as waving to them both before reaching a point two thirds up the pathway, when he can no longer see them – his smile disappears.

Indoors, Mr Rimmer sits quietly in his favourite armchair for a short while; he drinks two cups of tea before he decides that a phone call is not necessary – he will just relate to Jennifer that he made a complaint and add that a phone call from the inspecting officers had followed apologising profusely for their impertinent and thoughtless actions. 'That should do it.'. Mr Rimmer mumbles to himself.

Mr Rimmer is now eating a healthy Caesar salad at the kitchen table. He is sitting on the chair with the crimson-coloured velvet seat and looking outwardly into his luscious green garden – the swing is moving a little. Even from this distance he can just about make out the doll house at the centre of the granny house. Mr Rimmer pushes habitually his glasses back onto the bridge of his nose.

No, he cannot sit back and not make the call. If anything, it will only raise suspicion from the investigating officers themselves, if he is not seen to act, when he is clearly being harassed without justification. Half an hour later, Mr Rimmer is thinking about the conversation he has just had with a very helpful and supportive Chief Superintendent at Southport Station.

Looking back now, he has done the right thing. He reflects on the Superintendent's reassurance that the Inspector and the Sergeant would not be putting him in such a compromising situation again. The words seemed pregnant with the unspoken promise that an apology would follow.

48

CHIEF SUPERINTENDENT REID'S visit had been unexpected. Inspector Folkard and Sergeant Shakespeare had headed heartily to the office in order to meet up with the officers who had recently interviewed the Manning family, when suddenly, they noticed his familiar outline at the Inspector's desk. He seemed to be carefully studying the unauthorised whiteboard ahead of him. They were sure he had now noticed them. Upon entering, he said nothing. It was as if he was waiting for an answer to a question that had not been asked.

Confidently, Inspector Folkard related their new line of enquiry. As well, she spoke of the recent discovery that Mr Rimmer did indeed have a friend that lived out in Blackpool – one that apparently he visited frequently - he had until recently denied travelling out to Blackpool, stating he had not been there for numerous years. She added that this very afternoon they were going to re-interview him in the light of this new information. They were confident a more solid link would soon follow.

Chief Superintendent Reid stood up and quietly walked towards the window. He related the details behind a complaint made by Mr Rimmer earlier that afternoon. Mr Rimmer was clearly agitated because of their visit to Miss Dwyer. He did not directly say that he was being harassed but had requested that they were more sensitive with their enquiries. He had stated that in a profession like teaching, reputation was everything.

Chief Superintendent Reid turned around and looked momentarily at Inspector Folkard. He knew all his Inspectors well; some were better than others. If anyone could get a result, Hermione Folkard could. He was keen to be kept abreast of any progress made in the next twenty-four hours. He wished them both luck and with that he exited the office. Inspector Folkard went on to reassure Sergeant Shakespeare that his silence on the matter was a good sign – he was trusting them to come good with the right result. Just as the Lexus pulled away from the station's car park, P.C. Clark entered the office followed closely by P.C. McKenna. The smile on their faces said it all, although they seemed confused by the startled look on Sergeant Shakespeare's.

Events related once more, notes were made on the whiteboard under Mr Rimmer's name and Alice's. Inspector Folkard directed Sergeant Folkard to organise a follow up interview, as soon as could be arranged. Luckily, Mr Rimmer had picked up almost immediately. He had been expecting a call; he was expecting an apology. He had been feeling quite upset following their pointless visit to Jennifer's household. What did they think they were doing? Where they intending on visiting his work next? It certainly felt like harassment. Moments later the telephone line was terminated. Yes, he would be happy to receive them sometime after six .

Yes, it was obvious from Mr Rimmer's face that he had been expecting some sort of an apology. Sitting around the coffee table, a nice plate of garibaldi biscuits at the centre, they all smiled politely until Inspector Folkard spoke. She wanted to first apologise if there had been any misunderstanding following their recent visit to the Dwyer household. Unfortunately, recent information has come to light and they had had to make further enquiries – these had been extensive. In fact, this was the purpose for their visit, Inspector Folkard explained.

Mr Rimmer, who had been sitting forward in his favourite chair, settled himself; he sat back before he placed a palm onto each leg. Mr Rimmer appeared to clear his throat before he spoke. Of course, he would be happy to oblige in any way he could, but really, he didn't know what else he could do to help them. Mr Rimmer went on to say that if they were in his shoes, they too might feel a little uncomfortable. 'Like I said on the phone, teachers work daily with the threat of a false accusation hanging over them. What starts as a rumour can get out of hand; I have seen first-hand what a false accusation can do to colleagues – their lives, all be it temporarily, ruined.'. Already Mr Rimmer felt he had said too much.

Sergeant Shakespeare opened her notebook in order to refer to the details in the yet to be compiled report from D.C. Clark and D.C. McKenna. Inspector Folkard watched Mr Rimmer carefully as she spoke of the visit to the Manning household. When Sergeant Shakespeare related what the grandfather had said, Mr Rimmer involuntarily moved his right hand across his lap in order to hold his left. Mr Rimmer said nothing in response. He looked blankly at them both. For a moment he didn't seem to be there.

Having reminded Mr Rimmer of his previous statement, Sergeant Shakespeare asked if he still remained certain that he had not visited Blackpool in the last few years. Mr Rimmer nodded. Eventually he spoke whilst leaning forward and retrieving his tea-cup. What the grandfather had related was partly true. His own grandfather did work at Southport Pier, for many years in fact – and yes, he did not in particular like fairgrounds – they had always made him nauseous. 'Like Eva's school, St Williams has for years taken pupils to Blackpool, on reward trips or at the end of the year but I had not attended any of these – not my cup of tea. But I did not relate to Eva that I have a friend in Blackpool. As I have related to you previously, I have not been to the resort for many years.'. Moments later he added that he was not saying that the family were lying, but he was surprised by Eva's take on the conversation they had

had – maybe she was confusing him with someone else who had related something similar.

Inspector Folkard thanked Mr Rimmer for his time. She was sure he could appreciate why any leads, whether true or false needed to be followed up. In turn Mr Rimmer nodded before giving them a rehearsed half-smile. Inspector Folkard added that they had also called in on him to ask if he would take the time to show them the views from his mother's bedroom of his next door neighbours' gardens. She could not relate the reasons behind this enquiry but that they would very much appreciate his discretion on the matter: a single snap shot of both gardens would do. His assistance in this matter would be very much appreciated.

It took seconds to photograph either garden. Inspector Folkard was sure to stand at such an angle so that Mr Rimmer was completely satisfied with the shots she had taken. After each shot, Inspector Folkard showed Mr Rimmer the photograph. A smile revealed at each point that he was satisfied with the photograph taken – in fact, as she took a photograph of the right garden belonging to the Conways, Mr Rimmer pointed out that it was blurred and that it needed re-taking. It was at this point, as his back was turned on Sergeant Shakespeare that she skilfully retrieved some black hair from the antique hairbrush on Mrs Rimmer's dressing table.

Mr Rimmer's dormitory door was firmly shut. The hallway upstairs seemed more contracted with the lack of light. Together they moved downstairs, Mr Rimmer behind them both. For a moment or two Inspector Folkard could hear his steady breathing behind her, his left palm squeaking a little on the wooden stair rail as he descended step by step.

Upon reaching the bottom of the stairs Inspector Folkard made a comment about the cold weather. It would be winter next month, and Christmas. Mr Rimmer nodded solemnly. He stated that he did not like Christmas. Life without his mother had never been the same. He imagined it would be so in the Chambers household this year. In the case of the Mannings, one could only hope and pray she would be safe back home by then.

The three nodded at once. Sergeant Shakespeare made for the door just as Inspector Folkard asked about his mother's funeral. She added that it was just the wrong time of year to bury a loved one. She imagined her funeral had been well attended. Not so, related Mr Rimmer. There had been only himself at the time, that was, himself and the priest. Looking back he could have done it all so differently but he was probably in shock, had no family to lean on. 'A terrible shock.'.

Later that evening, the small team spoke at length of the day's events. Mr Rimmer had dealt with their line of questioning like a professional playing dodgeball.

P.C. McKenna shared her belief that something about his mother's death did not seem right. Sergeant Shakespeare agreed. When asked who had attended his mother's funeral, he replied that only himself had been present. 'It didn't seem right.'. P.C. McKenna stated; it seemed strange that his mother had not been buried with her husband – the plot had been purchased and was big enough for two further caskets. The 'owner' of the plot was officially recorded by the council as being Mrs Rimmer.

Had they even considered that Mr Rimmer, upon discovering his mother's overdose, had kept away, gone supposedly to town and deliberately allowed her to die. ' I mean, who goes shopping at a time when your mother is suffering with depression? Surely he could have taken her with him for a day out?'.

Having said it now, it all seemed possible. And if so, they had a motive. They debated for a while what could have triggered the overdose before they were back to the coincidental absence of Mr Rimmer at a time when his mother could have been possibly saved. Inspector Folkard added that the world had for many years offered many theories behind the subject of homicide. 'Wives and husbands killed one another with surprising frequency, lovers and ex-lovers were not far behind in the league. In recent years more parents were killing their own children – even in the last decade, mothers killing their offspring was on the up. But few, very few children, especially sons, killed their mothers.'. Inspector Folkard found herself recreating the scene. No-one had seen neither mother or son before Christmas Eve. She could have been dying for days. Inspector Folkard shook herself violently at the thought.

49

IT IS WEDNESDAY evening and the sky is dark by the time Mr Rimmer gets home. The recent visit from the Inspector and her Sergeant has affected him greatly. A solitary voice frequently reminds Mr Rimmer of the staff night out next month on the fifteenth. This cheers Mr Rimmer up. Mr Rimmer is looking forward to spending some quality time with Jennifer. It has already been agreed that he will escort her there and back home. He isn't interested in having a drink – Jennifer should be the one to relax and let her hair down. She has worked very hard to get where she is. Mr Rimmer looks at himself in the full-length mirror that is on his wardrobe door. He wants to look his best next month; he is still losing weight – there are times now when he even forgets to eat.

Yes, Mr Rimmer knows, especially following recent events, that Jennifer is an important person in his life. She is loyal, hard-working and decent. She did not reject him following the officers' visit. If she had wanted to, she could have chosen to keep quiet about their visit or even details of the conversation. She could have, as most people do anyway, avoid him, or like others he has known in his lifetime, use him in order to get where they want to be. Yes, Jennifer is different. Mr Rimmer looks at his mother's portrait opposite his bed. His mother is smiling – he knows she would say that he should count his lucky stars.

Mr Rimmer leaves his bedroom and is about to head immediately downstairs, when he sees to his left, his mother's empty bed. It has been impossible to move the position of the bed despite all of the years that have passed. The moment he moves the bed will be the moment his mother will disappear. As things stand now, he can see her lying there as he passes her door, lying on her back, looking away from him towards the nearest window. Mr Rimmer traces back a step or two and moves to the doorframe. He would give anything to bring his mother back. He hates himself for having let her die. 'I could have stopped her,' he mumbles. 'I could have fixed everything if I'd really wanted to.'.

Mr Rimmer falls to his knees. He now sees his mother as she was then. He will never be able to forget her grey face with blue lips and grey eyes. They were wide

open and had risen slightly, as if in prayer. Although he didn't want to admit it, her eyes looked haunted, and forlorn. He had never seen anyone look so desperately alone. She had died miserable, rejected and tormented. Had she called out for him, he would not have heard.

Hours have passed now and Mr Rimmer wakes up downstairs in his favourite chair. He feels quite weak and tired. He looks at the clock on the mantle place – it is almost eight o'clock. Mr Rimmer wants to go back upstairs, he wants to go to bed but instead he gets up and puts the television on only to turn it off ten minutes later. He would give anything just to not see another N.S.P.C.C. advert ever again. Usually, the only way to get through Christmas Day was to distract himself with the television but the adverts have a habit of reminding him of what he desperately wants to forget.

Mr Rimmer is making himself a cup of tea. He is looking out into his back garden; it is very dark and very little is visible. Despite this, he continues to stare outwardly. Suddenly, he remembers the photographs taken by Inspector Folkard. He thinks long and hard about the possible reasons behind taking them. He had after all seen every photograph. Not a single photograph had captured any part of his own back garden. Moments later Mr Rimmer is smiling a little as he concludes that the officers are barking literally up the wrong tree. The officers are clearly desperate and have no concrete evidence based on any of the latest suppositions made by relatives. They will not find Eva to corroborate the grandparents' story.

Mr Rimmer has decided to lock up early. He firstly heads for the front door – the porch is always closed. Despite this, a draft can be felt from the letterbox; it has the latest rendition of the Southport Visitor folded and clenched in its wide mouth. Mr Rimmer decides to take the paper with him and read it in bed. He tucks it under his armpit and heads towards the back door before going up. A final glance at his mother's portrait is taken before he turns the light out on her.

Bedroom door closed, Mr Rimmer places the newspaper onto the foot of his three-quarter bed before he begins to undress and put on his nightwear. It is not like Mr Rimmer not to wash before bed but the desire to clamber into his is great – it has been a long day. Surprisingly the sheets are already warm although he cannot remember putting the electric blanket on. Upon turning the newspaper over Mr Rimmer is shocked by the rhetorical headline: SERIAL KILLER AT LARGE? It is a while before Mr Rimmer can bring himself to read the article.

The article is in fact, not as bad as he thought. It has been based on what seems to be a short interview with Liam Manning, Eva Manning's father. In it he speaks briefly about his relationship with Eva, sharing his dread that she is also dead and possibly by the hands of the same killer as Mary-Eloise's. Mr Rimmer shakes his head from side to side before turning the page over. Twenty minutes later, Mr Rimmer is about to turn off his floral green bedside table lamp off when a familiar name catches his eye. It is his old school friend Thomas Dutton. A medium sized notice announces that alongside his wife Paula Dutton, they are celebrating their 30th wedding anniversary. The public notice has been placed by their four children who love them 'and always will'. There is also a mention of two grandchildren.

The photograph that appears above the notice shows the couple on their wedding day. It is similar to the one he keeps in a draw of his own parents – blissful.

Mr Rimmer feels tired; his head is hurting – his left arm has been tingling on and off all day. For a few brief moments, he contemplates how little he has achieved in his life. It is a cold night. There would be many more of these to come. Mr Rimmer looks to his mother for a long while but she is silent. He turns the floral bedside lamp off before he begins to cry.

50

THE REVELATION THAT the hair from the antique brush belonging to Mrs Rimmer had belonged to a wig came as a shock to all but Inspector Folkard. Although the hair had seemed real enough – forensics were easily able to differentiate between the two possible outcomes. Although the wig had been made up of human hair, the lack of natural oils showed the hair to be 'dead' despite its appearance – this type of hair would frizz up easily when wet – much drier. It was also obvious from the dexterity and type of strand that it had once belonged to a female, most likely a child and most probably Russian.

Even more interesting was the further revelation that although Mr Rimmer's DNA was present on all of the strands of hair belonging to the wig – so were the oil residues typical of the type excreted from any scalp. This could either indicate that Mr Rimmer had either touched his scalp extensively before touching the wig or that he had in fact worn the wig himself. In reality, they would need to find the wig in order to confirm either supposition. The excitement felt by the eager team was obvious when Inspector Folkard revealed that the report had also shown that small traces of blood spatter had been found on a few of the strands. Unfortunately, the blood belonged only to Mr Rimmer himself.

A lengthy conversation took place that afternoon between the team. Mr Rimmer, if pushed, would be likely to admit his mother had a wig but how easily could he explain traces of his DNA on it? And the blood spatter? Sergeant Shakespeare suggested that if the blood was related to one of the attacks then it had to be to Eva Manning's. Alice and Mary-Eloise had been strangled from behind. Their bodies had been found. There appeared to be no struggle – quick deaths.

Somehow Eva's death may have been different. From their time-line, she was probably killed in his home – there was no evidence that his car had been anywhere – there was no disproving that she had called round to see him. Maybe Mr Rimmer had invited her in as he saw her pass by his window bay – she was clearly on her way somewhere. Hadn't Eva's mother said something about not receiving a birthday card? Eva Manning could have been on her way to the newsagents in Churchtown village, or even the Co-op half-way up Marshide Road, to get a belated birthday card.

P.C. McKenna then added that most likely, Mary-Eloise had probably been killed at his home too. 'He is unlikely to place her in the marshland as well – would raise suspicion – too much of a coincidence.'. The others nodded in agreement, although Sergeant Shakespeare's head shook from side to side – her mouth raised on the left. She shared her frustration at their inability to warn others of their suspect, especially Jennifer Dwyer, who spent time with him every day, unaware of their strong suspicions. 'How could they look her parents in the face, if anything should happen to her?'. Inspector Folkard and the others nodded in agreement.

She knew there was nothing she could do. She had tried to inadvertedly warn her but Jennifer had spoken to Mr Rimmer about their visitation. Who knew what he would do next time if he were approached again by Jennifer, following another visit? They themselves could be blamed for whatever harm came her way.

Inspector Folkard nodded before she rose and moved towards her office window. Moments later she directed P.C. Clark to apply for a warrant in order to search the home and gardens of Mr Bernard Rimmer. 'Try one of the younger judges' she added, 'it's always worth a shot – maybe mention Christmas and the urgent need for a result, closure even, you know, in order to put the families of the deceased and missing, out of their misery.'. Nodding, P.C. Clark left with P.C. McKenna in toe as Sergeant Shakespeare joined her colleague at the window.

Inspector Folkard looked at her colleague; they knew the warrant would most likely be rejected. She turned back to her window and together they gazed at the wind turbines in the distance. When Inspector Folkard spoke, they both moved away and positioned themselves before the busy whiteboard. Mr Rimmer had mentioned to Eva that he had had a friend, whom he often used to visit, in Blackpool. It was time to subtly circulate photographs of Mr Rimmer and Alice – a couple of officers would do. They should ask specifically if anyone had ever seen Alice with Mr Rimmer.

He had denied ever knowing her. He had denied having been in Blackpool for a while, years. But how many times had it been true that the odd looking couple had drawn attention from others because of their difference in appearance and age? Alice had a face, that if seen, would have not easily been forgotten. They should knock on every door and explore every avenue – there was no need to go anywhere in the vicinity of the Lau household.

51

'Remember, remember the first of December

the trees stand naked and tall

the cold clutches and crackles

the snow gently falls

just in time for the Weihnachtsmann to call.'

JENNIFER IS READING out loud two of her favourite poems about Christmas. She is wearing a pair of tinsel-like earrings with Rudolph the Red Nose Reindeer hanging from one and Father Christmas from the other. Mr Rimmer is meant to be observing her lesson from the back of the classroom. He is meant to be making detailed notes on an official form. Instead, Mr Rimmer looks attentively at Jennifer - she looks a picture in her knitted white dress, she is wearing her dark hair down today.

As the second poem ends, Jennifer shares with the year seven class that she loves Christmas and that one of her favourite Christmases was spent in Spain, as a child, with both her parents and grandparents. 'Can you believe that, although Christmas Day is also celebrated on the twenty-fifth, the children have to wait until he sixth of January to receive their presents?' Like Mr Rimmer, the children are hanging on every word, waiting like expectant parents. Jennifer goes on to tell that on that particular Christmas, when she was about six or seven, her parents had split her total gifts in two, letting her believe that Father Christmas had especially visited twice, once on the English Christmas Day, and again on the Spanish Christmas Day!

Everyone except Jennifer is applauding now. Mr Jessop, who has been watching them both for the last fifteen minutes, stands in the shadows outside the classroom window. The bell for break-time will ring any minute now; he wishes to speak to them both. Jennifer has now successfully passed her teaching practice and he is wanting to offer her a teach first undergraduate temporary contract at the school from the January term to the end of the academic year – there is even a chance that in September a permanent post may become available.

Almost immediately after Mr Jessop has left, Jennifer launches her arms around Mr Rimmer, tears welling up in her eyes – she is so happy, and so relieved that it is all over now – she cannot thank him enough. Mr Rimmer is elated too, although a little taken aback. On the spare of the moment he suggests that they go out for a meal, tomorrow, on Friday, and celebrate. Without any hesitation Jennifer agrees.

Although there is only ten minutes left to have a cup of tea back in the staffroom, there is still enough time for the many staff, who have grown fond of Jennifer, to congratulate her on her appointment. Marcos Kennedy in particular, is very pleased for her. When the bell rings he is still talking to her; his left arm has been resting on her right shoulder for far too long. Mr Rimmer feels deflated; he gets up to wash both their mugs in the sink as a distraction. He tells himself he has nothing to worry about. He is turning them over onto the metallic draining board when he overhears Marcos' suggestion that they should go out for a drink to celebrate.

Mr Rimmer feels a little nauseous now. He begins to move away and cross the staff room – he does not want to be late for his next lesson. Like a loyal canine, Jennifer follows. She is now apologising to Marcos - she cannot accept his kind invitation as she is celebrating the good news with Bernard tomorrow night – he is after all her mentor, has been since she was his GCSE student. As they are about to exit through the door, Marcos reminds Jennifer of the Christmas night out insisting she has a drink with him then. Jennifer laughs. As Mr Rimmer turns to let Jennifer through the door first, he notices her flush a little. The nauseousness returns.

Walking later that night, Mr Rimmer is feeling a lot better. He has taken a long stroll this evening and ended up somewhere a little out of the way. It is cold now and the frost fastens on his face – the wind is icy and relentless but inside the homes of the dwellings he passes, the rooms look warm and welcoming. Some of the homes in this neighbourhood still have coal fires. Through the window of one home in particular, a middle aged woman, not her mother, is leaning protectively over a pretty child in a silver dress as she blows out the candles on her birthday cake. She is holding back a mischievous dark strand of hair whilst singing with the rest of the gathering.

Much later, when Mr Rimmer moves back a little, he sees the child standing at her bedroom window – candy stripped curtains at either side. He smiles and waves, and in return, she waves but she does not smile back. Mr Rimmer steps back in the shadows. He does not have to wait long before the child's mother enters the room. Twenty minutes pass before she finally sees him move away from sight as he casually walks away via the unlit walkway between the many trees on the other side of the gated garden.

52

UNSURPRISINGLY THE MUCH needed warrant had been dismissed. Inspector Folkard was feeling frustrated to say the least. Almost a week had passed and no headway had been made. Although Mr Rimmer's and Alice's photographs had been circulated by officers for days and mostly in the rain, there had been no luck finding any link to what Eva had related to her grandparents – it all seemed to have been communicated in vain.

Chief Superintendent Reid had made it quite clear earlier that afternoon, that tomorrow, Friday, was the day to pull out any officers meandering about in Blackpool, back to the station. They were three weeks from Christmas and burglaries were on the 'up', as was their time apparently. The stick of rock he had spotted on the desk of one of the trainee officers hadn't helped either.

It was unusual for the Folkards to entertain on a mid-week evening but the youngest and the most impatient of the Folkards would not hear of celebrating her birthday at the weekend. Like all of the women in the Folkard household, Zita Folkard had a mind of her own. Dressed in her silver birthday outfit with shoes and a crown to match, she blew out her seven candles and made a wish whilst Bernard Rimmer looked on from outside. Catherine Shakespeare had managed to pull back a single hair strand that almost caught fire just in the nick of time; she had remembered that two years ago, on her fifth birthday Zita Folkard had somehow managed to burn her fringe across the left side – caused a right panic - an awful smell too.

It was also the first time the Folkards had met her partner Wendy. Like her, she had shoulder length dark hair and blue eyes, although Wendy looked a little older. They were an attractive couple and seemed well matched. Hermione Folkard smiled at Walter when she saw them holding hands. It was time Catherine had some luck, settle down, maybe even start a family – who knew?

Equally as pleasing was the more settling sight of Harry laughing whilst holding his small son in his arms. Soon enough they would be celebrating his first birthday, their eldest and thankfully for now only grandchild. Although they were all smiling, Hermione Folkard, as most officers had from the beginning of time, was secretly struggling with the whole idea of happy families. In reality she lived with the constant fear of what lurked out there in the real world, the probabilities and chances and statistics that reminded her daily how lucky she was to have it all.

Nearly eight years ago, when Walter had spoken of a third child and the many more that should follow, Hermione had quite firmly said the word 'No.'. More children equalled a greater risk in her eyes – how could they keep an eye on them all? No. The world was too dangerous – Harry and Darcy were enough. When Hermione Folkard fell unexpectedly pregnant two things happened: Walter was elated and Hermione was sterilised.

Hermione Folkard was kissing her youngest daughter goodnight when she noticed a drawing by her bedside, of Walter in the garden. Hermione picked it up and smiled; yes, he had put a little weight on recently. Walter was wearing his glasses and was waving at her with his right hand. She wasn't quite sure why the picture seemed odd. Maybe it was because he had never appeared alone in any of her pictures. Zita was fast asleep now. Her face didn't smell of soap. She had cake between the gap of her two front teeth. She almost always lied when asked if she had washed her face. If she had actually washed her face, it was rarely with soap – if she had brushed her teeth it was a miracle. It was too late to wake her now.

It was when she was about to draw the candy stripped bedroom curtains closed that Hermione Folkard was sure she had seen the figure of a man looking up at the window as he casually walked by on the unlit walkway between the many trees on the other side of their gated garden. The wind was blowing louder now. It had all happened so fast, and it was so dark, that she could not determine if the familiar outline belonged to whom she believed was their only suspect in their latest homicide investigation. Hermione Folkard went back to Zita's bedside table and picked up the drawing – the three crayons used to draw the picture where beside her bed.

Hermione forgot to knock on Darcy's door before she entered. 'What's up mum? 'asked Darcy perceptively. 'Do you by any chance have an idea when Zita drew this picture?'.

'Yes.'. Darcy responded with confidence. 'She was drawing it on her bed whilst you were both downstairs clearing up. Why mum? What's wrong?'.

53

ALMOST TWENTY-FOUR HOURS have passed; Mr Rimmer is now sitting outside Jennifer's home waiting for her to come out of the house. He is running late. In her last text, Jennifer had insisted he call for her early so that he is able to meet once more with both of her parents – it has been a while since they last saw him – at least five years – they wish to thank him for all he has done. Mr Rimmer has toyed with the idea ever since.

Despite arguments for and against the meeting, Mr Rimmer has settled on the decision to not see them despite agreeing to do so. He has since texted to apologise and explain that he had clean forgot he had little petrol and is now running late - the restaurant will not hold their table for longer than fifteen minutes. He explains he will see them next time, or maybe even on their return – could she please wait outside the gate?

Mr Rimmer is still waiting five minutes later. He is about to call Jennifer when she spills out from the front porch. Thankfully she is alone. Jennifer momentarily turns to wave and blow a kiss to her mother who stands at the window waving in return. It is dark inside his car. Mr Rimmer feels comforted in the knowledge that Jennifer's mother cannot see him. He does not want to run the risk of be judged in any way. Although he has lost almost all of the weight he set out to shed, he is still very self-conscious, he is no spring chicken.

Jennifer's mother is still at the window when she reaches the car. He is about to get out, in order to open the car door for her, when she signals for him to remain in the car. Relieved, he leans over to the left and opens the door from the inside. Jennifer quickly gets into the car whilst at the same time profusely apologising for her lateness - she had misplaced her handbag and had been looking for it when her mother called upstairs to say a car had arrived and that he was waiting outside. Jennifer smiles. For a few moments Mr Rimmer is struck by the whole moment. Here he is, about to go out with someone whom he really likes and admires – how lucky he feels right now - and how happy.

The ride along the coastal road is pleasant. The car is already warm. The colourful bright lights reflecting onto the dashboard from the bridge and retail park, remind them both it will soon be Christmas. Already the shop windows promise this year's main event will be the best yet. The rest of the journey is done mostly in the dark. There are very few lights on the undulating coast between Birkdale and Ainsdale. It is as though they are both sitting side by side at the cinema, except that now they are totally alone. Mr Rimmer glances across and looks at Jennifer for a split moment; she is smiling, her crimson lipstick makes her mouth look wider.

Mr Rimmer tells Jennifer that he rarely comes to Formby. He shares that once, on a rare night out with his mother, Mr Rimmer had dined at the Shala Lingra Indian restaurant. His mother used to love Indian food. Last night, when Mr Rimmer texted Jennifer asking what food she preferred, he was delighted to hear that she liked Indian food too, although she later added that she liked Chinese as well.

Now in Formby, Mr Rimmer begins to tell Jennifer about the Shala Lingra. It is on a road called School Lane; this is because the restaurant was formerly a small primary school – 'once known as St Dymphna Catholic Primary'. As the car approaches the decorated village, Jennifer exclaims with delight at the sight of the tall and wide Christmas tree at the centre of the roundabout. To their immediate right is the restaurant. How quaint the cottage-like school is – how odd to have converted it into an Indian restaurant.

The restaurant is only half full, despite it being Saturday night. Three members of staff immediately approach them as they begin to take their coats off. Nothing has changed inside. It is a plain restaurant. The red carpet brightens the yellowish wallpaper. It is sparsely decorated but the staff are friendly and helpful – certainly the food smells delicious. Mr Rimmer turns to take Jennifer's coat from her and stops momentarily to look upon her. 'How beautiful you look. You look a picture dear.'. Jennifer blushes a little before they are shown to their table in the far right corner of the restaurant, a small quaint window to the side.

Mr Rimmer is trying to locate the exact table where he once sat with his mother when he realises he has missed what Jennifer has just said. A look of confusion dawns upon his face which gives him away. 'I said, it's lovely in here – really nice Bernard.' Mr Rimmer smiles back and apologises. 'I'm glad you like it. I knew you'd like it. 'Moments later they are seated opposite one another – him facing the back wall and her towards the front of the restaurant; they are soon talking like old friends. How at ease he feels in Jennifer's company.

When the elderly waiter with skin like dark leather asks what they would like to drink, Mr Rimmer replies that he is not quite sure. He asks Jennifer what she would like and quickly she responds by stating that she likes to drink Rose wine, 'if that's ok with you'. Mr Rimmer smiles; he announces he is driving, so although he will join her in a small glass, he will drink water for the rest of the evening. The polite waiter nods before taking their drinks menu away. His half-smile and retreat by taking a backward step from the table, makes Jennifer giggle a little. She is clearly relaxed and enjoying herself. How beautiful and radiant Jennifer looks tonight. The amber candle at the table lightens her face upwards and enhances all of her best features, especially her dark, wide eyes. The dark blue dress she is wearing is shimmering in the light – it matches her high heeled shoes perfectly. Her ears are each adorned with a single white pearl. She looks a lot older with her dark hair up.

An hour has passed now. Jennifer has been telling various tales about students she has met over the last twelve months – her enthusiasm permeates and is certainly catching, Mr Rimmer cannot remember when he last enjoyed his career as much, before Jennifer came along. He shares this with her and she smiles. Her cheeks seem redder now. When Mr Rimmer offers to refill her glass for the fourth time, she politely refuses stating she has already had too much.

Mr Rimmer is looking outdoors; he is looking at a young man walking a dog on the other side of the road. His hairstyle and height remind him of someone they both know. Marcos Kennedy has been at the back of his mind all night. 'Are you alright Bernard? You looked like you where miles away then.' He is about to speak before He changes his mind. Jennifer smiles before leaning forward. 'Come on, talk to me. You know you can talk to me. About anything.'

Jennifer's head is now tilted sideways. Her eyes are wide open. She is waiting for him to respond. Her offer seems genuine. Mr Rimmer is worried that if he were to speak of his feelings, his concerns, Jennifer might not like it – it could spoil things – the whole evening, everything. 'Marcos Kennedy'. Mr Rimmer's outburst is almost a whisper. 'I am concerned about Marcos Kennedy.' Mr Rimmer is so embarrassed that he fails to see Jennifer's reaction.

For a moment Mr Rimmer does not raise his head. Jennifer blushes before she laughs nervously; she then lightly places her hand upon his. As soon as it is there, it is gone. Jennifer laughs again, this time a little louder. 'Marcos is alright you know. Harmless. There is no need for you to worry. I'm a big girl now and I can handle the likes of Marcos Kennedy.'.

The word 'alright' resonates; he finds himself feeling something between anger and rejection. Mr Rimmer habitually pushes his spectacles back onto the bridge of his nose before speaking again. 'He uses women. He is a chancer. I don't want you getting hurt.' Mr Rimmer lowers his voice before apologising. 'I'm sorry. I don't want to spoil our little celebration tonight. I just don't trust the man'.

Jennifer's smile widens. She pauses for a moment. Her hand reappears; this time it remains on his a few seconds longer. Although her smile is reassuring, her eyes are not. Jennifer seems distracted a little now and looks towards the front of the restaurant, the exit close-by . Mr Rimmer asks Jennifer if she would like some desert but she does not – she is watching her figure – wants to look her best on the staff night out.

Mr Rimmer wanders whom will be watching her figure then – his left arm is hurting a little. It's time to go home.

When the second waiter approaches, he asks for the bill. Tossing an unmovable thick flick of glossy jet-black hair, he retreats in the same fashion as the last – this time Jennifer does not laugh. They remain silent until the youngest of the waiters arrives with the bill on a small silver plated tray with four *After Eight* chocolate mints. It is now after ten.

Jennifer excuses herself and rises before heading towards the ladies toilet. Mr Rimmer is arrested by what he then sees; he watches her every move. After a couple of seconds, he becomes aware that the eldest waiter, the one with skin like dark leather is watching him. Embarrassed, Mr Rimmer looks to the outdoors for a solution, any solution. Frustrated and confused by Jennifer's mixed signals, Mr Rimmer decides that on the Christmas night out he will come clean – tell her everything – tell her how he feels. He is expecting to be rejected, of course, but the phrase *Carpe Dium* has been at the back of his mind for the last few days. And cease it, he shall.

When Jennifer returns, Mr Rimmer is stood by the reception desk paying the bill. Jennifer seems more relaxed – she is smiling again – she has reapplied her crimson lipstick. Mr Rimmer bids the youngest of the waiters farewell. As he passes through the restaurant door, the cold air smacks at them and they quickly head towards the road. Jennifer thanks Mr Rimmer once more for the meal, 'In fact, for everything.'.

Mr Rimmer is feeling melancholic; the Christmas lights all around them cheer him on. They cross School Lane, walking quickly towards the far end of the supermarket car park where Mr Rimmer quickly identifies his classic car. As he approaches it, he suddenly feels a growing dislike for the vehicle. It is as if he is looking at himself in the mirror – old – classic – undesirable to most.

Mr Rimmer is holding Jennifer's car door open for her when she suddenly and affectionately begins to stroke the roof of the car with her right hand. 'I'd love one of these classics as my first car. I think I'd like one just like this, but in cream. I'm hoping to start driving lessons after Christmas you know?'. Mr Rimmer smiles.

Before they know it, they are heading home and talking away about driving lessons. Yes, Jennifer would be grateful if he could spare the time for the odd lesson or two. Jennifer shares that in the recent past she had upset her father by getting out of the car and walking all of the way home. She was sure Mr Rimmer would be a much better teacher. Her father rarely shouted but on that day he shouted at her several times – she was still shaking when she reached home! Mr Rimmer is now laughing. They are both laughing now.

Almost half-way home, Mr Rimmer takes the opportunity to raise the subject of the Christmas staff night out. He understands perfectly if she does not want to accompany him – she must begin to make new friends of her own – but the offer is there if she wants it. 'I really don't think I will be drinking and the taxi fare from the city to Southport will be even more extortionate, because of the time of year. The lift is there, both to and from the city if you want it.'

Jennifer pauses for a few moments before thanking him. 'How kind. Yes, I would be very grateful for the lift. Thank you Bernard. Thank you very much.' Feeling more content now, Mr Rimmer tells Jennifer about his overall experience learning to drive. His father had taught him – he passed first time. Although he struggled at first, he soon got the hang of it.

But it was his mother that taught him how to ride his first bike. He can still picture her now, back then when he had first fallen off. As he looked back, he saw her laugh loudly; that was before he fell. She ran to him overly concerned; she held him in her arms before encouraging him to try again. For a short while he just kept falling off. All he could hear was her mischievous laughter. 'You loved your mother very much'. Jennifer's comment brings Mr Rimmer back from a memory he had almost forgotten. 'I did.' He replied, 'I still do now.'

The lights are still on in the front lounge of the Dwyer household. Missy the cat is waiting outside the red door. Mr Rimmer is relieved not to be asked indoors. Instead, Jennifer leans over and kisses Mr Rimmer lightly on his left cheek before thanking him and exiting his classic car. Mr Rimmer is speechless. He waves in return as Jennifer passes the front of his classic vehicle, then watches her enter the porch before fumbling for a while in her handbag. As the downstairs hall light comes on, Mr Rimmer heads off in the opposite direction.

Inspector Folkard is now back home. Mr Rimmer stands in the shadows for a long while watching the coming and going about the house. Although it is raining lightly now, he is fully sheltered under a large, silver birch tree – only the cold is unbearable. He is there for almost an entire hour before she finally sees him.

54

ON A COUPLE of occasions that Friday night, Hermione Folkard had entered the bedroom of her youngest, in order to peek out from between the candy striped curtains. It was raining now, and it was late - almost midnight. When she looked for the final time that night, she did not expect to see anything at all. But there he was. There he was, standing behind a tree, sheltering from the rain.

Hermione Folkard was stunned. When he knew that she had seen him, he retreated: had stepped back into the shadows that had brought him there. Then, he literally disappeared. He had waited for her to see him; she was sure of that. He had done it deliberately. There she stood, much longer than anticipated, her right hand now holding back the curtain.

Later outdoors, Hermione Folkard walked down the path towards the gate. It was freezing cold – the rain fell heavily. Cautiously she stepped forward. She felt foolish somehow but not defenceless – she could not allow herself to be drawn out from her home. She could not take such a risk. Despite the training, despite her gut feeling, despite the risk, Hermione

Folkard stepped forward towards the spot she had first seen him. Her annoyance grew with every step she took. And despite looking for several minutes, she could not find him, he was gone. If she had left then, she could have reached his home before him, caught him out. But what of it? He could have claiming he had been out visiting friends. Any excuse would have got him off the hook. She could prove nothing.

Hermione Folkard returned to her home. She double checked the doors and windows before going upstairs where everyone was now asleep. From her briefcase she retrieved the drawing and looked at it a while. She could not say for certain that the unwelcome onlooker had worn glasses – she could not say for certain it was even been the same man. The stature and chosen position amongst the trees was all that they had in common. He was not an intruder; he had stayed on the right side of their gate. It was not a crime, to wave at a child as one passed by.

Her uncertainty bothered her – it was a grey area. Home stayed at home and work stayed mostly at work. In her significant career, Hermione Folkard had never really felt any concern for her family's safety. She needed to talk to Walter, they needed to be more vigilant, especially with the children. Hermione Folkard looked at the dogs asleep by Walter's side of the bed. She was grateful they had dogs. Any intrusion would not go unnoticed.

Lying in bed now, Hermione Folkard thought about Mr Bernard Rimmer. She was sure the stalker, if that is what he was, was him. As Bernard Rimmer he did not really pose a threat. But as another identity, who knew what he was capable of? He had after all, covered well his tracks – been lucky, if she was to be honest with herself. Was he threatening her? Was it a cry for help? Whatever the reason behind the visitations, she would not ignore them.

Sleepier now, Hermione Folkard had come to the decision that she should speak to her team, Catherine first. The wrong approach could trigger a chain of events that could result in the investigation imploding before their eyes. They had all worked extremely hard to get as far as they had. Seven months had passed since the initial murder of Mary-Eloise but Hermione Folkard was sure they were close to catching her killer.

The wind had picked up now and the shadows from the trees made patterns across the carpeted floor; as the wind grew more aggressive, they climbed onto the covers, their lanky fingers feeling the faces of those who slept. But Hermione and Walter Folkard were fast asleep now, dreaming of a time gone by.

Next door, the youngest of the Folkards was dreaming of Christmas and of the time when Santa would call in the middle of the night. How lovely where the gifts he had brought for her. This time, in this dream, she had caught him downstairs leaving via the chimney. She called for him to come back but he did not reply. He was leaving before he had drank his sherry and before he had eaten his mince pie.

55

ALMOST TWO DAYS have passed since Mr Rimmer's outing with Jennifer. It is Sunday evening. Mr Rimmer is sitting back in his much-loved armchair, palms down on both his legs – he is very much looking forward to the third season of The Manhattan Murder Trials. The advertisements are playing on the television. As Mr Rimmer awaits for the much anticipated first episode to begin, Mr Rimmer begins to dwell once more on the tender kiss from Jennifer. Like a mother's kiss, it has reassured him that she has some feelings for him. Although she sent a text that Friday evening thanking him for the evening meal, he waited until the afternoon of the following day before he replied.

Mr Rimmer blows his nose before turning the sound up on the television. Although he does not feel unwell, he has a small cold; he has been sneezing a fair bit the last two mornings. Advertisements over, the dramatic music begins and the recap of last season's finale captivates his full attention. Mr Rimmer pushes back his spectacles back onto the bridge of his nose before rubbing his palms together.

It is during the second interval, whilst Mr Rimmer is making himself a cup of tea, that he finds himself reflecting on the character of the perpetrator. It is all too often these days, that the murderer in a series such as this one, is shown in a more attractive manner – almost part of the director's purpose – the viewer possibly bonding with him or her. It is quite clever of the writer to present a character such as this man, as one who has been a victim in the past. In a strange way, Mr Rimmer does not want him to be caught.

By the end of the first episode, Mr Rimmer is feeling tired; he is shaking his head from side to side. The episode has been disappointing - he has looked forward to the new season since it had been announced, and like many things in life did not live up to his expectations. Twenty minutes pass and Mr Rimmer is already in his bed. Mr Rimmer has got into the bad habit of not showering before bed. It is so cold and he feels quite cold, shivery even.

His mother is looking down upon him. Her eyes don't look as soft today. For a moment Mr Rimmer feels the urge to pray – all those Sundays in church have left a lasting and desperate impression. Mr Belchier at work often refers to it as *the catholic guilt*; his brother is a priest but he doesn't attend church either. Mr Rimmer wishes there was someone actually out there to help – there are lots of different things bothering him right now.

The memories of Jennifer's company cheers him on. Like the last two nights, he takes the story further as he goes to sleep – drifting happily, feeling a lot warmer. How long he has been asleep he is not sure? Suddenly, the story that became a dream has gone horribly wrong. The others have started screaming from the back of the garden and Jennifer has heard them. Panic written all over her face, she looks to the door just as the sound of steps can be heard descending the stairs.

Mr Rimmer wakes suddenly. He puts on his glasses and goes downstairs to get a tall glass of water. His left arm is hurting; sweat is dripping from his forehead. Mr Rimmer sits up for a few moments before getting out of bed. As he passes the bottom of it, he finds that he cannot look at his mother; maybe it is time to move her. Downstairs, he looks out of the kitchen window. It is so dark that he cannot even make out the outline of the granny house. The darkness is uncomfortable, anything could be lurking out there, hidden amongst it.

Twenty minutes pass and Mr Rimmer is feeling a little better. More settled now, tired even, he goes back upstairs and heads for bed. Mr Rimmer pulls the dark florid green quilt back, only to discover that the bottom sheet needs tidying; his restlessness during the evening has disturbed almost every corner – even a pillow has found its way onto the floor at the far end of the room. Mr Rimmer is now tirelessly tucking the pale green bottom sheet under his side of the bed, when two of his right fingers come across something. Mr Rimmer pulls a medium sized see-through bag out from under his mattress before he sits down.

Through the gossamer-like sack, he clearly sees a collection of long strands of hair, in different bunches, each tied at the top with a different coloured ribbons. There is a new addition; it's dark brown hair is tied with a pale blue ribbon. Mr Rimmer bites his bottom lip before quickly hiding it back under his mattress. He looks to see if his mother has seen him, but by the look on her face she already knows.

56

SERGEANT SHAKESPEARE SAT quietly for a few moments before speaking. She was about to say something when she fell silent again. The look on her face was one of disbelief. 'Really? Are you sure? – Are you 100% sure?'. 'I could not swear by it,' replied Inspector Folkard, both hands at her hip, ' otherwise I would have acted upon it. Here, look at this. 'Sergeant Shakespeare's mouth opened slightly.

'At first I thought Zita had drawn a picture of Walter. I even put the picture up!'. Inspector Folkard walked towards the window – it was dark now. She paused for a moment before adding, 'I haven't said much about it all to Walter – but I know he's worried – I'm worried.'

'And how do you know he hasn't been watching for much longer?' Sergeant Shakespeare joined her at the window before passing the picture back to her. 'I don't.' Inspector Folkard replied coldly. Inspector Folkard sat back behind her desk. After looking at the drawing of their unwelcome visitor once more, she opened a draw to her right and placed it inside. It was a rare sight for Inspector Folkard to openly share her growing frustration with anyone outside her home. 'We're two weeks from Christmas and still no further. Until now, I have always waited patiently – known it's always a matter of time – a quiet certainty within me. I'm not sure how patient I can be in this case, the way things are. Him out there.' Sergeant Shakespeare looked upon her colleague for several moments; she dearly wished she had an answer for her. The silence that now presented itself in the room, brought no comfort to either of them. It was late now – time to be heading home.

'I'm off shopping tonight,' announced Inspector Folkard, 'I can't leave everything to Walter'. Sergeant Shakespeare nodded before turning the light off in the office. Together they headed for the half-empty, half-full car park.

It was a dry night but extremely cold too. Inspector Folkard half-waved towards her colleague before getting into her car – there was plenty of shopping still to be done. How cheery were the dazzling lights that adorned the many lined trees along Lord Street: electric blues, crimson reds, golden yellows, bright whites, fuchsia pinks and purples, emerald greens. How welcome they were, especially on such a night.

For a moment, Hermione felt a little lonely; amongst the crowd, various couples had passed her, holding various plastic bags and carriers. Unlike the advertisements on television, most of these looked tired - the strain and pressure apparent on their faces.

One older couple that passed as she entered a store, was holding hands. From their outfits, matching scarves and hairstyle they seemed to have somehow morphed over their many years together; Hermione was sure that underneath their coats, was a pair of matching jumpers.

It was whilst Hermione Folkard was toying with the idea of buying for her grandson a white snow globe, one with a reindeer to the centre, that she thought she had spotted a familiar face. Moments later, the familiar face of Kenneth Chambers came into view. How confused he appeared, disorientated. Within seconds he was joined by his wife, Kate. From the anxious look on her face, they had probably become separated in the store.

The Chambers moved in unison amongst the ignorant crowd. Kate appeared to be talking about each item she held; in return, Ken listened and nodded – sometimes he appeared to speak a little. How changed they were. In the last six months, they had aged in what seemed to be years. It was difficult to ascertain whether the change was due to his advancing Alzheimer's or to the effects of having lost their only child – maybe possibly both.

Somehow, Hermione Folkard found herself feeling more fortunate than she had in the last few hours. There was so much to look forward to this Christmas – her entire family would be sat around the large dining table. What a difficult time it would be for those who had lost loved ones, especially recently – what a loss – what for them now? Twenty minutes had passed and Hermione Folkard had selected many items for purchase – amongst them was the snow globe for her dear grandson. She was at the till in a queue when the Chambers, in a world of their own, passed close by. Their basket was still empty.

On the following Saturday morning, the Folkard clan headed for a much needed walk to the nearby Botanical Gardens. Hermione had linked her son's sturdy arm from behind; in turn he smiled – a broad, grown-up and handsome smile, quite arresting. She listened attentively to Harry who was speaking off the expectations from the P.G.C.E. course he had embarked on. How different he seemed – a typical student one moment and next, a future teacher of Maths . He seemed strangely confident, energetic, enthused and unfazed by the endless demands made by the education system – and a father too.

Mark was laughing heartily in Walter's arms; soon he would be one. He kept pointing at Zita who was feeding quite courageously the many advancing pigeons. Darcy walked ahead of all the others. No doubt she was thinking on what her mother had said earlier, about putting an end to her newly acquired relationship. Maybe her mother could have worded things better. Looking back, the word 'desperate', seemed a little harsh. It was unthinkable for Hermione Folkard to accept, that a boy who was clearly punching well above his weight, could treat her daughter in such a manner – ashamed to tell his friends that they were dating – in Hermione Folkard's opinion an unworthy coward.

The large Victorian tea-room come glass-house was warm for the time of year – in the corner stood a large Christmas pine tree decorated solely with baubles and striped candy canes. How busy it was; despite the largeness of it, there were few spare tables. The ceiling windows were covered with various plastic toys. Together they possessed a desirability that was quite inexplicable; separately, aside from one another, they looked like the type of toy that would last, at the most, a week. Darcy was smiling more now. A glance from father to eldest daughter had convinced her to go easier on her mother.

Fifteen minutes later and the clan had habitually begun walking around the wide and murky lake; they were heading now towards the sandy playground. Hermione handed Mark back to Harry before she linked Darcy's slender arm from behind. Both smiled and looked somehow relieved that the war was over. Darcy kissed her mother's left cheek before it was returned – no words were exchanged – peace warming them like a thick blanket.

It was difficult to isolate each child's laughter as they swirled by on the roundabout. Darcy had a protective arm around Mark, whilst Zita kept changing seat for the fun of it. Hermione Folkard pushed the arc of the roundabout's metallic blue bar every two seconds – push – push – push – round and round and round they went – faster now. Spinning so quickly now, it was difficult to see the physical decay of the roundabout. When it came to a halt, it was obvious – the colours peeling away from the surface, the triangular wooden planks were faded too. As the ride came to a halt, Hermione noticed a new addition to the many words etched into the wood: *'not worth sleeping here'.*

Harry leaned forward and picked up Mark. Although laughing still, he was clearly struggling to stand without falling – that made them all laugh. Darcy and Zita had ended their ride with their back to their mother. Zita stood and turned to be helped off by her father. Darcy turned to do likewise. But her mother's frown had returned – a look of horror upon her face.

Hermione Folkard signalled for Walter to move the party ahead towards the swings. Sitting on a bench for a short while, she watched the hungry birds being seduced by the breadcrumbs from a child in a nearby pushchair. Soon they began to circle her feet as a wayward piece of bread landed close-by. It was time to take action. It was time to head home.

Feeling less nauseous now, Hermione Folkard walked deliberately behind the tired party, now heading back towards the car park. She scanned the park once more as she dialled Catherine Shakespeare's number. 'What did you just say?' came the reply. 'I said, Darcy has a chunk of hair missing from her crown. I have no idea when it happened nor how it happened – but I'm going to catch that bastard if it's the last thing I do.' A short conversation followed before they both hung up.

A couple of hours later, Darcy related to her parents, who were looking far too worried for no apparent reason, that she had felt a tug at her hair whilst on the bus from school to home. She added that things like this happened all the time – had happened to other girls before – that some of the lads in her year had even pinned one of their friends down on the floor during a party at the weekend and shaved an entire left eyebrow off – his mother was livid. Darcy contained her laughter – her parents weren't finding any of these revelations funny.

Later that evening, whilst Zita slept soundly, both parents looked thoroughly through her mop of hair. Satisfied no hair had been taken, it was obvious from the chunk that had been removed from Darcy's, that a pair of scissors had been used. It was time to speak to her superior – what he would have to say about her superstitions was anyone's guess. For the first time in her career, in her life, Hermione Folkard was stuck between the devil and the sea. What she could do and what she wanted to do, where two very different things.

57

A SUBTLE AND indescribable aloofness has grown between Jennifer and Bernard. In Mr Rimmer's mind, it has grown from a molehill into a mountain. Jennifer has only texted three times this week; two of them were in response to his own. Mr Rimmer is contemplating the reasons behind this strangeness, whilst he is outdoors in his neglected front garden. He knows Albert and his mother are sitting at the window but he ignores them; after a short while, he has even forgotten they are there. 'There are many possible reasons behind a person distancing themselves', he states out loud – Mr Rimmer does not like what he hears in return. Maybe, he ponders, maybe he caused the friction between them – made his feelings for her too obvious.

Almost all of the summer flowers are dead now – only the odd lilac geranium plant survives in each window box. In reality, they have lasted much longer than expected. Looking aside, the paint is beginning to flake from the ornamental window shutters too – the paint he acquired from the DIY store is still there, in the garage. Despite the time of day, Mr Rimmer finds himself unable to keep the winter's sun glare out from his eyes – his efforts seem somehow pointless.

In a few days, Friday night, and the week before Christmas, he will pick Jennifer up once more in order to attend the Christmas night out. Mr Rimmer is determined not only to look his best but to be the perfect companion. He knows he must not allow thoughts of Marcos Kennedy cloud his mind and bring him down. He must be polite and present himself in the best possible way. Moments later, Mr Rimmer is filled with dread once more; he wishes he could laugh more heartily – mingle more comfortably. Socialising has never come easy to Mr Rimmer. If he had attended more social events, instead of avoiding them, then maybe he would not be having this problem right now.

Mr Rimmer has now tidied all of the window boxes to the front of the house. At first he thought he'd leave the geraniums alone – the boxes could look unusually nice for the time of year – he could plant some colourful heathers between them. Then suddenly, Mr Rimmer decides there really is no point leaving them in – they would soon die anyway. Having been thrust into the wheelbarrow, they now lie dejected and rejected despite their greatest effort to please and survive.

Later that evening, Mr Rimmer is about to go to sleep, when he remembers the linen bag under his mattress. He looks towards his mother, then bites the bottom of his lip before feeling for it. Relieved it is no longer there, he is about to move his hand away when he comes across the tip of it, just as he slides his hand out sideways. Mr Rimmer looks to his mother for help. His left arm is hurting now – it has been bothering him on and off for days.

Determined to rid himself from it, he takes the bag carefully out from under his mattress and heads downstairs to the back door – wellingtons on – down the side path adjacent to the right hand side of the bungalow, passing the elongated Victorian greenhouse on the left to the bottom of the garden. There, Mr Rimmer stops and listens for a while, ensuring he has not been seen by anyone. He heads across the bottom of the garden and to the granny house, where inside, Mr Rimmer returns the linen bag with its contents, back to the pit where it belongs.

Mr Rimmer's left arm is hurting even more now – his smallest finger is tingling. He stops for a few moments before he leans against the sliding door of the greenhouse. Despite the darkness, he is able to see the outline of the mother-in-law pointing at him from a nearby shelf. Mr Rimmer feels nauseous and sick inside, faint even.

Back indoors, Mr Rimmer can hear his mother calling from upstairs. Despite covering both his ears he can still hear her, loud and clear – there's no escape. He knows he will be in no fit state to take Jennifer out despite his best efforts. Tomorrow he will call in sick to work. He must now go and attend to his mother.

Days pass. Mr Rimmer has not returned to work. The end of term has been and gone. Unfortunately, Mr Rimmer has had to give the night out a miss, his stomach is still very unsettled – a nasty bug. Jennifer has texted every second day since his absence – she hopes he is feeling better. Her father dropped her off in town – he was missed – different colleagues asked after him – it was a great night out – she wishes he would have been there, 'is it ok if I pop in for a visit?'. Raymond Belchier has texted too; he has included in his messages some of the sordid details of the evening's events. Amongst them, was the news that Jennifer had left with. Marcos Kennedy later in the evening, 'has since looked like the cat that got the cream – methinks all his Christmases came in at once!'.

Mr Rimmer has deliberately not replied to any of the texts, not even to Jennifer's. Despite the news, Mr Rimmer is now feeling better, stronger even. His left arm has stopped hurting – he hasn't even used his inhaler for days. Mr Rimmer decides against clipping his hand nails – he hasn't shaved for days. Looking in the mirror, he decides he will grow a beard this Christmas.

58

LOOKING BACK ON the conversation that had taken place earlier that week with her boss, Inspector Folkard could not help but agree that she should have involved him a lot sooner. Professional to the last, Superintendent Reid had confirmed all of her suspicions: there was no action that could be taken against Mr Rimmer at that present moment in time. However, patrol cars would as often as possible circuit in the vicinity of her home and the girls' schools, at least until the threat lessened, or even intensified. The appropriate action would be taken as soon as any concrete evidence came to light, 'in a nutshell Inspector, the earlier the bird catches the worm, the sooner it can be eaten.' At no point had her superior questioned her judgement. If anything, he had reassured her. Smiling now, Inspector Folkard herself that there had been no more visitations, at least not to her knowledge.

The following day, and on the afternoon of Christmas Eve, P. C. Clark knocked and entered her busy office – her face alight; she held a piece of note paper in her right hand. It was obvious from her face that she needed Inspector Folkard's attention right away. Inspector Folkard stepped out from her office. P.C. Clark related with some obvious excitement in her voice, that the owners of an ice-cream shop, Rossi's, in Blackpool, had telephoned the station a number of days ago. The message had been passed to the wrong team and had lay in Constable Wiggings' in-tray for days. Upon his return, he passed the relevant information on.

P. C. Clark had only just finished talking to Mrs Rossi on the telephone. She related that her son Virgilio, had seen a man, like the one described to him from the photograph, the one shown to them weeks earlier, with Alice. 'They'd been sitting round the table talking about Alice's murder, when their son, who was home for the Christmas break, interrupted and asked about our recent visit.' It seemed that, on both occasions when the police had visited, he had been away from home, a university student, now in his third year.

Virgilio Rossi had said that an older man, fitting Mr Rimmer's description, had been seen by him, coming from her flat on a couple of occasions, 'both Sundays'. P.C. Clark explained that at the time when Alice had been murdered, Virgilio was home from university, at the time in his first year. He helped cover a few shifts at the shop whilst two of the girls were on holiday. He said that he remembered Alice, a girl of mixed race – an Asian girl. He got on well with her – had even walked her home, back to her flat – had assumed the older man had been her father.

The Rossi's had in the past met Mr and Mrs Lau. They had visited the shop a few times since her death; had even introduced themselves, but had never actually stopped and bought ice-cream. They knew the man in the photograph was not her father. They didn't even realise Virgilio had spent time with Alice.

P.C. Clark was heading off to meet with Virgilio. She waved the photograph before adding that she would get a statement from him If he positively identified their suspect. She would then ask him if he would agree to a line up. 'Within the hour boss, we might have glad tidings!'. Inspector Folkard was not entirely sure whether to allow herself the glimmer of hope that this was the moment she had been waiting for. She instructed her eager P.C. to wait for Sergeant Shakespeare's return from a burglary case earlier that day. P.C. Clark looked fit to burst.

By four p.m. there had still been no phone call. Inspector Folkard regretted not having travelled personally to the Rossi household; she tried to keep busy, but kept finding herself staring at the incident wall. Another half hour passed before her office phone finally rang. Inspector Folkard was surprised by the knot that had formed right below her stomach. She let the phone ring twice before she picked it up. It was Sergeant Shakespeare. Virgilio Rossi had identified Mr Rimmer from the photograph shown to him. He was pretty sure, having now seen the photograph, that this was the man he had seen on at least two occasions with Alice Lau.

Inspector Folkard was speechless. She thanked her Sergeant before quietly putting the phone down. An image of Mr Rimmer holding a pair of scissors in his hand formed inside her head, he was sitting on a bus behind her. He began cutting Darcy's hair without her knowledge. Inspector Folkard could see his face clearly now. He was standing outdoors looking up at her daughter's bedroom window.

59

CHRISTMAS DAY HAS almost been and gone. Mr Rimmer has not even left the house. He has been tidying this and that in the back garden – moving a few things around the house. Later in the evening, Mr Rimmer is lying across the settee looking through a photo album – many of the faces are unfamiliar now. Mr Rimmer's thoughts turn to a familiar photograph. In it, Mr Rimmer's mother stands not far from the front porch. The house is in need of a lick of paint; the ponds look like they have been filled with a variety of common manageable plants. In it, a child, Mr Rimmer, is clinging to his mother's skirt – in turn she holds him close but her eyes are not upon him – she is smiling at someone else. She is smiling at someone over the garden fence. She is smiling at Albert Conway.

Mr Rimmer remembers something Albert Conway said many years ago – something distasteful – something Mr Rimmer deliberately ignored. He looks at the portrait on the television for a few moments before putting the album down on the coffee table. It is time for bed. Mr Rimmer looks about the place before going upstairs. He enters the bedroom, before pressing on the light switch. Mr Rimmer is now comfortably in bed; he reads The Southport Visitor for a short while before turning the main light off.

Despite the darkness, the room is faintly alight with the evening moonlight. Mr Rimmer looks to the wall opposite him before turning over. The portrait of Mrs Rimmer is gone. Instead, there is a large rectangular stain on the wallpaper. She is lying face-up on her bed now – her head on the pillow, her eyes wide open. Like the Mona Lisa, she is not exactly smiling. Before long, Mr Rimmer is sound asleep. He still lies on his side with his left hand below the pillow - the linen bag now safe within his clutch.

Outside the wind is blowing fiercely. A snow-storm is coming. Jennifer's text on the following morning, Boxing Day, arrives earlier than expected. Mr Rimmer ignores it. He continues to vigorously scramble his eggs; he is feeling hungry. Today he is planning to visit the Folkard household – the girls will be at home. Although watching from a greater distance, it is obvious that the youngest of the two spends a considerable amount of time in the back garden, regardless of the weather. Mr Rimmer begins to whistle a happy tune just as another text arrives. Mr Rimmer plates his breakfast and scoffs a mouthful before reading the short text. Jennifer is on her way round.

Mr Rimmer has only just finished his breakfast when the main line telephone rings. For a moment Mr

Rimmer is taken aback; the main phone rarely rings. It rings persistently for quite a while. Despite it being in the sitting room, and behind a closed door, the sound of it begins to irritate him. Mr Rimmer continues to ignore the call. Eventually it stops ringing and peace is restored.

Barely an hour passes when there is a faint knock at the front door. Mr Rimmer waits a while before getting up from the settee. The knock is repeated; this time it is a lot louder – more urgent. Mr Rimmer unlocks the front door, then the porch door. All the while, Mr Rimmer has avoided looking up and directly at Jennifer. He knows it is her from her hands and feet – her shoes have some snow on them. In one of her hands she is holding a Christmas gift bag, in the other she is holding a mobile phone. The sound of a car pulls away, probably a taxi.

'Hi, Bernard? I've been worried sick about you. You haven't answered any of my texts. Are you ok?' Mr Rimmer nods, giving Jennifer one of those smiles where the lips cling together and the teeth never show. In the meantime, the front door is held open and she passes indoors; she is still talking. Mr Rimmer subtly locks the porch door before he closes the front one. Outside it is snowing lightly now – how pretty it looks outdoors – how cold it has grown. 'Have I done something to upset you?' Jennifer continues. 'Can I sit down?' Mr Rimmer nods, 'Of course. Would you like a cup of tea?'. Jennifer nods before nervously asking if he has any mince pies going.

For a moment Mr Rimmer is taken aback, 'I have no mince pies – in fact, I am sure of it.'. For a moment Jennifer stares at Mr Rimmer, almost confused by some small change in him – what it is, she cannot put her finger on. She is about to speak again when Mr Rimmer adds, 'but I did spot a pack of biscuits in the back of the cupboard. I'll fetch those.'. Jennifer is about to get up to help Mr Rimmer when he gestures for her to remain sitting. 'Won't be long Jennifer. Back in a tic.'.

Moments later, Jennifer's is talking again. Her conversation revolves mostly around what she did with her family yesterday, on Christmas Day. Mr Rimmer isn't really listening, he is fishing inside the deep cupboard for the packet of biscuits. Eventually he reaches them and brings them with him. He holds two mugs of tea in his left and the packet of plain biscuits in his right. 'Haven't had a Nice biscuit in years. I love these!'. Mr Rimmer is aware that Jennifer is watching him intently. He is sipping his tea when she speaks. 'You know, you suit a beard. I wouldn't have thought so, but you really do. Are you growing it?'

Mr Rimmer cradles his chin with his right hand; his thumb sustains the right side of his face whilst the first finger sustains the left hand side. Mr Rimmer moves his hand up and down his chin a couple of times before speaking. 'How was the staff night out?' Mr Rimmer leans over and picks up a Nice biscuit.

Jennifer looks a little uncomfortable. Instinctively, she sits back in her chair – she is still wearing her coat. Her face is a little flushed now. Mr Rimmer is smiling. 'Bernard. Bernard I am sorry you didn't make the staff night out. Everyone had a lot of fun.'. Jennifer is about to add something when Mr Rimmer interrupts, 'and did you have a lot of fun Jennifer?'. Jennifer stutters a little before replying. 'Yes. Yes, thank you. I did.'. Jennifer looks like a child that has been caught stealing sweets in a shop. 'Are you upset with me Bernard?'.

Mr Rimmer's smile has now disappeared. His Nice biscuit has disappeared too. 'A little bird told me that Marcos took you home that night.'. Jennifer's face is scarlet in colour. She is still to drink most of her tea. Jennifer leans forward and places her mug down. Her eyes look about the room. The room seems very different somehow. Jennifer looks again at Bernard Rimmer. Mr Rimmer is drinking from his mug once more; he is looking directly at her. She has never noticed him slurp before. His hand nails look oddly long. Jennifer begins to get up. Mr Rimmer, who has since been watching her intently, places his empty mug down on the coffee table. 'Sit down dear.'.

Jennifer is standing now. She is not sure why, but she dare not take her eyes of Mr Rimmer. She is feeling hot. And a little dizzy. For some reason, memories of that police sergeant come flooding back now – the one who seemed overly concerned. Mr Rimmer suggests she has another sip of tea. Jennifer is thinking about saying she has to go but something tells her she should not. She sits back down and drinks a little more tea before she speaks. 'Bernard, Marcos only took me home. Everyone else had been drinking, had you been there, I would not have left with him.'. Mr Rimmer has nothing to say. 'I know you worry about me,' she continues. 'You warned me about him and I listened.'.

Mr Rimmer is about to speak when Jennifer's mobile begins to ring. For some reason Jennifer ignores it; but her handbag is on the coffee table and the device has lit up. The name Marcos is on the screen. A look of alarm spreads on Jennifer's face as she leans over to enter her pin and turn the device off. As she does so, Mr Rimmer leans over too; he waits for her to enter her pin before casually removing the mobile from her palm.

Jennifer is feeling quite sick now – her throat feels dry. She looks to Bernard but he is ignoring her. Instead, he is reading all of her texts from Marcos. For some reason she is now unable to move. Mr Rimmer is now staring at her somewhat astonished by what he has read. He pauses for a moment before he leans forward and grabs her by her hair.

The house phone has been ringing on and off throughout the afternoon but Mr Rimmer is ignoring it. Mr Rimmer is packing a few things into a canvas bag. He takes the scissors from the kitchen draw before he zips it closed. Mr Rimmer's knuckles are bloody; he needs to clean himself up. He is taking a shower when the doorbell rings. The house is silent for a while – as is Jennifer. Jennifer is now below with the others. The doorbell rings again.

'RING IT AGAIN.'. Inspector Folkard's face wore a look of practised neutrality. 'I know he's in there,' stated Sergeant Shakespeare ',and from the sound of the water exiting the drain to the side of the house, he is probably in the kitchen.'. For another short while, the house was silent. Inspector Folkard and Sergeant Shakespeare waited patiently. Then suddenly, through the patterned glass of the front door, the familiar silhouette of Mr Rimmer approached. The door opened. He was not smiling.

From his uncombed hairstyle, it was now obvious he had been taking a bath, or a shower. Dressed in blue jeans with a shirt and jumper to match, he looked at them with what appeared to be a strong distastefulness for them both.

Sergeant Shakespeare informed Mr Rimmer that they had been trying to reach him all morning. Mr Rimmer said nothing. He appeared unmoved by her statement: 'And what can I do for you?'. 'May we come in?'. Again, no response. Mr Rimmer looked at Inspector Folkard for a short while before stepping aside; his hand gesture invited them both in, then showed them to their customary seats. 'Would you like to sit down?'. 'Yes, thank you,' replied Sergeant Shakespeare. Mr Rimmer walked between the settee and the coffee table before sitting himself in his customary seat. Leaning forward now, with his hands clasped together, he looked attentively at them both sitting side by side.

Sergeant Shakespeare, sitting within close proximity of Mr Rimmer, now pivoted herself round to the point where she was looking directly at Mr Rimmer. 'A witness has recently come forward and identified you as the man seen with a young woman named Alice Lau. Alice Lau was murdered last year.'. Sergeant Shakespeare paused for a few moments. 'We would like you to come along with us, to the station for an identification parade.'. This time, Mr Rimmer seemed a little more responsive. His eyes blinked quickly in succession before he sat back in his chair – his hands parted now – palms down onto the thigh of each leg. 'We would be grateful if you could assist us further with our enquiries in order to ascertain the truth behind this allegation.'.

For a moment Mr Rimmer seemed to look incredulously at them both. He looked at Inspector Folkard first before laughing a little; he then looked at Sergeant Shakespeare and laughed a lot louder. 'You cannot be serious. I have already told you that it has been years since I stepped foot in Blackpool.'.

'You are not being arrested Mr Rimmer,' began Sergeant Shakespeare, 'under Code D of the Identification Process we can offer you a form of video identification, if that is what you would prefer. Or we can also offer you the standard Identification parade. Either way, it is paramount that you co-operate with us at this point in our investigation.'.

'Am I being arrested?'. Inspector Folkard looked long and hard at their suspect; she thought that Mr Rimmer seemed strangely calm under the circumstances. 'No.'. replied Sergeant Shakespeare. 'Although a refusal to co-operate at this point in the investigation would unavoidably and regrettably lead to you being arrested. Once at the station we will explain the procedure.'.

Mr Rimmer said nothing more; he stood up before and turned before walking towards the kitchen. He picked up a brown leather jacket that was loosely hung onto the shoulders of a kitchen wooden chair with a velvet-like red seat and put it on. He looked to the back door before going to lock it and with that he was ready to accompany them both.

'The portrait of your mother?' enquired Inspector Folkard, 'it is gone.' 'Yes.' replied Mr Rimmer. Inspector Folkard was surprised by his aloofness. The portrait's absence seemed significant somehow – wrong even. Looking about the room, there was something about the place that had altered – even Mr Rimmer himself seemed different, less pleasant, less likeable, less transparent. Upon their exit, Inspector Folkard noted the two Conways watching the three exiting together via the wide metallic gate. Although it was impossible to see Albert Conway now, Inspector Folkard was sure he would be leaning forward, close to the glass of the bay window, his mouth gaping open.

Inspector Folkard sat in the back of the unmarked vehicle whilst Sergeant Shakespeare drove. All the while neither spoke to one another. It was difficult for Inspector Folkard to strike a conversation of any sort. The journey was taking longer than usual – the brightly lit streets busy with traffic and eager buyers hoping for a bargain. Only ten years earlier, Mr Rimmer had taken himself off shopping, whilst his mother lay dying in her bed. Inspector Folkard grimaced at the possible coincidence. The missing portrait was still haunting her. She was sure, the Mr Rimmer they knew would have under any circumstance been a lot more accommodating – would have never removed his mother's portrait. For a moment she looked at her suspect. Whom exactly did she have sitting in the back of the car?

Forty minutes later and Inspector Folkard found herself stood at the back of the plain pale blue rectangular interview room whilst Sergeant Shakespeare explained the identification process. She was seated with her back to the Inspector. Opposite her, sat Mr Rimmer. How calm and cool he appeared in the light of this new information. It seemed strange that he had made such a small protest – even stranger, he was yet to ask for a solicitor.

'During the identification parade,' began Sergeant Shakespeare, 'you will be accompanied by seven other adult men who will resemble you in age, height and general appearance. For example, all of the men will be wearing glasses.'. Mr Rimmer said nothing. 'Neither myself nor Inspector Folkard need be present during the process. If you do not object, we will be in the room where the witness shall be present.'. Sergeant Shakespeare paused for a few seconds. Mr Rimmer continued to look towards the back of the room. 'I have no objections.'.

'In a few moments you will be taken to another room where the identification parade will take place. Please inform us if you have any objections to the arrangements or the participants in the parade. If you do not, then you may choose your own position in the line. You will not be able to communicate with the other participants. You will not be able to see the witness. A video recording will be made of the identification parade.'.

Sergeant Shakespeare spoke a little louder now, 'if you are ready now Mr Rimmer, we will proceed.'. For a moment it seemed as though Mr Rimmer was not going to stand. He seemed rooted to the spot. Inspector Folkard stood up. She followed Sergeant Shakespeare out from the room, in turn she had followed Mr Rimmer.

Back along the grey painted corridor they had first entered, and in less than a minute they all came to a halt outside a dark grey door. Before leaving Mr Rimmer, Inspector Folkard passed a form to the two plain clothed officers who took over. As they walked away, neither could help feel some dread at the possibility that Virgilio Rossi may not identify their man. They had only to wait five minutes before they were called into the adjacent room. The identification parade was ready.

As they entered, they both nodded courteously towards Virgilio Rossi; they were both unsurprised to see Chief Superintendent Reid sitting at the back of the room. He nodded too; he looked rather serious. Inspector Folkard knew that only a positive identification could secure a warrant now. It was frustrating that even a this did not necessarily secure a prosecution - but a warrant was all she needed, she was sure of that. Without it, the case would be on-going. Inspector Folkard was sure Chief Superintendent Reid was on the verge of reassigning her last two officers to another case.

The likeness between each 'suspect' seemed great. They were are all about five feet ten inches tall, wore glasses, even their clothes had a likeness about them. How unlikely it seemed now that he would pick the right suspect. After all, he had only seen him twice, and from a distance of about fifty feet. In that time, Virgilio Rossi could only have seen him clearly for a very small amount of time, seconds likely. Inspector Folkard's stomach was tied up in knots now.

Virgilio Rossi looked calmer now. He was reassured once more that nobody from the identification parade could see him – would even know he was the witness that had come forward. His attractive olive complexion and light-brown hair complemented what was probably a new set of Christmas clothing. Dressed in light blue jeans and a white tee-shirt with matching hoodie, he stood rooted to the spot, looking carefully at all of the suspects. After a minute or so, he took a step forwards, then one sideways; he continued to do so, pausing from time to time.

At first, he stopped to look at suspect number two. Seconds later he paused by suspect number six. Lastly, he paused before suspect number eight. He looked at them all for another moment before saying that he thought suspect number six was the man he saw with Alice Lau. Sergeant Boardley asked Virgilio Rossi if he was sure, 'Sir, I need you to confirm that this is the man you saw with Alice Lau on the two occasions you have referred to in your statement. You must be completely sure.'.

Sergeant Shakespeare looked over to where Inspector Folkard stood. The look on her face said it all. For a moment it was as if the world had stopped spinning. Virgilio Rossi did not answer Sergeant Boardley's question straight away. He looked to the suspect he had picked out from the parade just a while longer. As he did so, Mr Rimmer lifted his right hand and proceeded to push his spectacles back onto the bridge of his nose.

'It's him. Suspect six. It is definitely him. ''Thank you sir,' continued Sergeant Boardley, 'an officer will be with you shortly. He will take you back to the room where your family is waiting. You may go home then. Thank you for your co-operation'.

Inspector Folkard and Sergeant Shakespeare afforded a wide smile as soon as Virgilio Rossi was escorted out of the room. It was the Superintendent's presence that stopped them from clasping one another – the relief evident in their faces. Across from them, the parade was being shown out from the room. Mr Rimmer strolled out calmly; he looked like a man who was about to walk away Scot free.

61

MR RIMMER IS thinking of the girl that is below with all of the others. Although she was still breathing when she was tied and thrown in – it will not be long until she dies – dies slowly like his mother did, ten years ago to this day.

The pale blue room with its grey furniture is depressing to say the least. Inspector Folkard whispers something into Sergeant Shakespeare's ear. Mr Rimmer is now listening attentively. From the look on both their faces, it is impossible to know whether he was successfully identified by the unnamed witness. Despite this, Mr Rimmer is feeling strangely calm, confident even. Although he has never been in this situation before, he has watched enough crime drama to generally guess what might be coming next. Mr Rimmer is observing Sergeant Shakespeare closely. She looks more hostile with her hair tied back – not as feminine as she did on the little one's birthday.

Sergeant Shakespeare pulls up a chair and sits opposite him, whilst Inspector Folkard stands behind her, to the side, not far from the door. 'Mr Bernard

Rimmer, I am arresting you on suspicion of murder. You do not have to say anything. However, it may harm your defence if you do not mention when questioned something which you later rely on in court. Anything you do say may be given in evidence.'

Mr Rimmer takes a deep breath before closing his eyes momentarily. He then opens his eyes before looking about the room. From the look of confusion on his face, he is not entirely sure what exactly is going on. Mr Rimmer asks for a glass of water – his throat is dry – he could really do with a cup of tea. 'Are you alright Mr Rimmer?. Inspector Folkard looks concerned, even curious. ' Do you feel alright?'. Feeling quite nervous now, Mr Rimmer cannot even remember how he got to the station in the first place. 'Did I drive here?'. Mr Rimmer's left arm is hurting a little now. He pushes his spectacles back onto the bridge of his nose before leaning onto his forearms on the table, hands clasped as if in prayer.

Inspector Folkard is now speaking to Sergeant Shakespeare at the back of the room. Sergeant Shakespeare sits opposite him once more before speaking again, 'Mr Rimmer, you are now in police custody and will later undergo an interrogation. Sergeant O'Leary will now take you to a room where an inventory of possessions will be conducted. A booking procedure will then take place. We will ask some basic information from you before we fingerprint and photograph you.'

Mr Rimmer sits back in his chair. For a moment he thinks he is going to cry. He has a horrible feeling that something has happened to Jennifer – he is not entirely sure when he last heard from her – he is thinking about this, tracing back the last few days when Sergeant Shakespeare speaks again. 'Mr Rimmer, Would you like us to notify anyone of your arrest? Would you like some legal advice or assistance whilst you are being detained?'.

'No.' Mr Rimmer is deep in thought. 'I don't think so.'.

62

INSPECTOR FOLKARD LOOKED kindly at Mr Rimmer before lowering her voice and speaking to Sergeant Shakespeare. 'Get in touch with Merseyside MIND and the Community Mental Health Team. We need to deal with this sensitively – possibly we will need to detain him under Section 136. Let's make sure he has the support he needs before we interrogate him – they're likely to recommend a full assessment as well as the support from an appropriate adult. And let's get him a solicitor.'.

'OK. I'm going to get him a hot drink – a nice cup of tea. He looks distressed.'. Sergeant Shakespeare paused before she went on. 'I don't know what it is, but he seems more like 'our' Mr Rimmer now.'. Inspector Folkard knew what Sergeant Shakespeare meant. 'How long for the warrant?'. 'It's been hard getting hold of a judge – Boxing Day and all that – could be tomorrow.'. Let's hope not. The sooner it's issued, the better. It'll be dark soon and I'd like to start work at the house first thing.'.

A few hours later the warrant had been granted. The property search would begin the following morning, first daylight. Inspector Folkard and Sergeant Shakespeare headed home not long after eight that evening. The anti-climax shared by them both had affected them in a unusual way. Somehow the much anticipated elation from having caught their man was hanging in the balance – what the search would reveal, they were not sure.

Equally, the interviews were still to follow. At present they could link him to two, possibly three deceased women; they would need some concrete proof before they could detain him further, before they could even charge him. Certainly they both agreed, that earlier on that day, when they spoke to him in the comfort of his own home, he did not seem the same man they had spoken to on previous occasions. The earlier Mr Rimmer seemed aloof, aggressive even, cocky too.

'Good night Hermione.'. 'Yes. Good night. See you first thing. God knows what we'll find there.'. The two women looked at one another – they were both thinking of Eva Manning. And with that the two quietly folded, almost simultaneously, into their individual vehicles. Christmas behind them and the New Year ahead of, maybe there would be something to celebrate after all. Certainly, providing closure for the families, providing them with some answers, was at the top their priority list, that, and putting away somebody they suspected was extremely dangerous.

63

MR RIMMER HAS been sitting in his cell for a few hours now – it is late into the evening. Earlier on, he could not eat his dinner – his stomach felt tight, much like his chest. Mr Rimmer has been feeling anxious for most of the day. No matter how much he tries, he cannot fully recall what happened to Alice – Alice with the small feet. An elegant female officer brings him a hot drink of tea before the main lights are turned down – he manages to eat a bourbon biscuit, it reminds him of home.

Asleep now for two hours, he is dreaming of a time when his mother sat with him for hours making Christmas cards. She has a large box of festive rubber stamps and a large variety of block coloured inks that she had collected over the years. A few of her favourite stamps had been bought from a narrow store in London, near The Russell Hotel where they had once stayed when he was much younger. There they sat cutting and printing, sticking and shaping. There was a time when his mother used to successfully sell the cards in the local newsagents in Churchtown. It all stopped after father died. One of the houses on the front of a card looks like the converted primary school that is now an Indian restaurant in Formby.

Mr Rimmer is now dreaming of Jennifer; they are outside the Indian restaurant. They are both talking to one another whilst leaning on the opposite sides of the car bonnet. He is so pleased that she would like him to teach her to drive. She is smiling. Her crimson lips are so beautiful – she is very beautiful. Suddenly, and immediately behind her, a man who resembles one of the men who participated in the line-up, touches her shoulder. Jennifer turns around; she looks frightened. She clearly recognises him. He is wearing a familiar brown leather jacket and blue jeans. His smile is disconcerting – ugly even.

Safely in the car now, Jennifer seems a lot calmer – the familiar man disappears as she looks back through the gap between the two front seats. As she turns to speak to Mr Rimmer, a look of horror spreads once more across her face. Her eyes widen like a frightened child and her wide mouth opens aghast. Jennifer is now glued to the back of her car seat, edging even towards her car door, her hands clutching her handbag. Mr Rimmer looks outside his window; he cannot see anyone. He looks into the side mirrors, nothing.

Mr Rimmer pulls over – he does not understand what she is frightened of. As he turns to speak to Jennifer, he catches a glimpse of his mother in the rear-view mirror. Mr Rimmer is horrified. She is wearing her curly dark wig and her pale blue dress, the tessellating brooch at her breast. Mr Rimmer does not notice at first that Jennifer is getting out of the car. Mr Rimmer reaches out to stop her – who knows who could be out there?, but as he touches her lower left arm, he notices that protruding from the left sleeve of the pale blue dress is his own arm, followed by his own hand.

Jennifer is gone now. Looking in the mirror once more, Mr Rimmer sees that it is not his mother in the mirror, it is himself. Although he is not wearing glasses , he is dressed in his mother's clothes; he is wearing her red lipstick. Panic ensues him. He calls after Jennifer but she is running away. She keeps running and doesn't look back. Mr Rimmer continues to cry in his sleep. He continues to cry until he wakes up sobbing. He isn't quite sure how he knows, but he is sure Jennifer is in danger – possibly now with the others.

Confused and struggling to clear his mind, he finds rocking himself forward and back to be of some comfort. Something, he is not sure what, or even someone, he is not sure whom, tells him that Jennifer may still be alive. But he cannot be the one to save her. He is locked inside. So anxious now, his chest is beating hard, Mr Rimmer feels sick – he can see green spots ahead of him before the light disappears and everything is calm once again.

64

INSPECTOR FOLKARD'S MOBILE rang six times before she finally picked it up. It was when she heard the name of the missing woman that she rose quickly out of bed, an incredulous look upon her drained face. Bed light on, her husband continued to sleep soundly on his back – Zita curled-up like a quaver in his arms.

Only a few minutes earlier, just after 7:00 a.m., a Mr Jacob Dwyer had telephoned the station, concerned because his daughter was yet to return home. Jennifer Dwyer had not been seen since she had left their household, in a taxi, at about ten thirty in the morning. She was heading to her mentor's house, Mr Bernard Rimmer, Marshide Road – had gone to both visit him and deliver a Christmas present. The taxi firm confirmed that she had been dropped off outside his house; the driver was able to recall a blue car on the drive at the time.

Jennifer had led her parents to believe that she would be home for dinner – would call a taxi for the return. Both parents had remained home all day. Jennifer never arrived home. Both parents had rang her several times, left several messages. Mr and Mrs

Dwyer firmly believed that if Jennifer could, she would not have ignored their calls – she would have replied. The familiar voice of Police Constable Stanfield added, 'Jennifer has been missing nearly twenty-four hours.'.

'That's not long after we picked him up.'. Inspector Folkard replied. She unconsciously swept the back of her right half-open hand across her forehead. 'Yes,' replied Police Constable Stanfield 'and there's more. Mr Dwyer went to Mr Rimmer's house twice that evening, at first about nine in the evening, then just before midnight. On the second occasion, one of the neighbours came out and informed him that Mr Rimmer had left with two police inspectors.'. Inspector Folkard couldn't raise a smile even if she wanted to – Albert Conway – President of the Neighbourhood Watch. 'Thank you, Omar. I'll be setting off to the station in the next half-hour.'.

Sergeant Shakespeare's car was already in the car park when Inspector Folkard arrived to the station. Team ready, six officers had already gathered in the incident room whilst four others awaited their arrival outside Mr Rimmer's property. 'Briefing in five,' announced Sergeant Shakespeare as she followed Inspector Folkard into her office. 'You got Omar's call then?'. The look on Sergeant Shakespeare's face said it all. 'He's had a restless night in custody our Mr Rimmer – crying relentlessly at one point in the night – shouting in his sleep.'.

'Any news on MIND?'. Inspector Folkard's voice showed some concern for their troubled suspect. 'Yes, they're with him now. A psychiatric assessment will be carried out this morning – we should be able to interview him sometime this afternoon.' 'Ok. Briefing then we go. You have the keys?'. 'Yes.'. Sergeant Shakespeare paused before adding, 'it was strange you know – he raised no objections when we asked for the keys – just nodded. As we were leaving he added something along the lines of, not forgetting the one with the bull and the Spanish cathedral on it. No objection at all, almost as if he wanted something or someone to be found. Do you think we'll find Jennifer there?'. 'If we do, let's hope she's still alive. To be honest, I really don't know what we'll find.'.

Fifteen minutes later, Inspector Folkard emerged from the stark building and headed for the car park. She got into a maroon coloured vehicle car before the rest of the party arrived. How dark the sky was at that hour – and how cold it was. It suddenly dawned on Inspector Folkard that today, the twenty-seventh of December, was her father's birthday. Although it was unlikely she would get the chance to call him until much later in the evening, Inspector Folkard suddenly craved for some much needed father-daughter time; she could always talk openly with him. It wasn't easy keeping the harrowing details to herself, specifics that at times kept her awake late into the early hours. Although living abroad in the Canaries now, his warm voice and composed nature had a way of still infectiously altering her mood for the better – a phone call later, and she would be ready once more to take on the world.

Sergeant Shakespeare opened the vehicle's door, 'I'm driving then?'. Her warm smile was infectious too. It wouldn't be long before she made Inspector herself – she'd rarely met in her career a sergeant that was more dedicated and professional in their duties – kind-hearted too. Seatbelts on, their unmarked vehicle followed the search team out from the station, the sleepy town of Southport blissfully unaware of the missing young woman, the arrest of Mr Bernard Rimmer and the impending charge.

Although it was much lighter now, the journey along the coastal road was bleak, to say the least. Usually, and at such a time in the early hours of the day, the view could be counted upon to be nothing but splendid – a radiance warming the marshlands. Today, everything was grey; grey for as far as the eye could see. Disappointingly, only the tip of Blackpool Tower could be seen across the water today. At least there had been no recent rain – searches involving gardens were never easy when it rained. No matter how hard teams tried, mud managed to get everywhere.

The post-Christmas mood wasn't helping either. For as long as Inspector Folkard could remember, the post-Christmas misery had clung on psychologically for days; at such times it was a relief to keep busy at work. Today was not necessarily one of those times. A day like this called for sitting by the fire, avoiding getting dressed, eating countless shortbread biscuits, watching television, drinking lots of tea, cuddling and tickling the children, returning back to bed with Walter.

Turning right from the coastal road, they meandered dutifully towards the dwelling that had remained in the Rimmer family for generations. It seemed a pity to interfere with the sculptured nature of the property, the gardens in particular. But such was the nature of the job. They would enter now, and unfortunately leave unable to hide from what they had disturbed for ever, unable to leave like thieves in the night.

Sergeant Shakespeare opened the wide, metallic mustard gate. She did so as she glanced towards the Conway household. It struck her that this was the first time she had seen the downstairs bay window curtains shut. Certain that their arrival would invite Albert Conway to leave his warm and safe bed in order to interconnect in some way with them, they entered hastily into the porch, the cold taking hold of them in a vice-like grip.

Forty minutes had already passed when P.C. Clark approached Inspector Folkard in the kitchen; in her right hand she held a medium sized see-through bag, tied firmly at the top. Inspector Folkard looked at it incredulously. Through it, various bunches of longish hair lengths could be seen, each tied at the top with what seemed to be a different coloured ribbon.

Unable to handle the evidence, Inspector Folkard was sure she could identify two of them at least – tied with a blue ribbon, one darkish length looked very much like Darcy's hair, auburn flecks melded. Another, a medium blonde length this time, tied with a yellow ribbon, looked much like Mary-Eloise's had on the day she had accompanied the Chambers for the identification. How strangely fascinating it seemed that hair itself could retain such life within it. Nothing seemed to have faded, nor wilted, as most things did in life.

Inspector Folkard knew, that despite what it looked like, possibly some or all of the hair, could belong, like Darcy's, to other girls who were not deceased. 'Get them to the lab – and have the DNA looked at, as soon as.'. Seconds later, and another officer coming from indoors, approached her with a bag containing two pairs of unwashed female underwear. 'Found these under a mattress. His mattress, I think.'. Inspector Folkard signalled for P.C. Clark to take them too.

It was evident after the first hour that Mr Rimmer had not much else in the house – no wigs to speak of – nothing. At that point, it was impossible to know whether the items seized so far would in fact connect him to any of the crimes – the hair after all, could belong literally to anyone. Certainly there seemed to be no sign of Jennifer Dwyer. Although another coincidence seemed impossible, Jennifer could after all, and it was still the Christmas period, have stayed over at a friend's house – could presently be on the verge of contacting her parents – had most likely lost her mobile somewhere along the way.

Inspector Folkard was upstairs in Mrs Rimmer's bedroom watching through the right window the small team working around the elongated Victorian greenhouse at the far-right of the garden. The striking mother-in-law plant, perched on a shelf in the nearest corner, had caught her eye – her longest tongue was pointing across the bottom of garden. At such an angle, Inspector Folkard noticed that it looked like the likeable monstrosity was sheltering the quaint small fuchsia under its widest wing, the infantile houseplant that they had once all gathered around and affectionally admired.

Suddenly, her attention was drawn a sharp left to the bottom of the garden, towards the wooden granny house. Sergeant Shakespeare was shouting something – she was shouting loudly from somewhere inside the wooden enclosure. Outdoors now, she was waving her arms to the others working around the greenhouse. Inspector Folkard opened the window, the pale muslin curtains exiting at the same time as her head protruded forwards. Inspector Folkard heard her clearly then. 'Call for an ambulance! And get the Inspector!'.

At first it was difficult to comprehend what was being photographed for documentation. Upon Inspector Folkard's approach, Sergeant Shakespeare looked visibly shaken at what was concealed directly underneath the doll's house, it's characters leaning forward from their upstairs windows. 'Bag everything up carefully. Everything. Then shift it all out of the way, hurry up!'. The stench coming from the dark hole below the hatch was intoxicating – the evidence of death concealed below what seemed to be the evidence of life.

Jennifer Dwyer sheltered her eyes, her entire face, as a torch beamed it's light down upon her and, what looked like the remains of several corpses below - some wrapped in tarpaulin. Curled like a foetus, she remained still, bound and gagged. A dark curly wig was visible on her head – with it a pale blue dress with a tessellating brooch pinned to it. Visible too where several mobile phones, a handbag, several items of footwear – amongst them, a recognisable pair of wellingtons belonging to Zita, the peach sheepskin slippers, the dressing gown.

The ambulance had arrived now. Within half an hour, Jennifer Dwyer had been removed and freed from the coffin that had enslaved her – the hole that was to surely to become her grave. Items where gathered carefully in evidence bags, some inexplicable to say the least – a red lipstick, possibly his mother's. The arresting portrait of his mother, that had been unfaithfully removed from the top of the television set, was also there.

Outside now, Inspector Folkard ended the call she had made to Superintendent Reid not long before Sergeant Cummings ended hers. Sergeant Shakespeare stood beneath the weeping willow looking rather perplexed, sombre even. She looked to Inspector Folkard before speaking out. 'Bernard Rimmer is dead. Died twenty minutes ago – of a coronary heart attack.'. Sergeant Shakespeare paused for a few moments before continuing. 'He'd not long been returned to his cell following a conversation with a psychiatrist from MIND – had shared details of persons and personalities – four apparently. He became distressed when speaking of his mother. He was returned to his cell for a break – died soon after.'.

Inspector Folkard could not hide her frustration. There were so many unanswered questions. She looked about her, surveyed the scene closely; there was still a lot of work to be done. She needed to stay focused. Inspector Folkard looked into Sergeant Shakespeare's dejected face. Despite having found Jennifer, despite having caught their man, despite having brought some closure to the families who had lost loved ones, a wave of loneliness and despondency gripped them both – as if astonished by the morning's events.

'I'm going to the station. You ok to continue here?'. 'Yes, sure.'. Sergeant Shakespeare managed a half-smile. Inspector Folkard looked to the back of the house before glancing instinctively upwards. The curtains blew freely and outwardly from Mrs Rimmer's right bedroom window now, the same window she had opened at the point when she first heard Sergeant Shakespeare's cry. An unmistakable pallid face looked directly at her now; she was dressed in red, pearls about her neckline – her dark hair was visible over her shoulders. It was difficult to grasp what was happening at the time, for in a moment she was gone.

But her attractive smile was unmistakable, bewitching even. It was the smile of a mother at peace, she was sure of it – the smile of his mother.

About the Author

SALLY-ANNE TAPIA-BOWES IS an author who graduated at Hope University with a degree in English Literature and Contemporary Art. HIS MOTHER is her debut novel with sequels HER FATHER and THEIR PARENTS to follow. Themes in this series include dysfunctional families, mental health, loss and regret.

She lives in England with her husband and three children. Her official website can be found at www.tapia-bowes.com

Printed in Great Britain
by Amazon.co.uk, Ltd.,
Marston Gate.